NO RIGHT, NO WRONG

He didn't have to open his eyes to know she was crying, he could feel the tears on his face. "Bastien," Libby said, her voice full of uncertainty. This was madness, he could tell that she knew it as well. She sat up. When she was no longer touching him the world went cold.

Bastien moved to kneel beside her. There was nowhere for her to retreat to in the tiny hut. She looked trapped, not by him but by her own demons. The look she gave him was one of entreaty. It told him how tired she was of always being in control of herself, of the situation. It begged him to make the choice for them both. He moved closer, so that the heat of their bodies met and mingled though they didn't quite touch.

"There is no right or wrong here," he told her. "There is just us." He knew what she needed, so he held her face between his hands as they looked deeply into each other's eyes. "It is time," he said, "to let the madness rule."

"Simply wonderful . . . a delight for lovers of time travel, or anyone who appreciates a terrific book. Susan Sizemore is one of the most inventive and talented romance writers."

—Anne Stuart, author of *Nightfall*

"I had to finish *After the Storm* in a single sitting. The book is fun, fast-paced, and witty."

—Jody Lynn Nye, co-author of *The Ship Who Won*

Books by Susan Sizemore

Wings of the Storm
My First Duchess
My Own True Love
In My Dreams
Nothing Else Matters
After the Storm
*The Autumn Lord**

Published by HarperPaperbacks

*coming soon

Harper
Monogram

After the Storm

♦ SUSAN SIZEMORE ♦

HarperPaperbacks
A Division of HarperCollinsPublishers

This is a work of fiction. The characters, incidents, and dialogues are products of the author's imagination and are not to be construed as real. Any resemblance to actual events or persons, living or dead, is entirely coincidental.

HarperPaperbacks   *A Division of* HarperCollins*Publishers*
10 East 53rd Street, New York, N.Y. 10022

Cover illustration by John Ennis

First printing: February 1996

Printed in the United States of America

HarperPaperbacks, HarperMonogram, and colophon are trademarks of HarperCollins*Publishers*

❖ 10 9 8 7 6 5 4 3 2 1

For Mom, and Mary, and Elisa Isabelle
—Love, Susan G.

Prologue

"Ladies and gentlemen, the Middle Ages."

"Yep, that's what it looks like, all right," Libby Wolfe answered Joe Lario's comment. A moment before they'd been standing in the blue transport chamber, now she and Joe and Ed were in a different time and place, dressed for the period and ready to begin their assignment. She walked across the creaking wooden floor to look out the small arrowslit window. A breeze ruffled her veil as she breathed the clean air of this distant era. "We've arrived on the second floor of the tower. I hope they don't send the horses and baggage through the same coordinates they sent us." She glanced at the arched doorway that led to a very narrow spiral staircase. Downs Tower itself was the only working timegate in this part of Britain, the transmission equipment built into its very walls. The worn stone stairs, however, were probably as hazardous as they looked. "Can you imagine trying to get a packhorse down those?"

Joe chuckled, then unsheathed his dagger and spoke into the hilt. "TS1, team Lilydrake is clear. Adjust coordinates for supply shipment."

"Copy, team Lilydrake," a voice replied from the dagger. "Stand by for one more gate-crasher." Communication would not be possible once they were away from the transmitter in the tower, but for now they were linked to their own time. When she heard the news, Libby wished they weren't.

"What?" Libby asked. She turned from a view of spring green forest and distant fields. Before she could say another word she caught a blue shimmering in the air out of the corner of her eye. Then a woman of medium height stood in the center of the circular stone room. The newcomer wore a yellow and brown gown which showed off lush curves. She had auburn hair beneath a sheer veil, blue eyes, a few freckles and the most sardonic expression Libby had ever encountered.

It took Libby a moment to recognize the woman, then she grinned. "Well, well, if it isn't Indiana Jones. I haven't seen you in about five years. Where's the bull-whip?"

"That's Marj Jones," the historian reminded her. "We named the dog Indiana, and the whip's in my other kirtle." Marj crossed her arms. "I've been told I'm supposed to baby-sit you three for the duration of the assignment. I'm supposed to make sure you don't make any anachronistic mistakes while dealing with the locals."

Libby felt like protesting, but she couldn't deny the wisdom of the Time Search History Department, which happened to be headed by her mother, in sending someone with them. Though she had spent some time among the local population as a child she really couldn't pass as a native for long without help. Medieval England wasn't her specialty. At least Marj was a friend, someone who shared her interest in old movies.

"Did Mom pull you from your research in Carmarthen for this? You are still researching Merlin, aren't you?"

"Yep. Despite Elliot Hemmons's efforts to curtail personal research I've been able to spend the last five years collecting folktales in a quiet medieval village."

Libby frowned at the mention of the man's name. "Hemmons is a major jerk. So's everyone on his Oversight Committee."

"Nobody in Time Search will argue that." Marj got back to business. "Never mind Carmarthen and Hemmons. My briefing was more than a little bit brief. What's going on?"

Libby, Joe and Ed looked at each other. None of them wanted to go over this ground again. "I think I'll go wait for the supplies," Joe said. "Ed?"

"Me too."

The men disappeared down the stairs before Libby could protest. That left her to explain the situation to their baby-sitter. There was one piece of furniture in the tower, a crudely carved wooden bench. She waved Marj over to it and sat down beside her.

"How old am I?"

Marj considered for a moment. "About twenty-seven, I think. I've sort of lost track of people the last few years."

"Twenty-eight," Libby told her. "My birth certificate tells me I'm twenty-eight, but *I* think I'm twenty-four."

She tucked her hands into the wide sleeves of her dark blue kirtle to keep from fidgeting nervously. "I can't tell you the exact details of the accident," she went on, "because I don't remember them. Not only don't Joe and Ed and I remember what happened to us at Lilydrake, the medical and psychiatric personnel who've been treating us won't tell us much about what happened." Libby tried very hard not to feel bitter about the walls of silence she'd been bumping up against for the last several months. She could fight off being bitter, but she still felt bruised. "What I do know is that the three of us were part of a five-person team that was using Lilydrake Castle as a base for a time travel experiment. It's several miles to the next settlement, so we had plenty of privacy."

"Privacy for what?"

Libby shrugged. "It was something to do with testing a radical new time machine called TDD in an isolated environment. It didn't work. The reason we know it didn't work is that when the thing got switched on two people disappeared and the rest of us got pulled back to Time Search headquarters with our memories scrambled. The damn thing stole time from us. Joe and Ed lost a year or so worth of memories, but the malfunctioning equipment sucked out about four years of my life. The shrinks don't want to tell us any more—if they even know any more—because they don't want to risk implanting false memories. We're supposed to get it all back naturally. So far we haven't remembered a thing. So we got permission to come back to Lilydrake, fix up the old place, do some research, and hopefully, get our memories back at the scene of the crime—as it were."

Marj was thoughtfully silent for a while before she let out a low whistle and said, "This is weird."

"Yeah," Libby agreed. "Tell me about it." She got up and went to the window. "The horses have arrived." She looked back at the historian. She tried not to show how restless and anxious and eager and worried she felt. She was trying to treat this expedition into the past in a calm, professional way. She wanted to run outside, jump on a horse and speed off to the castle that held her missing life. Instead she made herself say calmly, "Time to go. I think we can make it to the road that leads through Blean Forest by nightfall if we don't push the animals too hard. From now on I'm Lady Isabeau, come from my father's stronghold in Wales to fix up his ruined castle in Kent."

Marj stood and gave her a deep bow. "And I am your companion, Lady Marjorie."

Libby smiled. "Just don't let me forget who *I'm* supposed to be while I'm trying to remember who I really am."

1

"*What you need* is a husband, Lady Isabeau," the Sheriff of Elansted remarked as they rode down the forest track.

Libby stared at the craggy-featured man while Marj responded, "Are you offering yourself for that position, Sir Reynard?"

It was late April, the air was cool, but sunlight filtered through the thick canopy of tree branches. Spring was everywhere in bloom around them. Libby remembered spring in Kent, but as a child who visited with her time-traveling parents. It was a lovely day to be out for a ride, but Libby wished she had a few less people to share the scenery with.

Libby, trying to stay in character as Isabeau of Lilydrake merely gave the sheriff a slight smile in reply to his suggestion. Marj had decided that Isabeau should be the shy sort, so the historian was doing most of the talking. Libby knew she was anything but shy, but was trying her best to stay in character.

She would have sworn that Sir Reynard was normally a taciturn man, but he was making the effort to be charming to the ladies he'd put in his charge. Especially to Lady Marjorie, who was riding on a pillion seat behind Libby's saddle.

"Oh, no," he answered Marj's question with a low, rumbling laugh. "While the Lady of Lilydrake is lovely, I would not look so high for a maiden to wed."

Libby didn't turn her head to look, but she could imagine Marj tugging on her wimple while she looked the sheriff over. She guessed that there would be an amused but critical gleam in her companion's eyes.

"Then why did you bring the subject up?" Marj asked. She had a wonderfully rich, deep voice herself, did Dr. Marjorie Jones. She was a fine match for bantering with Reynard of Elansted. As usual her tone was laced with sarcasm.

"I was thinking of Lilydrake," he replied. "The countryside around the estate is in deep disorder, I've heard. The villages of the demesne are deserted. I'm told Sir Daffyd had virtually abandoned the castle even before the fire that gutted the hall last autumn. It would make less work for me if there were a strong man to hold the fief."

"Yes, 'tis true, the place needs to be put in order," Libby said. She tucked away the local information about the hall's having burned to think about later, and added, "A pity my father has no sons."

"Indeed," Sir Reynard agreed, then rode past them to take his place at the head of the company as the path narrowed once more.

Marj shifted her grip on Libby's waist. She leaned close to speak quietly in her ear, switching from

Norman French to English to say, "What about your two brothers?"

"I was the only one weird enough to get into the time travel business," Libby reminded her. "So, this is the forest primeval," she added as she looked skeptically at their lush, green surroundings.

"This is it," Marj agreed. "What do you think? Remember anything?"

"Nothing recent." Libby looked at the thick branches tangling together over their heads. The oaks seemed jealous of letting any sunlight reach the ground. "I think I'd prefer a bit less rampant greenery. I'm more of a city girl. I think."

"Not me," Marj said. "Carmarthen in the thirteenth century is a great place to get away from everything. Not much night life, though."

"That pretty much goes without saying." Libby chuckled. "You should try living in a yurt in Mongolia like I did."

"So the Horde Study got funding after all, huh? I thought Hemmons tried to kill the research as being unimportant."

Libby gave a grim chuckle. "He lost."

"Good. What's it like on the steppes?"

"I don't remember."

"Lucky you."

Libby started to shrug, but Marj's hand on her shoulder reminded her that it wasn't a common gesture for medieval ladies.

They'd been on the road for two days now, most of it in the company of Reynard of Elansted and his men. It was the sheriff who'd insisted on their joining his party for safety in numbers when they'd met him on the Blean Forest road. To have refused his offer would have been out of character.

"I wish there were still a timegate at Lilydrake."

"Couldn't have used it if there was," Marj reminded her. "Continuity Factor won't allow it if you're going to deal directly with the locals to do your research."

"There are too many rules to time travel," Libby complained. Some of them were the laws of physics, some of them were safeguards and obstructions imposed by the Hemmons Oversight Committee. Most of them were the laws of David Wolfe, the man who'd invented time travel. The Continuity Factor stated that one thing had to happen after another. Time Search personnel had to seem to take the same amount of time to travel from one place to another as everyone else. "It's not polite to freak out the locals, as my mother once told me. Our mission statement is not to mess up the past, the past did a perfectly good job of messing up on its own. We come back to observe, and we do it one day at a time, within the understanding of the people we encounter. So spake the great Jane Wolfe and her mighty consort. Never mind that they broke all the rules themselves back when *they* were having adventures. Back when dinosaurs walked the earth," she added sarcastically.

"Before Elliot Hemmons tried to take over Time Search, you mean," Marj chuckled. "Rumor has it they made up the rules after they had the adventures, including your birth in a drafty castle bedchamber."

"Technically, that makes me a local, you know. Maybe you shouldn't be interacting with me."

"It's too late for me to jump off the horse now, kid."

Personally, Libby wished she could just return to Lilydrake before the accident and prevent it from ever happening. The Continuity Factor covered that as well. Not only couldn't someone be in two places at once, it wasn't possible for time travelers to change their own personal history. It had been tried, it hadn't worked, no one knew why. Time travel did not allow second chances.

"This is inconvenient," Libby said, thinking mostly about the uncomfortable time she'd spent in the saddle recently. "But it does make sense. Wait a minute—I remembered." Libby jerked with surprise, which very nearly caused Marj to lose the grip she had around Libby's waist.

"What?" the shaken historian demanded.

"Mongolia."

"Keep your voice down," Marj warned in a stern whisper. "What about Mongolia?"

Libby almost laughed with delight, then tears that she wasn't sure were of relief or heartbreak blurred her vision. "Nobody told me I was in Mongolia. I remembered it. I just—remembered. All on my own." She glanced back at Marj. "How about that?"

Marj's grasp on her waist turned into a swift hug. "Good for you. What do you remember? Details."

Libby concentrated as she stared intently ahead, just barely aware of the horsemen and footsoldiers moving along the road with them. She stared, and she thought, but no details emerged immediately from the effort.

Then up ahead someone called out, "Wolvesheads!"

And just as her imagination began to sketch out the slender shadow of a man silhouetted against a stark Asian sunset someone jumped out of the woods and grabbed her horse's bridle.

"Oh, good," she said, looking down at the ragged man. "An outlaw."

He was hard-eyed, the stench from him nearly over-powering, but he was exactly the sort of person Libby was looking for. At least she hoped he was an outlaw. She reached down to slap his hands away from her horse. Surprised at her reaction, the man backed quickly away. He drew a knife and ran forward as another man stepped out of the woods. This one raised a bow.

"Duck!"

"What?" Marj shrieked. Libby pushed her off the horse.

As Marj hit the ground, Libby lifted her heavy skirts and kicked the man with the knife in the throat. She backed the horse up just as an arrow sped by its head. The arrow hit one of Reynard's footsoldiers in the shoulder. He fell to the ground with a muffled scream. Her horse made a similar sound, and tried to rear.

Libby looked around frantically as she fought to keep control of the animal. She saw the soldiers locked in hand-to-hand combat with the men who'd ambushed them. Marj had grabbed a staff tossed to her by one of their companions and had joined Joe and Ed in fighting off a pair of robbers. There were outlaw archers hidden among the trees, but Reynard of Elansted had bowmen of his own. Elansted's men had formed a circle to protect her and Marj. They were obviously better prepared for this fight than the men who'd attacked from the woods.

"Don't kill them!" Libby shouted as Reynard came riding toward her.

There was blood on his sword, but he answered as he rode past, "I'm not going to kill the wolvesheads. I'm going to see them properly hanged," he added as he wheeled his horse to shout orders at his men.

Hang them? *You can't hang these men*, she thought as the sheriff and his soldiers rounded up what outlaws they hadn't already killed. *At least not until I'm done with them*, she added as she remembered that the outlaws had been the ones who'd attacked them.

Her horse was still nervous, so she got down out of the high-backed saddle and stood on the ground, patting and stroking the animal to calm it. "Can I get you anything?" she asked, touching her cheek to the soft velvet of the horse's muzzle. "An apple? Some fresh grass? A sedative?" She was still exhilarated from the adrenaline rush of the fight. She supposed she should be ashamed of herself, but she had always had a weakness for adventures. She was glad she'd reacted automatically to the situation, just like she'd been trained.

"That wasn't so bad," she murmured as Marj came up to her. "Actually, it was fun. Which, is, of course, a very immature way of looking at it and I should be ashamed." She looked at the disheveled historian. "You okay?"

Marj nodded, then leaned close and whispered, "'Oh, good, an outlaw'?" Libby couldn't help but smile at the woman's outraged tone. "Just what sort of research are you doing in the thirteenth century, Wolfe?"

"I'll tell you later," Libby answered as Sir Reynard rode up once more.

He swung down off his horse to stand before them. He was tall for the era, so Libby had to look up a bit to meet his gaze. He had a hard-edged, ruthless look to him at the moment that reminded her a bit of her father. She shook her head at the notion of any resemblance. This man was a stranger. He'd told her that he was new to the area, on his way from London to take up his duties in the shire. She knew she was just grasping at any hint of might-be memory and would have to be careful not to make up her past life instead of actually getting it back.

Reynard gave her a perfunctory nod. "I'm sorry, my lady, but we'll not be going on to Lilydrake today." Before she could protest he gestured at the men his soldiers had captured. "I've got to lock this lot up, and Lilydrake's not fit to house prisoners."

"But—"

"We'll be turning aside for Passfair Castle," he hurried on past her faint protest. "I'm told Sir Stephan DuVrai has strong walls and a stout keep where my prisoners and you ladies will both be safe. In different parts of the castle," he added with a charming flash of dimples.

"But—"

"You know the DuVrai family, I think. I've heard that your families are closely connected."

The man had certainly researched his new job before leaving London. Libby nodded. "They're my godparents, but I haven't seen them in—"

"You'll be welcomed then." He gave her another nod and got back on his horse, the matter settled to his satisfaction.

Libby stared bleakly after him as he rode over to supervise his men while they tied up the prisoners. She didn't want to go to Passfair. She wanted to go to Lilydrake and get her memory back. At Passfair she'd have to continue playing the role of Isabeau, eat the local food, sleep on straw, put up with the damp, smoky rooms, the smells, endure the pure discomfort that was daily life in even a top-of-the-line medieval castle. Even if Lilydrake were a completely burned out ruin she and the others could break out their modern camping equipment and have some of the comforts of the twenty-first century.

She sighed, and tried to be philosophical about it. She wasn't going to Lilydrake, not yet. She was going to visit her godparents.

"Oh, goody."

"Please, God," Marj whispered, "don't let her say anything to him." She had no hope of her prayers being answered as the priest continued to drone on. While Libby was obviously trying to retain an expression of polite neutrality as Passfair's chaplain expounded his misogynist theories, her eyes glinted with the light of battle. Marj watched helplessly while the young woman's fingers plucked nervously at the bread trencher she shared with the DuVrais' oldest son, Henry. Father John had been talking to Henry throughout dinner while he occasionally directed a pointed glance at Libby. He was ostensibly instructing the young man, who was apparently due to get married soon, in the proper treatment of his wife. But his words were pointed at the castle's guest. He seemed to have taken a dislike to Lady Isabeau the moment he heard that she was heiress to the neighboring property. He had firm ideas about women having any freedom whatsoever. The evening meal was dragging on and on and the priest didn't seem to be winding down.

Marj did not blame Libby for her annoyed reaction. In fact, she would be happy to get up and punch the man out herself, but that would be interfering, and interfering was against the rules.

"Observe, don't impact," she muttered the History Department slogan to herself.

Sir Reynard, however, had very good ears. "What's that?"

"Excuse me?" Marj countered, hoping she'd spoken in Norman. She'd been speaking far too much English while traveling with Libby, Joe and Ed and was worried her own disguise might have slipped. Mostly because being around Reynard made her feel a bit giddy and reckless.

He was seated beside her at the high table, a large, masculine presence she wished she could ignore. Despite her efforts to remain an uninvolved observer there was something about the man that made her want to do far more than watch him interact with his environment. There was something about the twinkle in his bright blue eyes that frequently belied his serious demeanor. He was a raw-boned, craggy, graying inhabitant of another world whom she had no business being attracted to.

"You said something about observing," the sheriff said as he handed her the winecup they shared. "I think observation is a fine knack to have in carrying out my duties."

"In my own as well," Marj answered. "It's my duty to keep a close watch on my lady's needs and circumstances."

"Of course."

Their gazes met, and their fingers brushed as the wine was passed between them. The jolt of the contact almost made Marj forget what they were discussing. Fortunately, for her own presence of mind, if not for the good of the assignment, it was at this moment that Libby chose to speak to the priest—loudly.

"Do you really believe women don't have souls?"

Lady Sibelle had wondered just how long it was going to take her guest to react to Father John's ridiculous notions. Isabeau had the look of both her parents about her. She had Jehane's dark coloring and tall slenderness,

Jehane's dark eyes as well, and a more delicate version of Daffyd's strong nose and elegant cheekbones. She was a beauty, and, more than that, she was a woman of spirit. Oh, she seemed shy and spoke little, but in the few hours since her arrival at Passfair Keep Sibelle had discerned not only intelligence, but strength mixed with some deep pain driving her goddaughter.

"Well?" Isabeau demanded when the priest ignored her.

"I think I hear the buzzing of a little Welsh fly," was the only acknowledgment the chaplain gave to Lady Isabeau's words. "Or the buzzing of a meddling female." He gave a negligent wave of his hand. "It is all the same."

"What—?" Isabeau asked. There was a dangerous edge to the girl's voice. Sibelle half expected the contents of the girl's winecup to be flung in Father John's face. She half hoped it would be.

"Learn silence and humility, woman."

"I'd rather learn how to kick your black-robed bu—"

"My lady!" Isabeau's lady-in-waiting said as she hurried to Isabeau's side. Sibelle had watched Lady Marjorie's growing concern as well and was glad that she came to her lady's side.

"I have a headache," Isabeau said as she turned to Marjorie. She touched her fingertips to her temples. She had gone pale. "I don't know what I'm doing."

"Women never do," Father John said.

To Sibelle's annoyance, her son responded to this exchange with a cold laugh. "Stephan," she said in her usual mild way as she placed her hand over her husband's.

Stephan brushed his lips against her forehead. "Matilda is crying again," he observed before he straightened and looked sternly at the priest. "You disturb my guest, Father."

"Your guest has too sharp a tongue, my lord," Father John replied easily. "My duty is to correct such behavior, do you not agree?"

"Not at my dinner table, it isn't," Stephan responded sharply. "Henry," he added, "go to the chapel with the good father and pray."

"But—"

"Now. Take Matilda with you," he added as Henry and the priest got to their feet. "Spend time with your betrothed," Stephan commanded in a quieter voice as Henry moved past him.

Henry sneered and said, "Matilda has no place in my prayers."

Sibelle shook her head unhappily. She glanced at the end of the table where poor Matilda sat, alone, dejected and dripping with tears. Matilda had been crying since she arrived at Passfair the week before. Henry showed no interest in her, she showed none in him. He was rude, she was frightened. The situation was completely miserable.

Sibelle looked to Isabeau. Her friend's daughter did not look well, but she still looked in better condition than poor Matilda. Isabeau was a woman of vitality, Sibelle was sure of that. Like her mother, Sibelle thought, and glanced back at Matilda. And that child reminded her of herself all those years ago, when she'd arrived at Passfair confused and lost and in need of a friend. The sort of friend Jehane had been to her.

Sibelle stood. "Take Lady Isabeau to the guest bower. I'll prepare a potion to help her headache." And once her head was clear, Sibelle thought, she and Isabeau would have a little talk.

2

"*My mom's right,* I need a baby-sitter."

"I guess you do," Marj answered. "You feel okay?"

"No. But compared to the kind of headaches I had just after the accident I'm fine. I should have kept my mouth shut, though."

The guest bower was a small, dark room on the second floor of the tower. It contained one curtained bed and a long flat chest that doubled as storage space and somewhere to sit. Libby sat on the chest with her arms wrapped around her drawn-up knees. She watched as Marj moved restlessly across the room. She was miserable and confused and furious with herself for causing a scene down in the hall.

"Yes," Marj agreed as she paced in front of her, stirring up the scent of herbs in the dry rushes as she moved.

Libby winced at the sarcasm in the woman's voice. "I know that these people's opinions are none of my business. I didn't come here to cause trouble, Marj. I guess I'm not as prepared to interact with the locals as I thought I was. It's not easy."

Marj stopped pacing and turned on her. "I know. I've spent five years in the same village. It's been very hard staying an outsider, but it can be done."

"This is harder than I thought it would be. I haven't had one of these stupid headaches for a while. I guess I'm not as ready to cope as I thought." She sighed. "I remember that it was fun pretending to be part of this world the times I came here as a kid." She sighed again. "I'm not quite myself, you know."

"Then who are you?" Marj sounded both teasing and sympathetic. "You said you'd tell me about your research later. Well, it's later."

Libby welcomed the chance to talk about her work. She would like to think that it was as important as coming to the past to recover her lost memories. That wasn't true, of course, but concentrating on doing something useful helped keep her fear that she'd never remember those lost years at bay.

"About my research," she said rather than expose her demons. "I'm here to study outlaws."

Marj looked puzzled. "Can't you do that at home? As I recall, the crime rate in—"

"No, no, not criminals. Outlaws. The legends and popular, fanciful concepts, the whole Robin Hood schtick, that's what interests me. I want to know how it all got started. Everyone loves the steely eyed loner, the man outside the law," she went on. "Western culture's romanticized criminal behavior for hundreds of years. I came back here, to the place where the outlaw legends originated, to try to figure out why. Outlaw, wolfshead, brigand, bandit, those words are glamorous to us. I want to figure out what it is about Robin Hood that's translated into the popular outlook."

"Those men who attacked us weren't Robin Hood."

"Actually, Mom says Robin Hood lived up in Lincolnshire a couple of generations ago. But Blean's always been full of brigands and I have to work with what I've got right here."

"Oh, yeah?"

Libby nodded. "There's one that never got caught, Sikes. He's been operating in this forest for at least twenty years. I want to find out about him. I don't know if those were his men who attacked us, but I want to observe them as much as possible."

"Before they get hanged," Marj added bluntly.

Libby did not like being reminded of the brutal realities of this world. "Cold in here, isn't it?" she observed to change the subject.

It was cold, despite the fact that it was a nice spring night. She shivered despite all the layers of clothing she wore. The thick stones of the walls kept in the chill and damp, and there was a mustiness in the air. It didn't help that the smoke from the tallow candles lighting the room gave off the aroma of animal fat. She didn't even want to think about climbing onto the straw-filled mattress. She knew that it would be damp, and the blankets full of vermin. She hadn't minded the inconveniences of the days spent camping out as they crossed the countryside, but now that she was inside she was too aware of the discomforts of the time.

"Do you think there's mice?" she asked as she peered into the shadows near the walls.

"Of course there's mice," Marj answered blithely. "Rats, too, I imagine."

"Thanks."

Before she could suggest that they sneak off to sleep outside in a tent the door opened and Lady Sibelle entered. She was accompanied by the girl who'd been sitting at the far end of the high table during dinner. A pair of large dogs followed the women into the room.

The girl was Matilda, Libby remembered, Henry's betrothed. Matilda looked like she'd been crying. Libby thought that if she were betrothed to Henry she might be tempted to cry too. She wanted to smile at the girl and say something sympathetic, but remembered that she wasn't supposed to interact with any more people than necessary. So she focused her attention on Lady Sibelle as the dogs jumped up on the bed. Matilda hung back near the door. Her godmother carried a silver goblet full of some steaming liquid.

"I've brought you a posset, my dear," Sibelle said as Libby rose to meet her. "To calm you and help you sleep."

Eating dinner had been trial enough, Libby didn't think she could stomach taking any local medicine. "Thank you, my lady," she told her hostess, "but after all those lovely jellied eels I don't think I could manage to swallow another thing."

"Nonsense," Sibelle said as she took a relentless step forward. "You scarce touched your meal. Mothers notice such things, you know. And a godmother's care should be as loving and concerned as a mother's. Here." The silver cup was thrust firmly into Libby's hands. "Now, drink up and then we'll talk a bit while the potion relaxes you." Sibelle took a seat on the chest, folded her hands in her lap, and waited.

Libby looked desperately toward Marj, but all she got from the historian was an amused look. "Thanks a lot," she grumbled under her breath. She took a sniff of the potion. She smelled sage. "What's in it?"

"Wine, some herbs, egg yolk and barley water." That didn't sound so bad, Libby decided. She took a deep breath, closed her eyes, and swallowed the liquid in three long gulps, just as Lady Sibelle added, "And poppy, of course."

It was too late to spit the stuff out, so all Libby could do was stare at Sibelle in horror. "Poppy?"

"It will help you sleep."

Of course it would. "Opium's real good for that." Lady Sibelle smiled and nodded. Oh, great, her godmother was a drug dealer.

"I think you'd better sit down," Marj said as she took Libby by the arm and guided her to the bed.

The dogs moved aside grudgingly as she sat, then one of them immediately put its head in her lap. She began scratching it behind the ears automatically. "I've got a dog like this at home," she said. "Mother's been breeding them since—"

Maybe it was better not to bring up too much about her parents' lives in case she made some sort of disastrous slip-up. Lady Sibelle thought her old friends rarely visited because they had settled down to live in a far-off castle in Daffyd ap Bleddyn's homeland. Libby had to make sure she didn't do or say anything that made anyone suspicious of this perfectly reasonable explanation. The actual explanation was that her parents lived in Batavia, Illinois, eight centuries in the future, and were in charge of a time-travel organization. The castle in far-off Wales made a lot more sense.

"I remember her taking a brace of our deerhounds with her to Wales. These, too, are descendants of

Melisande," Sibelle told her. "Now tell me," the Lady of Passfair went on, "why are you not yet wed?"

This was the second person today who'd brought up the subject of marriage. "I—"

"Her betrothed died this last winter," Marj hurriedly explained. Libby gave the historian a grateful look.

Sibelle nodded and reached out to pat Libby's hand sympathetically. "Then I'll include the lad in my prayers. Still," she added, "I have sons other than Henry." The girl by the door made a sniffing sound. Sibelle cast her a brief glance, then went on, "Perhaps, your parents will look to one of my and Sir Stephan's boys for your husband."

"Husband?" The word came out a stunned squeak. "I don't—"

Sibelle waved the subject away. "'Tis a matter for my lord and your father to discuss, but I think it is high time you were wed. If you are to rebuild Lilydrake you will have to have a strong husband to guard it. The king will want to ensure the loyalty of a Welsh heiress by giving her an English husband. You could do worse than one of my lads. Far worse."

"Yes, ma'am," was the only answer Libby could manage. She was beginning to feel a little bit dizzy.

This conversation was very strange. And why was Lady Sibelle looking at her so intently? Libby had no defenses against the woman's searching gaze, the dose of poppy in her bedtime drink had seen to that.

"I see now what makes you heart-hungry, for it is a lost love you pine for."

"It is?" The world was getting very, very fuzzy. Hadn't Mom once said that Sibelle was the local wise-woman? "I do?"

"Aye." Gentle hands stroked hers. "You'll rest easy here with us, my dear, where we can share our troubles and cure them together."

"Right. Fine," Libby murmured. She sighed deeply as her eyes slid closed. "Rest here. I can do that." But first she was going to have to get some sleep.

Libby hadn't realized how haunted she'd been by forgotten nightmares until she woke up from a night free of them. In fact, she'd slept very well, even with the straw mattress and the dogs for company, one curled at her feet, the other stretched out along her back. In fact, sharing the bed had been so natural she wondered if maybe she missed not sleeping alone. But who was she used to sleeping with? A dog on the end of the bed, or something a little bit more human?

Something long-limbed and bony. Someone.

The thoughts jarred her completely awake. She sat up quickly and fought to shake off the lingering effects of the sleeping potion. She was twenty-eight, she reminded herself as she pulled back the bedcurtains to look around the dimly lit room. It would be very surprising if she wasn't used to having somebody in her bed at one time or another. Well, she hadn't been used to it at age twenty–four—she'd been saving herself for the right man. He'd probably come along at some point but she just didn't remember him. Yet.

She pushed a dog aside and threw back the covers. As she stood up she realized she'd slept in her clothes. Local custom was to sleep naked, but she thought getting out of bed in a cold castle without any clothes on was taking realism a little too far. Just having her bare feet sink into the rush-covered floor was uncomfortable enough.

Tripping over the person lying next to the bed was worse.

Libby swore as she fell forward onto her hands and knees. Then she whirled around to help the woman she'd fallen across to sit up. "Are you okay, Marj?"

"I'm fine," Marj said from across the room.

Libby found herself looking into the red-rimmed eyes of Matilda. "What are you doing here?"

Still wrapped in a tangled blanket, Matilda scrambled to her feet. "Lady Sibelle said I should attend you," she told Libby in a soft, hesitant voice.

Libby stood. She looked at Marj, then back at the girl. "Attend me?" Matilda nodded. "Why?"

The girl tugged on a long brown braid. "Lady Sibelle said there is much I can learn from you."

Libby knew instantly what Sibelle had in mind, but she also knew it wouldn't work. What skills did she have that she could pass on to a medieval girl? How to run an espresso machine? Program a virtual reality chamber? She wasn't like her mother who'd come to the Middle Ages with knowledge of embroidery and dressmaking and how to run a castle household, and had taught all that stuff to the teenaged Sibelle. Mom had made over an ugly duckling heiress into a swan. The last thing Libby needed was to take on a project like Matilda. The last thing she knew how to do was take on a project like Matilda. And she could tell from looking at the sad, bedraggled girl, that that was exactly what her godmother intended.

"Oh, no," she said, and went barefoot and rumpled in search of her hostess. Marj, Matilda, and the two dogs followed along behind.

Sibelle was in the great hall, lingering over her breakfast while the servants cleared away the trestle tables below the dais. She looked up with a smile when Libby approached. "Come, my dear, and welcome." She gestured toward some covered dishes on the table. "I've saved a meal for you, for I knew you would oversleep a bit." She gestured the others toward the far end of the table. "Lady Marjorie and Matilda, welcome as well. I would like to speak with Isabeau alone, please."

Libby exchanged a wry look with Marj before the historian moved past her. Then Libby sat down and picked up a spoon. She poked it into a dish that contained something white and squishy. She supposed it would be out of character to ask just what Lady Sibelle had saved for her breakfast. "It doesn't have opium in it, does it?" she did ask.

"Cheese curds? No, the flavors wouldn't mix well at all."

Cheese curds. Edible. Not like the sort one found deep fried at state fairs, but edible. Maybe. Libby was hungry, so she gave the cheese a try. "Not bad." After she'd taken a few bites she looked up and found Father John glaring at her from across the table. "What?"

"The Welshwoman doesn't see fit to thank God for her food, I see," he complained to the young man standing beside him. Henry.

Henry was looking her over with embarrassing insolence. He made her feel like she didn't have any clothes on. "I would thank God most fervently for a bite of the Welshwoman's ti—"

"Henry!" Sibelle rapped out. She pointed. "Attend to your betrothed. Father, attend to your prayers." The men glared, but they obeyed the Lady of Passfair.

Sibelle sighed once they were out of earshot and said, "My apologies for my son's unchivalrous words. It's Matilda," she went on before Libby could think of anything to say. "Oh, not Matilda herself, but the idea of marrying. Henry has some notion he wants to run off on crusade, or follow the tourney circuit, or do anything but marry Michael of Wilton's daughter. And Matilda does nothing to make him change his mind, the poor child." Sibelle's last words were said with more exasperation than sympathy.

Libby swallowed another bite of cheese, then said. "I really must go on to Lilydrake. My father charged me to rebuild the keep as quickly as possible."

"Of course you must go to Lilydrake, and soon," Sibelle agreed. "But not before Beltane, surely. Of course you'll stay for the May Day fair. It will give you a chance to hire workers and purchase new household goods from the London merchants who come for the fair."

Libby remembered the fair held at Passfair on May Day every year. Back before there had been so many rules about Time Search people not interacting with the locals the Wolfe family had spent quite a bit of time actually living at Lilydrake. There'd been a household full of creative anachronists, scientists and historians who'd used the place for research while playing dress up. Gradually research budgets had been pared and the rules of contact had become more stringent.

The change was due to the interference of a wealthy businessman who had initially approached her father about turning time travel into a public attraction and began making trouble when David Wolfe wouldn't go along with him. Nobody in her family actually came back to the Middle Ages for the joy of living in the period anymore. It was all pure, strictly monitored research these days. Though Libby thought Elliot Hemmons's interference had brought about needed regulation for the wrong reasons, she was glad that she'd had a chance to experience time travel when people were still allowed to have fun. She remembered trips to Passfair for the May Day celebration, and discovered that she was as eager for the festival now as she had been then.

"I loved the fair."

"Then it's settl—"

"You're ugly and stupid and I hate you!"

"Henry!" The voice that roared from the doorway was Sir Stephan's. Reynard of Elansted was with him, his hand resting on his sword hilt.

Libby watched, appalled, as the young man whirled on his father and shouted. "It's true! I won't have her." He pointed. "If I must marry one of your friend's daughters, I'll take the Welshwoman instead."

"Get out!"

Matilda was crying, shaking in Marj's embrace. Libby discovered that she was on her feet, shaking as well, but with anger. What had the girl done to deserve Henry DuVrai's shouting at her like that? And why did people keep talking about her getting married? Not that that was important right now. As Henry stomped out she went to kneel in front of Matilda. Something definitely needs to be done about Henry, she thought. She took the girl's hand in her own. Something needed to be done for Matilda as well.

"Why me, Lord?" she muttered.

"Runs in the family," Marj muttered back. "Are we staying?"

Before she could answer she heard Reynard of Elansted say, "You're right, my lord. It's best I and my men stay here until after the fair."

If Reynard was staying, she realized, so were his prisoners. She wanted contact with those prisoners. Maybe she could do something with Matilda, something that didn't break any Time Search rules, while she also worked on her own research.

She looked up at Marj. "Yes," she said. "We're staying for the fair."

May Day morning was absolutely glorious, bright with sunlight, green with spring, the breeze warm and scented with flowers, the crowd was full of laughter and good cheer. Libby, seated with Sibelle and her women on benches on the wide top step of the hall entrance, had a clear view of much of the activity. Colorful tents and stalls were spread through the inner and outer baileys and all the way down into Passfair village. Whenever the breeze shifted it brought the aromas of fresh-baked bread, honey cakes and roasting meat. Merchants and entertainers and townsfolk had come from the surrounding countryside, Canterbury, and as far as London. There was a tourney list set up, and targets for archery. The click and thud of the quarterstaff competition could be heard in the distance. A great pile of wood stood ready to become a bonfire come sunset, and a maypole was set up in the center of the inner bailey, decked with flowers and ribbons. There was a race going on involving relay teams carrying huge baskets of flowers picked from the fields at dawn. Flowers, in fact, were everywhere, worn braided in both men's and women's hair, carried by the children. Colorful garlands were hung on every conceivable spot.

A crown of gilded flowers and a hood of green rested on a length of red velvet on the castle steps, waiting to be awarded to a lucky couple at the end of the day. At Passfair, the most important part of the celebration was the crowning of the Queen of the May and her consort, the Hooded Man.

Libby looked fondly at her godmother. Just being with the serene little woman was helping her. While she'd tried to cope with Matilda and taken part in the life of the castle for the last couple of days she'd enjoyed Sibelle's maternal presence. Even while she hated living in a drafty castle and coping with snide remarks from the priest and clumsy passes from Henry, the time with her godmother had been restful.

Time Search people weren't supposed to have any more impact on the locals than was necessary to conduct research. Libby wondered if there were any rules about the locals having an impact on Time Search personnel. The thought made her turn her head toward the courtyard, where Marj Jones was talking to Sir Reynard. Marj did her best to avoid the man, but he was constantly seeking her out. Their gazes were constantly meeting from across a room. Marj looked haunted, and didn't talk about the sheriff. It was so hard to watch Marj reluctantly falling in love that it hurt.

"They make a handsome couple," Lady Sibelle said as she noticed where her goddaughter's attention was centered. "Of an age and of proper rank. They deal very well together."

"Hmm," was the noncommittal answer.

"Do you wish to discuss the match with Sir Reynard?"

Isabeau jumped as though she'd been struck. "What?"

"Perhaps I should have my lord discuss the subject, then," Sibelle suggested when she saw how startled the girl was at her suggestion.

"No, no," Isabeau told her hurriedly. "I don't think marriage is quite—. No." She cleared her throat. "It isn't possible."

Sibelle looked at the couple in the courtyard, oblivious of all but each other. She doubted very much that Isabeau was correct about the possibility of their coming together, but she said no more about it. Those two were old enough to make their own arrangements without anyone worrying about the formalities.

With marriage very much on her mind on this fire festival day, Sibelle glanced at Matilda. The girl looked handsome this morning, dressed in pale blue, her light brown hair combed out to hang loosely around her face. A wreath of bluebells that matched the color of her eyes crowned her head.

"You're beautiful, my dear," she said, patting the girl's hand. Her words managed to draw a shy smile from Matilda. She'd been smiling more since spending time with Isabeau and away from Henry. The problem was, the girl was going to spend the rest of her life with Henry. "Henry is down by the lists," she said, and stood. So was Guy. While Guy was supposed to be destined for the Church, Sibelle was considering him for Isabeau. She took her goddaughter by one hand, her future daughter-in-law by the other. "Come, ladies. Let us go see how my sons are faring in their practice."

Marj and the sheriff joined them as they crossed the courtyard. Marj put as many people as she could between herself and Reynard, and Libby heard her sigh. Libby gave her a sympathetic look, and sighed herself because she knew Sibelle was interested in her getting a good look at Guy's bare chest. The local custom was for the men to compete bare-chested. The local women no doubt thought it romantic. But she and Marj weren't local, and romance was the last thing either of them needed. Besides, Guy's chest was far from impressive. And he couldn't be a day over fifteen.

And speaking of bare chests, she thought as her attention was drawn to the clattering of quarterstaffs, *Ed needs to go on a diet.*

Ed Feldshuh was sparring with a tall, lanky stranger. Crossing quarterstaffs with a local in a contest was probably close to breaking the rules, but this was the sort of day where it was more conspicuous to observe than to interact. She started to call out encouragement to Ed, but then his opponent whirled around, dark hair flying. She got her first good look at the man as he knocked the heavy staff out of Ed's hands.

The stranger was fast as a cat, his sharp, predator's features intent on the hunt, the triumph in his eyes evident even at this distance. He was not fifteen. And his chest, dark-furred, covered in a sheen of sweat, was very nice indeed.

"Oh, my God," Libby choked out, and stopped dead in her tracks while the world whirled madly around her.

Marj was at her side instantly. "What?" she whispered, taking Libby's arm as she teetered dizzily. "Another headache? What?"

Libby blinked. Her friend was blocking the stranger from her sight. "Headache?" Definitely. Her temples were suddenly throbbing.

The sunlight was too bright, but the air was also full of gibbering shadows. Fortunately, the pain lasted only a moment. Sibelle put her arm around her shoulder, said something soothing, and the disorientation cleared. Libby blinked again, and managed a weak smile for the concerned women gathered around them. Today was May Day, time to party. She refused to go all weird and miss out on all the fun. She had no idea what had brought on the sudden fit, but she had no intention of letting it happen again. Maybe it had been Ed Feldshuh's flabby chest, because it couldn't have anything to do with the man he'd been fighting. She'd never even seen the other man before.

"What were we doing?" Libby wondered, then noticed Matilda. "Oh, yes, Henry." She took the girl by the hand. "Let's go on to the lists, shall we?"

Beyond where she stood the quarterstaff contests went on, but she didn't let her attention be drawn back to the clack and thunk of clashing wood. It was only a few feet to where another group of men were practicing with padded wooden broadswords and shields. Sir Stephan, his sons, his squires, the castle guards and most of the local noblemen were here, leaving the archery and staff competitions to clergy, commoners and women.

Libby took shy Matilda by the hand and stepped determinedly up to the group of men gathered on the edge of the lists. Lady Sibelle gestured her sons over while Libby vowed she was going to have fun, even if she had to do it at the side of the matchmaking mother of a fifteen-year-old. She shared a smile with Lady Sibelle as Sir Stephan and his sons turned their way. Then her determination was shaken within moments, as Henry stepped up to them. He looked sly and mean, expressions that didn't set well on features that were so much like his sweet father's. Libby barely managed to keep from sneering as he snubbed Matilda and gave her an elaborate bow instead. Just looking at Henry made her want to kick him.

"Surely Isabeau is the fairest lady in this company," he said. "No doubt you will be declared Queen of the May."

Matilda moved back, trying to conceal herself behind Libby. Libby, in turn, took a step to the side. "Not I," she said to Henry. "I'm told there's a competition for the honor, and that Matilda is the finest lute player in Kent. I have no such accomplishments." Henry frowned while she continued to extol the virtues of his betrothed. "Matilda has a fine hand with a needle, as her lovely kirtle shows, and she fashioned the wreaths we're wearing in our hair."

"And you have hair like black silk," Henry said. Then he added nastily, "While Matilda has hair like mud."

"My hair is brown," she told him sternly. "No different than Matilda's. Be nice." She glanced anxiously at the girl. Matilda was pale, but she wasn't crying. Not yet.

"Be good, Henry," Sir Stephan warned.

Henry hadn't taken his hot gaze from Libby. She was very aware of the crowd gathered around them even though he didn't seem to be. The whole courtyard had grown silent, even the clacking of the quarterstaff competition was stilled.

"I care not that Matilda's hands are clever for household tasks. I look at your hands and think how they would feel touching me," he added as he grasped Libby by the wrist and forced a kiss on her palm.

Libby kicked him.

She probably hurt herself more than she did the nasty young man, for her shoes were soft and his shin wasn't. His expression became fierce with sudden anger. His grip still tightened painfully around her wrist while he raised his other hand to strike her. Libby gasped as she tried to pull away.

"Henry!" Sir Stephan shouted.

"Hold!" the sheriff called.

The butt of a quarterstaff smacked solidly into the center of the young man's forehead before either of the men could come to the rescue.

As Henry's eyes rolled back in his head and he fell slowly to the ground, a small cheer went up from the watching group. Neither Stephan or Sibelle looked displeased at their son's being knocked unconscious. And Matilda, subdued, docile Matilda, actually gave a quiet giggle before settling dutifully on her knees to see to her almost-lord's injuries.

When Libby turned to thank her rescuer she found herself face to face with the man she'd last seen fighting Ed Feldshuh. He was leaning on the staff he used so well, gazing about him as though he owned the castle and everyone else's presence was a mere inconvenience. His eyes, Libby noted irrelevantly, were green. He was long-limbed and lean-muscled, with an angular face and heavy brows, his beaked nose and sharp cheekbones giving him the appearance of a hunting hawk. He was dressed in softly clinging deerskin braccos. He wore a knife on his belt and wide leather wrist cuffs to strengthen and protect his forearms when using the quarterstaff. Plainly, he was not a knight. Equally plainly, he was the most dangerous man at Passfair.

3

"Kill the peasant!" Father John snarled as he pushed Matilda out of the way to get to Henry. The girl made a frightened sound and fled behind Libby once more.

Sir Stephan crossed his arms and asked, "Why?"

"He struck your son!"

"So he did. Saved me the trouble of doing it myself," he added to approving laughter from the crowd.

"What cause had you to strike Henry?" the priest demanded. "What cause had any man?"

It was the sheriff who answered. "Well, it looked to me that the brat was going to strike Lady Isabeau."

"The Welshwoman had dared to raise her hand—"

"Foot, actually," Libby interrupted. Her correction earned her an acid look from the priest.

Father John pointed dramatically at her rescuer. "How could you allow this man to assault his betters. For shame!"

"Yes, isn't it?" Stephan replied dryly.

With a look of disgust, the stranger began to turn away. Libby would have tried to stop him, but Marj's hand landed warningly on her shoulder before she could get involved.

It was Sir Stephan who said, "Wait, good yeoman." The stranger turned back, one eyebrow raised with sardonic curiosity. "I know not your name, nor have I thanked you yet," Sir Stephan said as he stepped forward to offer his hand to the other man. The stranger hesitated noticeably before clasping Stephan's hand.

"Bastien," he answered. "Bastien of Bale."

He had a deep voice, with a lilt to his accent that made Libby think of Ireland or Wales or perhaps the highlands of Scotland. *He's definitely not from around here*, she thought as he turned toward her and his long, serious face was transformed by a smile. The assessing look in his eyes left her blushing all the way down to her toes. Not one to be intimidated, she looked boldly back.

"The archery contests are beginning. Come with me, *my lady*." He spoke as though she were the only person present, and the way he spoke her title left her confused as to whether the words were meant to be rude or possessive.

Since the man had just rescued her from a potentially humiliating scene she didn't mind how he used the words. "I'll gladly go with you, good sir."

"Not sir. I'm of good, common stock," he corrected as they walked away from the staring group. "Never sir," he continued loudly as people began to murmur behind them. "I'd hate to be a gentleman."

Libby could hear people following them, but she didn't turn around. Bastien also pretended there was no one there, but he did it with a smirk. Rude, she decided, and enjoying the license to be so. She slipped her hand from his. She didn't mind the rudeness, and certainly didn't blame him for it, but it wouldn't do either of them any good for her to go along with it. The Middle Ages were the pits for everybody involved, especially bad for anybody below the aristocratic class. Bastien here seemed to have that fact of life pretty well figured out, and he obviously didn't like it. His attitude was refreshing, actually, but dangerous.

"So," she found herself asking him as they approached the archery range, "what exactly does a yeoman do, anyway?" Yeomen, she knew, were peasants, but they weren't bound to an estate like serfs. They were small landowners who had more freedom in many ways than the nobles who were in power. Bastien, here, probably owned a nearby farm.

"Pay too many taxes," was his reply.

"Besides that."

They stopped walking and he leaned on his staff, his gaze on the archers rather than her. The swish, thwock of the contestants' arrows hitting straw-filled sacks set up as targets became background noise to their conversation as he answered. "Yeoman do what they can, and what the nobles will allow."

"Do you use a bow?" Libby asked as she found herself reminded of Robin Hood.

"I do, my lady."

"As well as you use a quarterstaff?"

He gave her a sidelong look, a definite glint in his narrow green eyes. "You could find out."

Women were allowed to compete in the archery contests. Libby grinned. "You're on."

"On?"

"You are suggesting a wager, aren't you?"

"With a noblewoman? Not I." His smile told her otherwise. "What would a lady wager a peasant with? What might you have that I would need? A poem? A song? A pretty piece of embroidery? What might I wager that you would want?" The look in his eyes told her exactly what he thought he had that she might want, and what he'd want from her.

She looked him over, she couldn't help it, he was lean, far too handsome for his own good, and probably hers as well. Despite the teasing, suggestive thoughts that came to her, she carefully kept them to herself. She should not have suggested a bet, it was totally out of character. Besides, time-traveling amnesiacs had even less business getting involved with the local peasantry than real noblewomen did. She refused to respond to the look he gave her, as she reminded herself that his behavior was completely improper for the period, even more than hers was. He shouldn't have the *chutzpah* to be talking to her.

"We don't have to wager anything," she told him. "Sir Stephan will award a prize to the winning archer."

"I want no prize from Sir Stephan."

Libby gave him a challenging grin. "Who says you're going to win?"

"See how she suffers from the sin of pride, as well?"

Father John again. Libby whirled to face the crowd and the sneering priest. She planted her hands on her hips as she declared, "Who says it's pride? Maybe I'm good at this. Maybe I can—" This was no time to mention the sudden vivid memory of shooting arrows using a recurved bow while riding on a galloping horse. "Use a bow," she finished.

"I can use a bow," Father John answered smugly, "but I do not have to brag about my prowess. Only a foolish woman would—"

"We can all use bows," Lady Sibelle interrupted. "Women and men alike are trained in my lord's household, are we not?" There were nods of agreement as the Lady of Passfair stepped forward. "Come," she said, "let us chose teams, women against men, Matilda, myself, Lady Marjorie and Lady Isabeau against my lord, Sir Reynard, Father John, and Master Bastien. What think you, my lord?" she deferred to Sir Stephan.

Sir Stephan nodded, and slapped the priest on the shoulder. The friendly looking gesture was hard enough to make Father John wince. "I've often heard you praise your talent with a bow since the king did me the great honor of sending you to serve as my chaplain, good father." He looked around at the other men. "How can we lose to mere women with John's prayers and sharp eye to lead us to victory?"

The only man who didn't laugh was Bastien. The only man who didn't quickly gather around the Lord of Passfair was the scowling yeoman. "I have no taste for the competition," he said when the knight gave him a curious look. "I would not challenge my betters," he added. His tone was polite, but his expression was not.

"Snob," Libby muttered under her breath. She was willing to bet he always had been. It was in the nose. It'd almost be a waste not to be arrogant and elitist with a hawk beak like that.

The silence that followed Bastien's words was tense and uncomfortable. It was broken by Sir Reynard slapping him on the back, about as hard as Stephan had jarred the priest. "Don't be troublesome, lad.

Archery's a common man's sport. Compete on your own ground."

"On May Day all are equal," Lady Sibelle added.

After a moment's hesitation, Bastien gave a slight nod, along with a dangerous smile for the crowd. "You are wise, Lady Sibelle, and Sir Reynard is correct. I will fight with the knights of Passfair for today."

"You speak as though you would fight against us on another day," Stephan commented.

Before Bastien could reply, Henry came stumbling up. He had a red knot on his forehead about the size of an egg, but didn't look too worse for wear. Pity, Libby thought, then noticed that he looked more embarrassed than in pain.

He planted himself in front of the man who'd knocked him out and said, "I deserved that." Then he turned to Libby and bowed. "My apologies, Lady Isabeau." His tone was gruff, but he seemed sincere. After Henry spoke to her he glared at the priest, continued to ignore Matilda, and asked, "What's going on?"

Libby exchanged a look with Marj as the challenge was explained to Henry. "What's with the brat?" she whispered to her companion.

"Maybe he needed to get hit on the head," Marj whispered back.

Libby gave a quick look back at Bastien, and the thick wooden staff in his hands. "Think it'd help my memory if I asked him to hit me on the head?"

"Might not hurt to ask."

She didn't intend to ask Bastien of Bale anything. She had the feeling that being involved with him in any way would be dangerous. He was too handsome, too masculine, and belonged to another time. She was glad the group had divided up into teams, that there was something to do besides talk to him. She had no business talking to him, and she didn't need his help with her memory, either, she thought.

Maybe she didn't need any help, at all. Hadn't she just recovered another one of her Mongolian memories without any conscious effort? She wanted to get her hands on a bow, to find out if the memory was as real as she thought it was.

The merry crowd was growing larger around the archery range, waiting for the men and women to begin. Wagers were being made, and loud opinions were being exchanged. Libby grew tired of waiting for Sir Stephan and Lady Sibelle to decide on the rules and went over to pick a bow from a selection being watched over by one of the castle guards. She picked one, waited impatiently for the guard to string it for her, then tested the pull.

"It will do." Her arms were going to hurt from the exercise when this was over, but she'd manage. "May I take a few practice shots?" she asked as the others came over and began choosing their own bows.

"If it's true the Welsh are the finest archers in the world, then it would be cheating for the woman to practice before she shoots," Father John protested.

For a moment, Libby saw red as anger very nearly overtook her. She'd had about as much as she could take of the man's—. Calm down, girl, she reminded herself as she clawed back from the ragged edge of fury. She would not lose her temper. She tried hard not to let him get to her.

In the short time it took her to get her fury under control, Bastien was standing beside her, an expression somewhere between humor and concern in his green eyes. He held an arrow out to her. "Why don't you try putting a practice shot through the priest's tongue?" he suggested.

Libby didn't know whether to be appalled or laugh at his advice. She knew she should be appalled at being tempted to take Bastien up on his words, but Father John was the worst pain in the butt she'd ever met.

"What have I ever done to him?" she asked Bastien instead. You weren't going to talk to Bastien, she reminded herself even as she spoke to him.

He flipped a bit of hair back off his shoulder, the casual grace of the gesture completely riveting Libby's attention. "Perhaps your beauty tempts him to forsake chastity, my lady."

She was so caught up in her fascination with the man that she didn't notice the compliment he'd given her for a moment. When his meaning did hit her she blushed, and turned away, feeling totally out of her depth in dealing with this handsome stranger.

Fortunately for her skittering nerves, Lady Sibelle raised her bow and said, "Let us begin, shall we?"

"They make an attractive couple, don't they?"

"No," was Marj's terse reply to the sheriff's question.

"Well, I think so."

Marj heard the amusement in Sir Reynard's tone, but she didn't see anything funny in the situation. She didn't know why he did, either, and didn't intend to ask.

"He's little more than a peasant," she pointed out. About the handsomest, most macho peasant in the thirteenth century, Marj conceded. And Libby's so much more than she seems, she added to herself. Including the boss's daughter. David Wolfe would not like it if his little girl got involved with anybody, let alone a local, which was against the rules, anyway.

"Heads could roll for this," Marj murmured as she watched Libby blush at something Bastien said. "My head, specifically."

Sir Reynard put his hand, his big, warm hand, comfortingly on her shoulder. "Daffyd ap Bleddyn's a long way away," he reassured her. "And he'd be a fool to hold you accountable for his daughter's actions. She's a woman grown, isn't she?"

Once again, he'd overheard her whispered words. He had excellent hearing, and she had a bad habit of talking to herself. She was acquiring a worse habit of liking the sound of Reynard's deep, rumbling voice. If anyone was breaking the rules here, it was her. Libby, after all, had just met this Bastien of Bale. All right, she was lit up like a spotlight and Bastien practically glowed with sexuality. Everybody in the castle was aware of the attraction. Hell, everybody within a ten-mile radius was probably aware of the attraction between those two. The air temperature went up several degrees when they so much as glanced at each other, but it really wasn't doing any harm. Libby would never see the man after today.

"Let the girl have her holiday," Reynard urged, as though he'd read Marj's thoughts. He gave her shoulder a gentle squeeze. "And remember that today is May Day yourself, my lady."

Marj handed the sheriff her bow to string. "Very well, if it's a holiday, let's get on with the contest."

"Are you any good with a bow?"

"Yes, I am."

"Well, I'm not," he admitted. "In fact, I expect the womenfolk are about to make fools of us men. Not that we don't need to be made fools of every now and then." He gave her one of his deep-dimpled smiles. "Perhaps I should name you my champion and you can wear my colors into battle."

Oh, to hell with Libby, Marj thought as she responded to the sheriff's charm. "Maybe I should."

She wanted to say to hell with the rules as well, but she remembered herself and instead moved away from Reynard of Elansted to take her place among the women. Lady Sibelle had taken her turn, hitting inside the target circle, but not by much. Bastien of Bale lifted his bow to shoot. Marj didn't watch him, she watched Libby watching him. Libby's concentration on Bastien was complete. Looking around at the crowd, Marj decided that Libby's attitude was not very different from that of anyone else at Passfair, though perhaps her flushed cheeks and bright eyes spoke of a bit more personal interest. Still, everyone was watching Bastien with silent intensity while Bastien paid attention to the task at hand. He moved with deliberate grace. The flawless play of muscle and flesh as he drew the bowstring slowly taut was sheer physical poetry. His expression was still, stone-carved, pure concentration.

"I think your lady is much taken with yon archer."

Marj discovered she'd been holding her breath. She gasped when Lady Sibelle whispered in her ear. She missed seeing Bastien release the bowstring as she looked at the woman who'd spoken. As the crowd roared she glanced back quickly to see that Bastien's arrow had buried itself just inside the green inner circle painted on the target.

"He's good," she said, and ignored Sibelle's comment about Libby's interest in the man.

The Lady of Passfair tucked her hands inside her sleeves. "I would be taken with Bastien of Bale myself," she said, "if I were young and ripe for a lover."

Marj looked at Libby as she stepped up to shoot. "She's not ripe for a lover," she told Lady Sibelle. *Not if I have anything to say about it*, she added to herself as Libby gave Bastien a challenging look. He stepped back, looking complacently smug, and leaned casually on his staff when Sir Stephan passed it back to him.

Libby didn't even seem to look at the target as she lifted the bow and shot. After her arrow thwacked dead center in the green circle, Bastien didn't look so smug, but he did answer the impertinent smile she turned on him with one of his own.

The crowd shouted their praise for the lady's skill, while Father John looked appalled. Lady Sibelle chuckled knowingly.

Marj said, "Oh, dear."

Libby wondered why her friend sounded so worried. "Was that too flashy?" she asked Marj as she made way for Father John to take his shot.

She grabbed Marj by the arm and moved back even further as the priest gave her a venomous look before lifting his bow. For a moment she thought he might actually fire the thing at her. He turned his aim on the target, but his hatred was disconcerting. He put his arrow into the target very close to hers.

"Maybe I shouldn't be so conspicuous," she said as she decided that her performance was what the historian was upset about. "I was just trying to show Mr. Bastien of Bale that he's not exactly God's gift to jockdom. He reminds me of my brothers." Actually, he wasn't at all like her brothers. He wasn't like anyone she'd ever known. "He's pretty good, though, isn't he?"

"He's looking at you," Marj said.

"I know." She could *feel* him looking at her, even though she and Marj had moved away from the archery range and there were people between them.

The intensity of the man's gaze followed her, penetrating and compelling. It sent shivers through her, it both warmed and warned her, it made her want to turn back and go to him and turn and run for safety. It made her wonder how long it had been since she'd been with a man, if she'd ever been with a man, and if there was any man quite like Bastien of Bale—in this world or the future one where she belonged. Bastien of Bale made her think of sex, and that was the last thing she needed.

She sighed. "I should not have gotten into this archery contest."

"No," Marj agreed. "What we need to do is get away from Passfair."

"You're right." She sighed. "I thought I could do some good with Matilda, but I haven't thought of a thing to help her. Maybe Matilda's good with a bow," Libby said hopefully. "Maybe she'll win the contest, and Henry will finally think she's wonderful and Lady Sibelle can stop worrying about the two of them ever getting together and then we can leave."

Marj arched one eloquent eyebrow in reply.

"It could happen."

"In your dreams."

"Right." Being taller than most of the crowd, Libby had no trouble watching the girl take her turn from the back. "We'll leave tomorrow," she conceded after Matilda completely missed the target.

"Good."

"Reynard's leaving with his prisoners then, anyway," Libby said. He thinks, she added to herself. In her pouch there was a key. Sometime today she was going to get a chance to use it. She had plans for Sir Reynard's prisoners that neither the sheriff nor Marj Jones would approve of. It was interfering, but there was no way she could stand by and let the men be taken to Reculver to be hanged.

"It's Sir Reynard's turn," she observed as she linked arms with Marj and made her friend move back to the front row of watchers. "Then yours." Marj made a face, but Libby wasn't sure if it was because of Sir Reynard or at having to shoot. Libby did watch Marj watch the sheriff. The historian's look was full of guarded pleasure, pride, and interest as Reynard drew and fired. He just barely missed the green inner circle.

As for herself, Libby firmly kept her attention away from Bastien even though she knew he was only a few feet away. She wondered what it was about these thirteenth-century men that two women of the twenty-first century found so fascinating. They were a pair of barbarians, brimming with testosterone and misogynist notions despite their tiny butts and killer pectorals. Maybe it's the costumes, she thought, maybe the clothes made everyone seem more romantic and desirable. It was like living at a full-time Renaissance fair. This was the sort of thing Elliot Hemmons wanted to provide to a future time, a flesh-and-blood entertainment reality to rent out to those bored with the virtual kind. He had no idea how dangerous these men really were. Libby knew she should be embarrassed that she was uncivilized enough to equate dangerous with sensuous when the words really didn't have anything in common, though her body told her otherwise.

Marj took her shot, also just barely missing the green. When Marj was done and the polite applause had died down, Sir Stephan stepped forward. He lifted a small embroidered pouch for everyone to see. "A dozen silver coins for the winner," he announced. He turned in a slow circle, jingling the coins as he did so. With his other hand he pointed at the archers. "Who shall receive the prize?"

Libby blushed as the spectators began to chant, "Isabeau! Isabeau!"

"Isabeau is Queen of the May," someone called out.

"Ooh, ouch," she muttered. She didn't mind taking the archery prize but she preferred another candidate for the beauty pageant. "Matilda is youngest and fairest in the land!" she called out. "I'll take the coins. Give Matilda the crown!" She grabbed the girl by the hand and pulled her forward. "Here is the May Queen, good people!"

"Isabeau!" was the loud reply from almost every voice.

This was not what she'd intended. Winning the archery contest had been fun, it had been something between her and Bastien of Bale, even if there had been fifty or sixty other people watching. Unfortunately the fifty or sixty other people hadn't known she hadn't been paying any attention to them. They'd been paying attention to her. Now her plans for Matilda were screwed up because she'd forgotten about the audience.

"This world's too damned interactive," she muttered.

When someone else called out "Bastien of Bale is the Hooded Man!" Libby glared at Bastien as though it were his fault he was being declared the most virile male in the vicinity. Much to her annoyance people began to call out "Isabeau and Bastien!"

When Bastien stepped up to her he wasn't carrying his staff. "Lady," he said, gently easing her grip from Matilda's arm, "I think we should accept this honor." As Matilda fled, Bastien's arm went around Libby's waist.

"Well, I don't—"

Her words sputtered to a stop as a knife appeared in his other hand. The knife rested at the base of her throat a moment later. She stared cross-eyed down at the weapon, and forgot to breathe.

"I'll take the lady's prize for myself," Bastien said as Sir Stephan hurried toward them. "And the lady's life as well," he added, "if I don't get what I came for right now."

4

Bastien answered the look of disbelief on Sir Stephan's face by pressing the tip of his dagger a bit deeper in Lady Isabeau's throat. Oh, not so deep as to break her fine, soft skin, but the action held enough menace to warn off the knight. Sir Stephan was a man who believed in some chivalrous ideal, while Bastien took a more realistic view of the treatment of noblewomen. He knew they didn't belong on pedestals. He also knew he wanted nothing to do with their kind, but that a few more minutes of having warm and shapely Isabeau of Lilydrake close in his arms would serve his purpose very well.

"What do you want?" Sir Stephan asked while the crowd gaped and murmured in consternation.

"My men," Bastien answered.

"Your men?"

"The men you're holding in your dungeon."

"The outlaws?" Isabeau asked. Despite fear, there was also curiosity in her voice. "You came for the outlaws? You're an outlaw?"

"Yes."

"Fascinating."

He tightened his grip and began to walk backward toward the keep, using her as both shield and hostage. "Don't faint," he warned as the crowd began to follow them.

"Or you'll be in big trouble," she responded.

"Yes," he agreed. "But remember that no matter what happens, you'll die before I will."

"Am I supposed to find that knowledge comforting?"

He could feel her trembling against his chest, but her voice was steady and full of sarcasm. He had to grudgingly admire even a noblewoman who could manage bravado despite being frightened.

Libby briefly considered driving her elbow into Bastien's flat, bare stomach, but decided that would be a good way to get herself killed. The man's grip was too tight, and the knife too closely pressed to her throat for her to take any risks.

"That dagger hurts, you know," she pointed out as they continued a slow retreat toward the keep.

"I'll try not to leave any scars."

"I'd prefer it if you tried not to leave me dead."

"I'll do my best."

She was oddly reassured by what was probably a lie. "Who are you?" she asked him. "Sikes? I thought Sikes was an old man."

"Sikes is an old man. And how do you know about Sikes?" And why was he having a conversation with this woman when he had a negotiation to get on with? "Reynard," he called to the sheriff, "release your prisoners or the woman dies."

He had not come alone to the fair. Five of his men

were imprisoned in the castle's deep undercroft, five more of his band emerged from the crowd as he approached the outer entrance to the storeroom with his prisoner. They'd done a careful reconnaissance of Passfair since they'd arrived that morning. Their escape plan was set and now they had the leverage to secure their comrades without using force. Bastien thought it was all going quite well.

Then he saw the priest lift his bow. Bastien shouted, "What are you trying to do? Kill her?"

Sir Stephan called a command, and the sheriff a warning, but the priest loosed the arrow anyway.

Bastien barely had time to drag Isabeau to the ground before the arrow whizzed through the air where they'd been standing. He felt the warmth of blood on his hand, for he must have cut her when they fell. A horrible anger at the priest raced through him as he dragged himself and the girl back up.

He continued to hold her before him. This was no time to examine just how badly she might have been wounded. Two of his men flanked them, swords held at the ready, keeping Stephan and the other warriors at bay. The priest was on the ground. Reynard stood over him, holding the bow and looking disgusted.

"Do you live?" Bastien demanded of his prisoner, though he could hear as well as feel her shuddering gasps.

"I'm going to kill him," was her furious answer. "I swear I'm going to kill that son of a—"

"Hush, gentle one. Be meek and obedient and we'll be done soon."

"I'm going to kill you, too."

He had no doubt this young lioness might well try. "Don't be foolish. You're already bleeding, let's not make it worse."

"How do you know you didn't slit my throat?"

"You're still talking."

"Good point. What do you want?"

They'd reached the door of the undercroft where the prisoners were being held. His men had already chased away the guard stationed there. He didn't answer Isabeau but directed his words to Sir Reynard. "I want my men released. It's as simple as that. Give me my men, I give you the girl."

"Now wait—" Sir Reynard began.

"Very well," Sir Stephan cut him off. He gestured the angry sheriff to silence. "Take your vermin and go, Bastien."

"Gladly. Give me the key."

Libby kept still. She nursed her annoyance, and ignored the sharp pain of the cut on the base of her throat. The anger stung more than the slight wound, she was almost more angry than she was afraid. She didn't like the idea of Bastien of Bale rescuing *her* prisoners. Why had she bothered getting the damn key if this discount store Robin Hood was going to show up and do her job for her? When she'd come here to study outlaws she hadn't planned on getting involved in a hostage situation. While the fascinated crowd stared at her and Bastien, Libby watched Sir Stephan hold his hand out to Lady Sibelle.

Sibelle said, "I'm sorry, my dear, but I don't have—I don't recall—Ah, yes, Isabeau has been taking meals to the prisoners. She's quite concerned for their welfare." Sibelle smiled brightly. "Isabeau has the key. How convenient for the swine holding her."

"You have the key?" Bastien whispered in Libby's ear. "I went through all this trouble, and you have the key?"

"You could have asked."

"Give it to me."

"Get it yourself." Libby was annoyed with herself for her own bravado. The man had a knife at her throat, for God's sake. Still, she couldn't help her reckless reaction. She did add helpfully, "It's in my pouch. Watch where you put your hands," she complained after he moved his hand from her waist and brushed her inner thigh before finding the embroidered silk bag hanging from her belt. The brief intimate touch sent a completely unexpected jolt of desire through her.

He moved the knife from her throat long enough to cut the pouch free, then tossed it to one of his men. "Hurry."

The girl reacted in the moment it took him to throw the pouch to Odda. She tried to escape, but he grabbed her by the belt before she could run. She swore in a most unseemly way as he pulled her back into his embrace. He didn't know whether to laugh at her spirit or threaten her with dire punishment for it. Before he could decide, the storeroom door was opened and his captured men came tumbling out.

"Up the south wall walk," he commanded, not giving any of them time to say a word. They weren't the brightest of men, but they reacted well to orders if they were given firmly enough. "Odda, Harald, show them the way." Once they were well on their way to the wooden walkway that circled the inside of the curtain wall he nodded to his remaining followers, grabbed his prisoner firmly by the wrist and ran for the stairs.

"Have you considered going out by the door?" Isabeau demanded as he dragged her to the top of the stairs.

"Too many guards on the gate. And it's the wrong direction," he explained as they raced along the walkway.

His men were already climbing down the ropes that had been secured around the central crenelations while he'd been involved in the archery match. The chance for the diversion had been a godsend, one that made him grateful for obeying the overpowering impulse to protect Lady Isabeau from the overbearing young noble.

The south wall faced the forest. They would have to cross the outer bailey and a deep ditch filled with sharp stakes. It was still a quicker, safer escape route than attempting the main gate and Passfair village where most of Sir Stephan's force was posted. Besides, the stakes faced outward to protect the castle from external attack, the defense would be easy enough to slip through going the opposite way. He also had archers posted at the outer edge of the forest as cover for retreat. He'd planned this escape very carefully.

At the base of the wall was a cart filled with a soft cushion of hay, left there in the chance that any the captives might be too weak to use the ropes. Fortunately, none of the men seemed so worse for wear that they needed to be tossed off the wall. In fact, he noted as he and his hostage reached the group by the rope, the fools who'd gotten themselves captured all looked remarkably healthy.

In fact, far from looking cowed and beaten, two of them went so far as to smile and give courteous bobs of their heads. Not to him.

"Good morrow, my lady," said Aethelstan as he climbed up on the flat section of wall between the high squares of the crenelations.

"Lady Isabeau," said Cynric. "You were right to say we'd see freedom today."

Bastien didn't know whether to glare at his newly freed second-in-command or the Norman woman Cynric seemed so friendly with. "Why would she help you?" he demanded. He gestured for the men to hurry. Aethelstan grabbed the rope and swung out over the wall.

"She has too gentle a heart to let anyone she knows hang," Cynric answered while he waited to take his turn climbing down. "Wanted to know all about our childhoods and such. She likes to listen, does Lady Isabeau. Saw we were fed well, too. Thought she might let us slip away when the bonfires were lit tonight." The older man narrowed his eyes questioningly. "You're not going to hurt the lady, are you, Bas?"

Libby could hear footsteps pounding up the stairs while the men talked. "Go," she ordered. Cynric went, leaving her and her captor the last ones on the walk.

"Who's running this rescue?" Bastien questioned indignantly as the last of his men disappeared over the wall.

"It could have been done with a little less flash," she countered with equal fire.

He thrust a finger under her nose. "I have this situation under control."

"Ha!" she said, and knocked the knife out of his other hand. He gaped at her as the weapon bounced off the wall with a metallic clang. Then, before she quite knew what she was doing, she twined her arms around his neck and pulled him forward. "For luck, as the princess said to the Jedi."

Overtaken by mad impulse she kissed him, her mouth pressing hard against his with swift passion and urgency. It lasted only a moment, it could only last a moment with his life at risk, but the stolen pleasure of it burned a new memory into her mind. The few wild seconds while her lips clung to his almost made up for some of what she'd lost.

When she broke the kiss she put her hands on his chest and pushed very hard. His hips hit the low wall, but the momentum was enough to carry him over the side. He swore at her as he fell toward the ground.

Libby paused only long enough to see that Bastien had landed in the haycart before she snatched up the fallen dagger. She tucked the souvenir from this escapade into the sleeve of her underdress as she turned to face her rescuers.

She knew why she'd helped with the escape. She owed Bastien a favor for his knocking out Henry. He'd saved her, now she'd helped save him. They were even.

She had no idea why she'd kissed him.

Still, she was smiling like a fool at the memory of it when Sir Stephan rushed up to grab her by the arms. "Are you hurt badly? No, it's just a scratch. We saw what you did."

She blushed. "You did?"

"It was brave of you to push the churl off the wall."

"Very," Sir Reynard said dryly as he turned from looking over the wall. "Might as well call your men off, Sir Stephan. It looks like they're going to make it into the forest before we can catch them."

"Pity," Stephan said.

Sir Reynard gave a laconic nod. "We'll get them eventually. And at least we know who the leader of this new band is. He's an interesting rascal, isn't he, my lady?" There was a glint of amusement in Reynard's eyes as he looked her over.

Libby thought he might be teasing her, so she lifted her head proudly, then touched the cut on her throat.

"Interesting isn't how I'd describe him, Sir Reynard. More like a ruthless menace."

"Uh huh." He brushed his fingers gently across her cheek. "Your lips are a bit swollen, my dear, but I didn't see him strike you."

She felt a strong need to get away from Reynard of Elansted's shrewd appraisal. The cut was still bleeding slightly, though she'd forgotten about the pain in the rush of the escape. She cupped her palm over it as she said, "I think I'd best have Lady Sibelle see to this."

"Of course," Sir Stephan said. "Come, let me help you down the stairs. You poor brave child."

Libby almost squirmed with guilt at her godfather's kind words, but she let him practically carry her down to the courtyard without saying another word. She was really glad that arrogant brigand Bastien had shown up at Passfair for May Day. She'd been prepared to help the prisoners on her own if Bastien hadn't taken the matter so dramatically in hand. That would have been a betrayal of the Lord of Passfair, and the sheriff, and, most importantly, the Time Search rules of non-interference.

Knowing the brutal fates of hanging or having their hands chopped off that awaited the outlaws if Reynard had taken them to Reculver had made her lose all objectivity once she'd gotten to know them. They had become people to her, not case studies, but men who'd been forced to try to eke out their existence on the fringes of their own society. While they had attacked her party she couldn't see that the punishment they would receive for it was equal to the crime they had committed.

Despite what he'd done to her, she was glad Bastien had shown up to take care of his own people. His men had been loyal enough not to breathe a word about their leader or their organization when she'd questioned them. Then he'd loyally appeared to rescue them. It would be valuable to study that loyalty. It was the stuff of folktales and legend. It was exactly the sort of thing she'd come here to investigate. He was the sort of man she'd come here to study: a legend in his own time.

"Or at least in his own mind," she muttered as she reached the bottom of the stairs and was surrounded by a gaggle of concerned womenfolk.

"Out!"

"What?"

"You heard me, priest. I want you away from Passfair before the bonfires are lit tonight."

Libby looked from the enraged Sir Stephan to the sputtering Father John who stood before him below the dais. She'd come down from the bower with Marj and Lady Sibelle after being bandaged and changing into fresh clothes. She'd walked in to find the household gathered in the ominously silent great hall. It hadn't been silent for long. As soon as Lady Sibelle joined him on the dais, Sir Stephan had shouted angrily at the priest.

Father John, who had been clutching the side of his head with one hand, drew himself up and pointed at the knight. "I was appointed by the king!"

"And you're being dismissed by me!"

"Why? What have I done?"

Sir Stephan put his hands on his hips. "You very nearly killed one of my guests today."

"I was defending your lands from outlaws."

"By trying to murder a hostage?"

Libby would very much have liked to jump in and ask that question herself, but she forced herself to be silent and let her chivalrous godfather deal with the nasty priest.

"The woman was of no—"

"The woman is my best friend's daughter, an innocent Christian soul, and was in danger enough without your interference. Aiming an arrow at her is unforgivable."

"I thought only to stop the wolfshead. I aimed for the outlaw's head." Father John waved a dismissive hand toward Libby. "I would not bring much harm to a valuable heiress."

"Much?" She couldn't stop herself from shouting in outrage. "How do you define 'much'?" The arguing men ignored her, but Sir Reynard gave her a wide smile before he turned his attention back to Sir Stephan and the priest.

"I mean what I say, priest." Sir Stephan pointed toward the door as two guards stepped forward. "Be gone."

The guards grabbed the priest by the arm. As he was hustled away he glared over his shoulder at Libby. "This is your doing, wicked woman. No woman should have power over men. I'll see you chastised for it, mark my words."

Libby watched in complete consternation as the man was dragged out the door. Much of the crowd followed, laughing and calling, treating Father John's banishment as another entertainment of the holiday. Libby just stood by the dais, shaking her head in confusion as the hall emptied. "What did I do to him?" she wondered. She'd asked the question before, and Bastien had answered with a compliment to her beauty. He hadn't meant his flattering words, of course. She knew that everything he'd done and said had been a lie, but she remembered his voice clearly as he'd answered her question. She remembered the look in his green eyes and the tilt of his head as he'd spoken. She remembered, and she blushed as if his assessing gaze were on her still.

Actually, it was a very good jailbreak, she thought as she pulled herself together and followed the crowd back out to the May Day celebration. Bastien organized a rather brilliant plan, she conceded. She didn't know why she'd criticized him when he really had had the situation well in hand.

Maybe she'd complained about his excellent strategy because she'd been a tad upset. She'd had a right to be upset, of course. But ever since she'd had amnesia she'd tended to mouth off at the least bit of stress. Hopefully this was a side effect and not a normal behavior pattern for her twenty-eight-year-old self. She doubted it, though. She already knew that enjoying adventures was a part of her personality. She could only hope that it was a part that had toned down in the years she was missing from her memory.

She decided not to brood about her behavior, or Bastien of Bale's, either, as she stepped outside. Today she was going to enjoy the festivities. Tomorrow she was going to bid a fond farewell to her godparents, go to Lilydrake, do her research, get her memory back and then go home.

"Everything's going to be just fine," she said as she turned her face up to the warm, spring sunlight.

"Lady Isabeau?"

She turned her head to discover Henry standing by her side. The round, red mark on his forehead went well with the sheepish look on his face. She didn't want to talk to Henry. "Yes?" she asked.

He gave her a jerky bow. "I want to apologize."

"You already did."

He looked even more sheepish, if that was possible, as he went on, "Not just about today, but about everything. I've been very rude and ill-tempered lately. I'm sorry. It's not my fault."

She glowered. "I hate when people say that. If you did something, it's your fault."

Henry blushed and looked away. "You sound like my mother."

He was so boyishly contrite that Libby couldn't help but smile. "No, I think I sound like *my* mother. Besides, you haven't been rude to me," she pointed out. "You've been rude to Matilda."

"There is no need to pay any heed to Matilda's feelings."

"Oh, really?"

He didn't heed her sarcasm. "It is you I have offended and your good graces I seek to enter."

Yeah, right. The kid might be contrite, but he had a convenient memory. "Why have you been rude, anyway?"

"Because of my father."

She had expected him to blame the exiled priest. "Sir Stephan?"

"When Father John was sent from court to be our chaplain Father didn't trust him. So he asked me to gain the man's confidence. So I did. I did what Father John told me, and acted the way he said I should." He looked around furtively, then added, "I came to enjoy the role I was playing."

"Oh?"

"Until today, that is," he hurried to add. "When I nearly struck you I realized that I'd gone too far, that

I'd become the man I was playing. I am so sorry," he said one more time, and went down on his knees in front of her. "Lady Isabeau, forgive me."

Libby looked around in embarrassment. "Gladly. Get up." People were watching, Matilda among them.

He stayed firmly planted on the ground before her. "I will make it up to you, I swear."

"Fine. Let's go look at the—"

"Marry me."

"No way." Her mother had not taught her how to say those words in medieval French, so when she spoke in English all Henry did was look at her and blink.

"Was that 'yes' in Welsh, my lady?"

The sardonic question had come from Sir Reynard, who stood nearby with Marj and Matilda. Matilda, of course, was crying. Libby didn't blame her a bit. Nobody deserved this kind of public repudiation.

She turned back to Henry and swatted him on the ear. "For shame!" she shouted at her underaged suitor. "How dare you speak so to me?"

"Lady, I love you. I would make you ha—"

"Silence! What of my honor? What of your betrothal? What of all I owe your parents? You offend them as well as me with such improper suggestions." This situation had to be resolved quickly, and there was only one way to do it. She backed quickly away from where Henry knelt, his mouth open in shock. "I will not stay under the same roof with a man who has no right to speak so to me." She looked at Marj. "Fetch Edward and Joseph. We're leaving for Lilydrake."

Marj gave a relieved sigh. "Yes, my lady."

"Right now," she added as the historian hurried away.

5

"*There's dried blood* on your chest, lad. Are you hurt?" Cynric asked.

Blood? Bastien touched the spot where his bare skin was stiff with the small dry patch of the stuff. Her blood. He hadn't meant to hurt the girl. He had never intended to do her any real harm.

"Damn the priest."

"Damn all priests, I say," Cynric answered. "But what about the blood?"

There wasn't much, but the sight of it was a caustic reminder. It almost burned the flesh where it clung. "It isn't mine."

He didn't explain further. Cynric seemed fond of the noblewoman, and the last thing he wanted right now was the sharp side of the old man's tongue. He didn't want to talk about Isabeau, but he couldn't help but think of her. He remembered her kissing him, the heat of her mouth, the soft curves of her body molded to his, and how his treacherous body had responded even in the midst of danger. It had been a long time since he'd been kissed. She'd set him on fire, then pushed him away.

He'd left Passfair dazed and still wasn't sure if it was from the fall or from Lady Isabeau's bold kiss. Had she meant to kill him or aid his escape when she toppled him off the wall? Not that he need think of it any more now that he was well away from the poisonous influence of her kind.

"Well, lad, are you hurt or no?" Cynric demanded.

"No. No more than usual." He would have shaken his head, but lights were beginning to flare behind his eyes and movement would only bring on the pain sooner.

Cynric's hand landed on his shoulder. "The headache again, lad?" he asked in a whisper.

"Not yet." The pain didn't come as often as it used to. He'd learned to anticipate just how much he could do before excitement and action brought on the murderous headaches. He could keep going for a while yet. Bastien pushed his friend's hand away. "Let's get back to camp." He wanted to lie down in the darkness of his hut, to be alone and free from thought and movement. "There's a feast of king's deer waiting for us," he added as they set off along the nearly invisible forest trail. "To celebrate your homecoming."

She was restless. Far too restless to just sit and stare at a bank of blank screens. The power pack was working, but the remote monitors were still dead. She was alone in a small, cramped building, but she complained out loud anyway. "It's very difficult to do psychological assessments of barbarian hordes when you can't see them. I thought somebody was supposed to come and fix this thing. It's been hours. Somebody ought to tell the new wonderkid in the physics department that his latest toy isn't working," she added as she lifted the entrance flap.

She walked outside to get some fresh air and turned to look back at the structure she'd just left. On the outside it looked like any other yurt, a round tent made of white felt squatting on the rolling grass plain. On the inside it looked exactly like what it really was, a high-tech observation post set up by Time Search. Libby found the dualism of the lonely structure fascinating. On the outside it blended perfectly into its ancient setting but held the secrets of the future hidden in its heart.

"Amazing, isn't it?" she murmured. *"And totally weird."*

"Yes."

She turned toward the sound of the agreeing voice— and found Bastien of Bale looking coolly at her from a few feet away. He was shirtless, leaning casually on his staff, his thick dark hair whipped away from his spare-boned face by the relentless wind.

"Oh," she said. *"It's you."*

"I've come to fix the monitor."

She eyed the outlaw skeptically. "What are you going to do, poke it with a stick?"

He shrugged. On him the simple gesture was a poetic play of skin and muscle. He looked her over with the most insolent expression she'd ever seen on anyone's face. It sent a rush of heat through her. A pleasant rush—until he put his hand on his dagger hilt and said, "Well, if that doesn't work . . ."

And terror drove her from sleep.

Libby woke up clutching the suddenly throbbing cut on her throat and biting hard on a scream. A whimper came out of the surrounding darkness, sounding over the wild pounding of her heart. Then something warm and wet scraped across her cheek.

It was just the dogs.

And it had just been a dream, she realized as the comforting presence of the animals on either side of her air mattress registered on her senses. It was just a dream, she reminded herself firmly, as her breathing calmed and the pain that was more imagined than real faded. A rather pleasant dream, actually, she decided. Until the outlaw showed up and spoiled—

She smiled into the darkness and scratched and patted the anxious dogs. "It's okay, Luke, Leia. I'm fine. And it wasn't a dream. It was a dream, but it was also another memory. I remember when the sensors broke down—only it wasn't Bastien that showed up, of course." The outlaw's sudden appearance had definitely been her subconscious's way of trotting out yesterday's traumatic events for examination. "So it was partially a dream. I remember the yurt and the sensor failure and that someone was supposed to show up to fix it." And why did she keep remembering things that happened to her in Mongolia?

She pushed off the warm cocoon of the sleeping bag and got to her feet, not with any help from Luke and Leia. In fact, it took a great deal of effort not to trip over the big, affectionate animals as she struggled into a pair of canvas shoes and pulled a long sweatshirt on over the underdress she'd slept in. She hadn't brought the deerhounds with her from Passfair; following her the few miles to Lilydrake had been their idea. They seemed to have gotten used to the sleeping arrangement they'd developed with her at Passfair and weren't about to give it up. They accompanied her now as she made her way outside.

The hall was a burned ruin, and all the outbuildings were in equally bad condition. The thatched roofs had gone up in smoke, their wattle and daub walls had disintegrated in the winter weather. The castle's wooden outer wall had been breached and the inner gate was gone. All that remained standing were the interior defensive walls and two towers. One tower stood next to the empty gate, the second in the center of the bailey. The destroyed wooden hall had been connected to the tower. When the hall had burned the three-story stone tower had remained, but not in very good condition. Ed and Joe had settled in on the tower's top floor, even though it lacked a roof. She and Marj had each claimed closet-sized quarters on the second floor. Fortunately for the horses the paddock fence had been easy to repair and the paddock itself was full of sweet, spring grass.

She picked her way carefully down the narrow, twisting staircase with the help of the beam of a flashlight and no help at all from the dogs. Once outside she found that dawn was pushing its way up the sky and that it was actually warmer outside than in. The thick stone walls held the darkness and the chill very well.

Ed and Joe were already up, sitting by a small cook-fire near the tower entrance. She went to sit with them the instant the smell of fresh coffee reached her.

"Thank God for a few amenities at last. Thanks," she said as Joe handed her an earthenware cup full of strong black coffee.

Joe Lario was a strong-featured, muscular man with a bald spot and artist's hands. Ed Feldshuh was shorter and rounder than Joe, puckish and playful. She had no idea how long she had known them, or how well, but she liked them in the here and now. She and Joe exchanged looks over the tops of their coffee cups.

"Remember anything?" they asked each other.

Libby looked around at the stone walls tinged with gray shadow and pink sunlight. "I remember how this place looked when I was a kid. And Mongolia. I keep getting images from about three or four years ago. I guess that's a start. You guys remember anything?"

"The place does look familiar," Ed said. "I think that's a good sign."

"I think the closer we were to ground zero the worse the effects," Ed suggested.

Libby felt a chill go through her despite the fire and the warm sweatshirt. "Ground zero? That's a grim way of putting it."

"People did die, Libby," Ed said. "Just because we don't remember them doesn't change how bad the accident was. Joe and I were luckier than you were. We weren't so close, so we didn't get as badly hurt. The aftereffects have faded, but I still want to know what happened."

Joe tossed the last few drops from his cup into the fire. As the liquid sizzled away on the hot wood he sighed and said, "I want to remember those people, so I can mourn them."

She shivered again as a knot of anguish tightened in her stomach. Though the day was growing bright with morning sunlight and the fire was a heated glow before her, her world was going dark around the edges. Ghosts of people she couldn't recall lurked in that darkness.

"I wonder what their names were?" Ed asked.

She shook her head, or would have if a wave of dizziness hadn't stopped her. She got the impression of a crowd of frightened people filling the courtyard. The images were all twisted and distorted. She could tell that the people were all dressed in medieval clothing, but she couldn't make out any faces. "Locals?" she questioned. "Were there locals here that day?"

"Maybe," Joe said. "I don't *know*, but my instincts tell me that we weren't alone."

"The one thing I remember clearly," Ed said, "is going up to the top of the outer wall to check the holographic programs."

Joe stood up and slowly turned, studying the bare stone of the outer wall. "That's right, the program had gone down. All the simulated images of guards and castle folk had disappeared."

Libby nodded. "Yes. But there were villagers or a group of pilgrims, or something, who wanted in." She pointed at the empty gate as confused impressions crowded into her brain. "There were some people who shouldn't have been here. At the gate—there was a woman—and I—" Her head was beginning to hurt. She closed her eyes, hoping to bring the distorted images into focus, but all she got was blackness and dizziness instead. "Damn," she said, helpless to stop what was coming, and passed out.

"Well," Marj said when she opened her eyes, "that was an exciting little adventure. Fortunately Ed and Joe were able to put you out before you went completely up in smoke."

Libby had no idea what the woman was talking about. Then she smelled burnt cloth. "I fell into the fire?"

"You fell into the fire."

Libby sat up slowly, and got enthusiastically licked in the face for her trouble. After she'd pushed the dogs away she looked around to discover that she was back in her room, lying on her bedding. Somebody must have carried her inside. She would have preferred being outdoors to the dim, musty dampness of the tower. She was distinctly uncomfortable with the dark closeness of medieval buildings. She stood up and stretched and said, "Oh, boy. Must have been the coffee."

"Yeah. Right," was Marj's caustic reply to her lame joke. She planted herself in front of Libby, with her hands on her hips. "You three were gossiping about the accident, weren't you?"

Marj's worried tone grated on Libby's nerves. She took a few steps toward the doorway, wanting to get out. "Yeah. So?"

"So, how many times have you been warned to take this whole thing slowly and carefully and not try to force the memories back?"

She gave Marj a hug. "I bet that if the stupid TDD project hadn't been so secret the shrinks wouldn't have been so close-mouthed about telling us what we don't know." She laughed again. "I bet the shrinks don't even know what was going on, and Dad wouldn't tell them. You've no idea how tight he keeps Time Search security."

"Oh, yes I do. I feel like I'm walking around blindfolded."

"He'd keep it all in the family if he could."

"I bet. Libby, honey," Marj added worriedly, "will you please take the rest of the day off from trying to get your memory back? You gave me one hell of a scare a few minutes ago."

Libby touched her temples. "I've got quite a headache," she admitted. It's worth the pain, she added to herself. She felt a little tired and a lot scared, but hopeful as well. As disjointed as they were, the memories were stirring. She was willing to ride the pain and confusion down the long, dark tunnel of her missing past. She'd do anything she had to to reach light and understanding at the end. "You're right," she said to the historian. "I won't push it any farther today. Today," she added with a smile, "I have an outlaw to go after."

Marj looked like she was going to protest, then after a few thoughtful seconds said, "Well, that is the research you're supposed to be doing. I assume that after yesterday you've lost all interest in Sikes?"

Libby brushed her fingers across the already healing cut on her throat. The image of a green-eyed brigand filled her mind. "Oh, yes."

"And just how are you going to track this Bastien down?"

Libby went to the pack she'd left sitting next to her bedding. She pulled out a pale yellow kirtle, a belt decorated with jewels and gold filigree medallions, a white silk veil, and Bastien's dagger. She held the dagger up in one hand and the belt in the other to show Marj. "There's enough miniaturized sensor equipment in the belt to track the man down over a hundred-square-mile area. After it gets enough readings off something he's been in contact with, that is. It's been taking readings from his dagger quite long enough."

"Ah, an electronic bloodhound," Marj said as she took the belt to examine. "What a clever family you Wolfes are."

"Yes," Libby agreed.

But a Wolfe hadn't developed the sensing equipment, she recalled even as she answered Marj. Not a Wolfe, but—. The memory slipped away before she could grab it. She couldn't recall who had once proudly handed the gold belt to her, and she had a sudden, bone-deep certainty that she should.

He'd had a wife once, Bastien knew, and she died at Lilydrake. That was all he did know. He lay in the darkness of his hut and tried to capture some old truth as he came fully awake. Confusion was all he got for his efforts, and a dull fading throb from the headache. He'd dreamed through a night of pain and hunted through his dreams for the answers that never came. Now he was awake, alone on a narrow pallet in a hut that bore no resemblance to a home, and he still didn't have his wife.

"I can't remember her face."

"I know, lad," Cynric spoke out of the hut's darkness. "I've heard it before."

The old man sometimes watched over him when he slept. It was meant kindly, so Bastien didn't reach for his dagger to emphasize that he'd rather be alone. He couldn't reach for his dagger anyway, he recalled. She'd knocked it out of his hand. For some foolish reason he found himself smiling at the memory of those last desperate seconds spent in Isabeau's company.

Lady Isabeau, he reminded himself bitterly as thoughts of yesterday replaced the unknown past in his mind. Isabeau was the Lady of Lilydrake. Lady Isabeau of the strong, clever hands, and odd, hard-to-understand way with the Norman's language. He had no reason to smile at anything any of that noble household did. It was their fault. Her fault even if she had never set foot in her father's castle before it was destroyed.

He sat up and ran his hands through his tangled hair. The pain and the dreams had left him sticky with sweat. "I need a wash."

"And some new weapons," the old man added. He shoved a sheathed dagger and an oak quarterstaff toward Bastien. "Don't know why you won't use a sword, lad."

Because he didn't know how to use one, Bastien admitted to himself. "I'm no nobleman trained to fight other noblemen."

"I'm no nobleman either, lad, but I'm good enough with a sword."

"You were a castle guard."

"Before I was turned out for being too old to fight." Cynric cackled. "I've shown 'em who's too old to fight. I've trained many an outlawed peasant to use a sword," he reminded Bastien. "You'd be easy to teach, as good as you are with every other weapon that comes to your hand."

Bastien shook his head. "A bow, a staff and a dagger's all I need." He unsheathed the blade Cynric had brought him. The hilt was finer than he would have chosen for himself, made of carved ivory and studded with jewels, but the double-edged blade was serviceable enough. "Who'd we steal this from?" he wondered.

"A bishop, I think. Hardly a proper toy for a churchman to be carrying."

"I remember him," Bastien said as he got to his feet. "The forests are full of thieves. Even churchmen need to be prepared for battle when they travel. This one wasn't prepared enough." The roof of the hut was too low for him to stand completely upright, so he went past Cynric to stand outside and stretch. When the old man followed him out he said, "I'm going to the stream to bathe. Have the men assembled for a little chat when I get back."

After a bit of consideration, Libby had decided that the yellow dress wasn't suitable attire for surveillance work. So she'd changed into a camouflage jumpsuit made of material that automatically changed colors to match any background. She'd brought as much gear from her own time as she could requisition for her out-law observing purposes. A matching hat covered her hair, while a little judiciously applied dirt on her face and hands served to complete the ensemble.

Marj and the men were back at the castle, and she was up in a tree across a stream from the outlaw camp, a pair of powerful but very miniature binoculars held up to her eyes. The tracking equipment from the belt was stuffed into a voluminous hip pocket, unused at the moment, because she had slipped unseen past several sentries and found her quarry.

He looked like he was getting ready to take a bath.

She'd spotted him as soon as he emerged from a shaky looking stick structure that she didn't quite want to dignify with the term hovel. She'd watched him look around the campsite, and even from a distance she'd noted the disapproving look on his sharp, raptor's face. When he'd started walking in her direction she'd nearly jumped out of her tree and ran for it. She'd relaxed slightly when he stepped off the main path and headed for a pool in the stream that was shaded by a gigantic willow tree. A new tension that was more

anticipation than fear filled her as he reached for the
string that fastened his tunic at the neck.

Libby let herself look at Bastien of Bale while he
took off his overtunic, but then she trained the binoculars toward the huts in the nearby clearing. She had
come here *not* to play voyeur, but to work. Besides,
she'd already been clutched to his nicely furry chest
and didn't need to take a look at it again. And she had
no intention of looking any lower than his chest. She
wasn't that sort of woman. At least she had no recol-
lection of being that sort of woman, though she had to
admit there was a certain temptation. She took a deep
breath, forced the glasses to hold steady on the distance, and concentrated on her work as she heard him
splash into the water not too far away.

Bastien's camp didn't look a thing like a movie version of *Robin Hood*. The half dozen huts were thrown
together out of sticks and bracken. She saw a couple of
smoking cookpits and the carcass of a deer hanging
from the low branches of a tree. The people who slowly
gathered in the center of the clearing wore ragged clothing, along with numerous layers of dirt. Gender was
hard to discern underneath hoods and loose, layered
garments but she thought there were several women in
the group of outlaws. She counted three toddlers and
four or five older children playing around the fires. She
was too far from the small settlement to make out any
conversations and didn't have any remote audio equipment with her to safely eavesdrop.

Nearby, interrupting her watchful silence, Bastien
began to hum. She automatically swung the binoculars
toward the sound. He was a tall man and it was a shallow pool. The water reached only to his lower thighs.

Seeing him naked made her realize one thing about herself. She knew that at some time in her lost years she must have learned a great deal about sex. Because as she looked at Bastien of Bale's long, elegant, beautifully proportioned, muscled body she knew exactly what she wanted to do with it, the places she wanted to touch and taste and hold. She found herself imagining wrapping her thighs around those narrow hips, her fingertips playing across the flat expanse of his stomach, her breasts pressed hard against his chest, her lips working their way from his lips to his toes and slowly back up again. She already knew the scent of him, the texture of his skin, the enveloping strength of his embrace, the taste of his mouth. Without conscious thought her imagination translated the knowledge she already had into a fantasy that left her shaken by desire. The intensity of her need surprised her, and she ended up making some small, frustrated noise in the back of her throat.

It was like the unfulfilled promise of a feast for her soul when she hadn't even known how deep-down hungry she was. It left her confused and trying to grasp memories of the reality she was missing. She was all too aware that while her imagination served up vivid details of sex with this virtual stranger who had no idea she was there, the reality was that she was hiding up in a tree. She was violating his privacy. She shouldn't be looking at him at all. She knew she should turn away, that she had no right to intrude on Bastien this way, but she couldn't quite bring herself to do it. While Bastien splashed and hummed and scrubbed himself clean she pressed herself against the tree branch and worked on calming the aching need that tried to consume her.

And then she went cold with fear as he looked up

and at the tree where she was hiding. Libby slammed down the binoculars and pulled her hat down to cover her face. The pounding of her heart changed to panic. It was the dangerous, cold glitter in his eyes that terrified her. She cowered motionless on the branch as she prayed that the angel-of-death look would pass her by.

The noise that had drawn his attention had sounded like a woman in need. It had been soft and demanding at once, a lustful call that was almost a whimper, not quite a plea, definitely an invitation. He felt as though he had heard it more with his flesh than with his ears and it must have been his imagination, for the soft sound had seemed to come from a tree across the stream. It could have been no more than the calling of a bird, or the wind in the willow branches. Yet, Bastien couldn't shake the feeling that he was being watched as he searched the nearby trees for a sight of what had made the odd sound. He'd been enjoying his privacy and the cool, cleansing water, but now he felt spied upon, vulnerable, more naked somehow. But he couldn't see anyone there. After a few moments of watching he got out of the water and hurriedly dressed. He couldn't shake off the feeling of being watched as he headed back to the camp.

Cynric was waiting for him at the edge of the clearing. He pointed toward the gathered people. "They're waiting."

Bastien nodded and moved forward to face the silent group. "Did you enjoy last night's feast?"

He was answered by nods, cheerful smiles and a few voices. What he remembered of the night before was being nauseated by the smell of roasting meat, and pain lancing into his temples with every laugh or shout from the revelers outside his hut. Sometime after the last roisterers had stumbled off to bed Cynric had offered him a flask of mead, but he hadn't been able to keep the honey brew down. He'd ended up stumbling outside to empty his stomach and interrupting a pair of lovers coupling in the glow of the banked cookfire. He'd hardly noticed at the time, but the memory came back to him now, driving home the point of just how much the lonely outsider he was among his own people.

For a few moments yesterday he'd looked at Isabeau of Lilydrake and been tempted by the seductive, false promise of her beauty. While they'd talked he'd pretended to be something other than he was, and while he pretended he'd almost believed she could offer him an end to his exile from passion. But that had been a dangerous game to save his people from the hangman.

He crossed his arms before him and said sternly, "I'm glad you enjoy being alive. Try to remember how pleasant the sensation feels the next time you consider walking into a trap."

"Trap?" Cynric asked. "What trap?"

He turned toward his second-in-command. "You of all people should have recognized what the new sheriff intended when he escorted Lady Isabeau through the forest. She and her riches were bait in a trap. An obvious trap." One Bastien wouldn't have put past the clever Isabeau having suggested to Reynard. She and Sir Reynard had seemed friendly enough. She'd been friendly with his men while they were captive as well. He wondered why. To his abashed men he said, "I told you to leave the sheriff's party alone before I went hunting. Why didn't you listen? Greed," he said before anyone could offer an excuse. "Pure, simple greed."

Cynric offered him a wide smile. "We knew you'd come for us, Bas."

"I don't know why I bothered. You deserved to be hanged for acting like fools."

"You wouldn't let that happen," Odda spoke up.

"You should have," a voice spoke up from the rear of the gathering. "Sikes would have," Warin of Flaye added as the crowd parted to let him through.

"Sikes can do what he likes in his part of the forest," Bastien announced as the other man came forward.

"That's so," Warin answered. "But it's well known that he considers all parts of the forest to be his."

"So he sends you often enough to remind us," Bastien said.

Warin was small and wiry, a quick-moving, rat-faced man with stringy yellow hair and watery blue eyes. Bastien noted that the outlaw had one hand on his sword hilt and grasped the neck of an earthenware jug in the other. Warin held out the jug to Bastien as he spoke, "Sikes sends me in friendship. Drink up, friend, and let us have a private talk."

Bastien looked the other man over with narrow-eyed suspicion. He still felt an invisible gaze on his back. They were probably safe enough but he felt that his camp was in danger even though Warin had appeared with one of his own sentries as an escort.

"Did he come alone?" he asked the sentry.

"I abide by the terms of our truce," Warin answered indignantly, while the sentry merely nodded.

"Of course you do," Bastien agreed affably. "Check the guard posts," he said to Cynric before he spoke to Warin again. "I'll take your drink, friend." He pointed toward his hut. "And we'll have our private talk about what Sikes wants in my part of the forest."

6

"You could have gotten me killed, you know that, don't you?"

The dogs just continued to lope happily along beside her horse, tongues lolling. They were obviously enjoying being out for a good run while Libby's heart was still pounding from her narrow escape from the forest. It would have been the stupid dogs' fault if she'd gotten caught. Bastien had not been looking happy when he disappeared into one of the huts with one of the other outlaws. She'd been able to tell that from a distance even though she'd put her binoculars away. His already dark mood wouldn't have improved if his guards had brought her into the camp. She'd already had one encounter too many with the leader of the wolvesheads. She wasn't ready for another, at least not yet, and not on his terms. She was glad she'd been able to get away with these idiot animals in tow.

The deerhounds had followed her trail from the castle and ended up sniffing around the base of the tree where she'd been observing the outlaw camp. If they'd started barking when they found her she would have been in big trouble. Fortunately, she and the dogs had managed to sneak past the sentries and back to the clearing on the edge of the forest where she'd left her horse hobbled.

"Don't do that again," she ordered the animals as the path bent and Lilydrake came into view. They ignored her, of course, and started barking as Joe stepped onto the path from the shadow of a tree. Libby quickly brought the horse to a stop as the big man held up a hand to catch her bridle. "What?" she asked.

He pointed toward Lilydrake. "You don't want to go in there dressed like that."

Libby looked up at the ragged crenelations of the castle wall. "Why not?"

"Company," he answered. "Hurry up, Lib, before somebody sees us."

Libby got off the horse and snatched the costume he tossed her. She went behind the nearest clump of bushes and hurried to pull off her camouflage clothing. "I should have carried a change of clothes with me."

"Yes, you should have. You left in way too much of a hurry. Did anybody see you?"

"Of course not."

She hadn't actually worried about being observed except for the few dicey minutes after the dogs showed up. The village nearest Lilydrake was as abandoned as the castle and the barely discernible track she'd taken into the dense forest could only be there for the use of outlaws and poachers. She would have faded easily into the green background if she'd heard anyone approach.

"I didn't think I'd have trouble getting back into my own castle." She emerged from the bushes clad in her yellow dress, the sheer white veil covering her braided hair. "Do I look medieval enough?"

Joe nodded. "And you've got me as an escort when we go in. So nobody's going to think that you've been riding around the countryside by yourself."

Libby resented that anyone would think to question her going anywhere she wanted, dressed any way she wanted, with anyone she wanted. But she also knew that the locals would think her being on her own was strange. It was a good thing Joe had been waiting for her. She had to play by this culture's rules no matter how much they grated on her. She had to try to lead the properly circumspect life of a medieval woman while she was here. Either that, or go back where she came from. "Right," she said after giving herself this stern lecture. "Who's our visitor?"

Joe took the horse's reins and they began to walk toward the gate. "You're assuming there's only one?"

"Lady Sibelle, and Matilda?" Joe nodded. She sighed. "Of course. I should have known I wasn't going to get out of baby-sitting Matilda that easily. Damn. We didn't come here to socialize with the neighbors."

"Yeah, but the neighbors don't know that."

"Time Search needs to do something to cut down on all this interacting. Maybe Mom should pass out copies of the rule book to the locals."

Joe chuckled. "That might work. We could get some monks to do it up with fancy calligraphy and illumination. Too bad hardly anybody back here can read."

"Yeah." Libby ran her gaze across the top of the wall as they neared the gate. "There's not a cloud in the sky, right?"

"Right." Joe looked up. "You're imagining seeing moving shadows on the wall, right? Castle guards?"

"Yeah. How do you know?"

"I've been standing in the woods for hours watching the same men-shaped shadows playing hide and seek in the merlons and crenelations. I think we're hallucinating."

Libby gave him a skeptical look. "The same hallucination? Do we get group rates on it?"

He shrugged. "We've got the same memories even if we don't know what they are. I think our eyes are trying to see what we remember being there."

"Ed's holographic guard images?"

"Those were the only guards the castle had. I remember looking up from the edge of the woods and watching them patrolling, and thinking that they looked as real as life. That was when we went on that pic—"

"—nic," Libby finished. She stopped in her tracks, heart pounding excitedly. Vivid images came as she spoke. "It was fall, late fall but warm. The leaves were gold and brown and red. There was champagne—we drank it out of wooden goblets. Blankets. On the ground right here. Red and blue and green plaid blankets, those scratchy, wool, handwoven things. We sat on them and wrapped ourselves in them when the day turned a little cold. It wasn't a picnic, it—"

"It was Thanksgiving. Back in the future it was Thanksgiving."

"Right. And we had a party. For—I don't remember what it was for. Not just Thanksgiving. We had a party." She looked at Joe. His eyes were as full of excitement as hers must have been. "I remember the party, but I don't remember you being there."

"I don't remember you, either. But I remember there was a party."

"And we—all five of us—spent a lot of time looking up at the marching holographic images and giving them names and histories and—" She closed her eyes and felt the bracing autumn wind on her cheeks and heard a rich, masculine laugh and her mouth was filled with the heat of a kiss that tasted like champagne.

As the princess said to the . . .

Pain lanced through her temples, driving the jumbled almost-memory into nightmare terror. Her eyes snapped open, and she took in deep gulps of warm, spring air to fight the threatening dizziness. The pain faded within seconds.

As it did she looked up into Joe Lario's dark, worried gaze. "Was it you?"

"What?"

"That kis—" Libby turned away. She shook her head. She didn't want to know. She didn't know what she didn't want to know, but she knew she didn't want to know it yet. She suddenly found herself in front of a doorway she didn't want to open. She was afraid there was something behind it she couldn't handle. It had to do with being kissed. "Why don't I go talk to Lady Sibelle," she said and walked hurriedly toward a meeting with her godmother to avoid thinking about a romantic entanglement she was terrified to consider.

It was worse inside the castle than she'd anticipated. At least twenty people stopped what they were doing to look at her when she walked into the inner bailey. She had no idea who all these strangers were. Nor did she care who they were when she caught sight of Marj standing firmly before the entrance of the main tower, blocking Lady Sibelle from going inside.

"Oh, dear." She hurried forward.

Lady Sibelle held out her hands to Libby as she approached. "My dear, you rushed off in such a hurry yesterday I was worried. Not that I blame you, of course." She shook her head sadly. "After Henry caused such a scene you did the only thing you could. I am so sorry for that boy's foolish words. So my lord and I decided that the loan of some of Passfair's serfs to you was the only possible way to make amends," she went on before Libby could get a word in. "As many as we could spare, to help rebuild and to get a garden started though it's late. Also a few maidservants for the hall and some fowls and sheep and people to look after them, of course. And a cook. You can't do without a cook, my dear."

"I can't?"

Lady Sibelle patted her hands. "Of course not. In truth, my dear," she went on while Libby gaped, "I've never approved of your father taking his serfs off to Wales and then leaving only a few guards to look after his castle. Look what came of it. I can't imagine outlaws looting the place if Sir Daffyd had been in residence."

It occurred to Libby that she was going to have to find out just what the local residents knew and surmised about the destruction of Lilydrake. First, however, she had to get her godmother to go away. "Yes, well—"

"I'd wager the guards invited the outlaws in and ran off to live in the forest with them, since no trace was found of the treacherous wretches." Lady Sibelle took her hand from Libby's long enough to waggle a finger under her nose. "You really should have brought more people with you."

"There's a war in Wales," Marj broke in to explain. "Lord Daffyd could spare no more men, and he trusted Lady Isabeau to find people to serve her at the summer fairs here."

Libby took a dazed look around the crowded courtyard. This was a disaster of monumental proportions. These locals did not belong here. How was she going to get out of this? She looked back at her godmother. "I'm overwhelmed by your kindness, Lady Sibelle. I'm sure you mean the best for me, dear godmother, but how can I accept such generosity? Surely, you need these workers for your own fields and household. I mean, with Henry and Matilda's wedding to prepare for and—"

"Ah, Matilda." Lady Sibelle waved forward the girl standing shyly in the background. "Matilda, of course, will stay here to attend you."

"Attend me?" Libby shot a panicked look at Marj. "Lady Marjorie and I—"

"Will teach the dear girl about running her own household as she helps you set your own in order." Sibelle patted Matilda on the head. "Won't you, my dear?"

"Yes, my lady," Matilda whispered. Libby was about to continue protesting, but then the girl gave her an imploring look from under tear-damp lashes. It struck her straight to heart. "I will serve you well. Please, Lady Isabeau, say I may stay."

Oh, hell. The kid needed somebody to love her. Libby didn't know how she could deny affection to someone who needed it that badly. Which was what Lady Sibelle must have counted on when she brought her future daughter-in-law here. There wasn't a Wolfe born that wasn't a sucker for lost puppies, whether the variety was human or canine.

Libby sighed. "Of course you may stay," she said to Matilda.

She looked at Marj again, and at Joe and Ed who had come up to see what she was going to do about the uninvited visitors. It was her call, she realized. She was supposedly in charge here, the Lady of Lilydrake as it were. What was she going to do? She was going to hide her comfortable air mattress and warm Thinsulated bedroll, that's what she was going to do. They were going to hide the coffee and the freeze-dried food and live on dried peas and wild game and other local fare. Yuck. And all their other modern equipment was going to have to be carefully put away—fortunately most of the things they'd brought with them were disguised to look like they belonged in the thirteenth century. The assignment could still be carried out as long as they were careful. After all, the most important reason they were here was to get their memories back. They could do that in the company of a group of locals and not change history in the process. Couldn't they? Of course they could. And surely she could manage to sneak off to study the outlaws without any of the locals observing what she was doing. This would delay rebuilding the timegate, but that couldn't be helped.

She turned to her companions. "Master Edward."

"Yes, my lady?" Ed asked after a moment's hesitation.

"Gather the appropriate materials and use as many of these men as you need to repair the buildings."

"My lady?" Marj said, her voice a high-pitched squeak.

Libby ignored her. "We have returned to Lilydrake

to rebuild the castle and rebuild it we will," she said decisively. "Master Joseph."

Joe was grinning. He said in English, "I guess we're not going to send out for Chinese tonight."

"Guess not," she replied in the same language. In Norman she said, "I appoint you seneschal to manage the fields and flocks and household."

He gave her a bow. "As my lady wishes." He actually seemed to like the idea.

She noticed that Marj had an appalled expression on her face. Libby started to take the suddenly pale historian aside to say something reassuring, then she glanced to where Marj's gaze was riveted. More newcomers had ridden into the courtyard.

"Oh, dear."

"Greetings, ladies," Reynard of Elansted called as he swung off his horse.

Marj sidled over to Libby. "What's he doing here?" she whispered without taking her eyes off the sheriff.

Libby would have shrugged, but a heavy, gloved hand landed on her shoulder before she could make the gesture. As Sir Reynard swung her around, he said, "How fair you look, Lady Isabeau." His gaze was on Marj as he spoke. "All you ladies are lovely today." He smelled of horse and leather and he wore a smirk beneath his luxuriant mustache. "I've come to stay for a few days," he told Libby. He waved back toward the four soldiers who'd ridden in with him. "I and my men."

Libby looked around frantically. "But—," she asked, "why?"

"After yesterday I grew worried for your safety. So I've come to protect you from the outlaws, of course," he answered cheerfully. "I'm sure your father would want me to take care of you. It's my duty."

There was a firm set to his jaw that belied the gently amused sparkle in his eyes. She could tell he wasn't about to be talked out of camping with everyone else in the ruins of Lilydrake. Libby just barely repressed a sigh. "How—chivalrous. And neighborly," she added with a helpless look toward Lady Sibelle.

How aggravating, she thought.

He didn't know if he wanted the nightmares or not, though they were the closest thing to memories he had. He did know he didn't want the skull-splitting pain that waking from the nightmares always brought. Bastien groaned and flung an arm over his eyes. His hand came down on the jug Warin had left behind. Wine, perhaps, more than dreaming, had brought on this morning's agony. He remembered that he and Warin had talked deep into the night, but he had no idea what they'd discussed. It was often that way with Warin. Sikes's man brought strong wine raided from French merchants as they traveled along the port roads. The potent drink always tasted foul, but it brought forgetfulness to Bastien. He didn't know why he was grateful for the wine's effect, since he'd forgotten enough for a lifetime already, but he always welcomed Warin into his hut.

Until the morning came tromping heavily on his head.

"There's a price to be paid for peace," he said, and was surprised that he had the strength to croak out even those words.

"Well, you look like you've paid enough for now," Cynric said from nearby.

Bastien was glad the old man was in the hut. "Is Warin gone?" he asked through the pain. The price for leadership was ignoring any hurt to body or soul. Especially hurt he'd been fool enough to inflict on himself.

"Warin left before the first light," Cynric answered. "I set Odda to follow him. He came back an hour ago."

Attention to details was another key to leadership. Bastien had been trying to find Sikes's camp for some time. It bothered him that the elusive old fox knew his band's whereabouts but kept his own hiding hole secret.

Bastien made himself sit up as he asked, "And?"

"And Odda lost Warin's trail near Lilydrake."

"Damn." Bastien scrubbed his hands across his face, scraping the palms on beard stubble. His mouth felt like something furry had used it for a den. When he looked up, Cynric's gaze was riveted worriedly on him. "Yes?"

"Did you dream, Bas?"

Shadow figures skittered and faded across his mind. No image stayed long enough to be securely caught. "I dreamed."

"Thought so." Cynric paused, then added, "You called out a woman's name."

Excitement rushed through Bastien's blood. He lifted his head eagerly. "A name? Who?"

Cynric cleared his throat, then he licked his lips while Bastien waited impatiently. Finally, he said, "Isabeau."

"Isabeau?" Bastien repeated the word, but it made no sense. He didn't know anyone named Isa—. "Oh, her."

He got up and walked from the hut. Cynric followed him out. The day was mercifully overcast, the breeze cool against his throbbing temples.

"Odda brought news."

Bastien turned his head at Cynric's words. "Of Sikes? You said he lost Warin."

"That he did. Near Lilydrake."

Bastien was tired of hearing the name. "What is Lilydrake to me?" *The place where my heart's buried*, he mourned silently. His heart and his sanity. The saints knew how he would have survived if Cynric hadn't found him as he wandered mad and feverish away from that cursed castle. He could remember being at the gate with a woman—his wife—though he could not conjure the image of a face and form he knew he loved.

"Lady Isabeau's in residence at the castle."

"The place is a burned wreck." It hurt to say the words in a calm, cold voice. He remembered fire, and screams, and running and running until his lungs nearly burst. He'd run away from Lilydrake. "The place is cursed."

"Perhaps, Bas, but the good lady is there. She has workmen repairing the walls. And . . ." Cynric paused dramatically.

"Out with it."

"The sheriff's in residence as well."

"Reynard? At Lilydrake? Not two miles from our camp?" Cynric nodded. "Come to hunt us down with the lady's help, has he?"

"Now, we don't know that the lady is helping him. She was friendly to us when we were prisoners, you'll recall my telling you."

"Aristocrats care nothing for peasants like us," Bastien reminded his friend angrily. "Nothing!" Heads turned their way at his shout.

Cynric held up a conciliatory hand. "As you say, Bas. Don't get your temper up. Stay cool. You're at your best when you think cool instead of hot."

That was true. It was better when logic ruled emotion. Bastien took a deep breath, ignored the pain and tried to use his mind. "So, Sir Reynard's come to hunt us, has he? Using Lilydrake as a base? We'll have to move the camp."

"That's sense."

"And we'll need to know his plans—how much time he can spare to search the forest, how many men he has, how Lady Isabeau and her stronghold figure into his schemes." He rubbed his hands across his bearded, rough cheeks once more. "We need a spy," he said. "Someone inside Lilydrake."

"And how do we do that?" Cynric asked.

"It's easily enough done," Bastien answered. "You said there were workmen repairing the castle."

"There are."

"Then all I have to do is join the work gang to make my way into the castle."

"You? You'll be recognized."

"I won't be recognized."

"You swore you'd never go near the place."

"I'm breaking my vow."

"Better if I go."

"You're too old."

"Odda, then."

"He's our best tracker. I want him to find Sikes's lair."

"Harald?"

Bastien put a hand on Cynric's arm. "You'll need Harald to help you organize moving the camp. Enough, friend. I know you fear the place will drive me mad. It won't."

Cynric didn't look happy, but he nodded. "You, then."

He didn't want to go back. He did fear for what sanity he had recovered. He refused to live in fear of a pile of stones. So he would go back. Better to ride the devil than let it ride him. It had been riding him long enough.

"Me."

7

Her hands landed *on his chest. They paused there, the palms laid flat across his nipples. The warmth from the contact singed into his skin, into his being. He didn't move, he didn't open his eyes, he just waited, breathless, anticipating, longing. All she was doing was resting the flat of her hands against him, but the surge of desire that moved through him was as powerful as from any caress.*

"Shh," she whispered, though he hadn't made any noise. Her lips touched the base of his throat, leaving one soft kiss before moving away. Her hands traveled slowly down to his stomach. They paused there while he longed for them to make their way down to his groin. While he held his breath in anticipation her lips circled one bared nipple. He gasped as the soft heat of her mouth touched him. She suckled for a moment, then gave one sharp nip. He nearly jumped out of his skin in reaction. So, she was in one of her wild moods, was she? He laughed, and grabbed her by the arms. They

wrestled for a moment, her skirts tangling around both of them, then he had her beneath him and he was kissing her. Her mouth was sweet and hot and fire danced between them. She moved eagerly beneath him as his hand found her breast. She was tangled up, wrapped in a cocoon of heavy cloth like a present to be opened. There were at least two layers of linen between his hand and the hard bud he sought. He teased and played with the hidden nipple, making her moan in pleasure and frustration while they shared a hungry kiss. Finally, he paused long enough to look into her eyes.

Her beautiful brown eyes.

Were her eyes supposed to be brown?

"Isabeau?"

She blinked. Her eye color didn't change. Her face was clear when he'd gotten used to seeing only shadows. "What?"

"What are you doing here?"

"Where?" She spoke in some foreign tongue, yet he could understand it.

"Here. What are you doing here?"

She gave him a wide, wicked, hopeful grin. "Having sex?"

Anger rose in him, killing passion. "Not with me, you're not!"

"But, Bas—"

"You have no business here! When she reached out to him he pushed her away. "No! I want my—"

"Wife," Bastien whispered into the dark as he woke from the dream. Nightmare. Who the devil was Isabeau of Lilydrake that she *dared* to intrude on his dreams? The anger that surged through him at the thought was as hot as the passion of the dream. Nobles were greedy. They'd steal anything they could from a man, including his dreams.

He found that his body was tight and aching, covered in sweat. In the dream he'd wanted his lover very badly, it had all seemed very real. In the dream there had been the promise of pleasure, completion, release. Now he was alone and still lustful. He deserved the pain, he reasoned, just punishment for dreaming about the wrong woman.

Isabeau of Lilydrake was to blame. What man wouldn't remember the feel of her soft skin, the clean smell of her, the sensuous shadow play of her body as she moved in her bright silk clothing? She was everything a poor man could dream of in a woman, forbidden fruit, all the more tempting for being so far from reach. But his arms had circled her once, and in those few moments she'd spun a web of desire with her kiss that he still hadn't fought off.

Just why was he really at Lilydrake? he asked himself as he lay back on the hard beaten earth of the hut. There were a dozen such structures hastily built for the workers who crowded into them to sleep. A short, fierce dispute during the evening meal had convinced the other peasants that he needed a sleeping place to himself, so he was alone. He was thankful that no one was there to witness his shame if he'd cried out the lady's name in his dream.

Right now he wanted Isabeau of Lilydrake.

He hated wanting her, but his body wouldn't let him deny it. That was why he was spying on the rebuilding of her stronghold, spying on her. She hadn't seen him as he'd mingled with the workmen, but he'd seen her often. Unreasonable as the drive was, he wanted to see her now.

He wished he had the will to stay put, to wait for the dawn, but he got up and left the hovel to move silently through the moonlit courtyard. The sheriff had men on patrol on the castle wall, but Bastien knew how to use the shadows well. No one saw him. Nor did the castle give up any of the secrets of his past to his searching gaze while he crossed the inner bailey. He'd had some faint hope that returning would bring back the memory of why he and his love had been at Lilydrake that day. In a way, it was a relief that the memories hadn't come back to distract him.

His goal was the central tower, the unguarded entrance to the lady's chamber, but the newly hung doorway creaked open before he reached it. Before anyone could come outside his back was pressed against the tower wall, his hand on his hidden dagger. The dogs came out first, their lean, alert shapes frosted by the moon. They stopped and looked his way, sniffed the air, but kept his presence to themselves. He smiled, satisfied that his efforts to gain the animals' trust in the last two days had not been in vain. He was no stranger, and they were too intent on some other mission right now to come to him for a petting.

"Go on," Lady Isabeau's voice called to them from the doorway. "Do your business. I want to get back to bed." The dogs bounded off into the darkness. "They need to be housebroken," she said to someone who had accompanied her. "Besides, I was having trouble sleeping."

"You were moaning in your sleep, my lady."

"I was not," Isabeau answered sharply.

"And twisting in a most unseemly fashion."

"I was just trying to get comfortable."

"And whispering about baring your breasts to—"

"Matilda!"

So, the lady was having restless dreams of her own, Bastien thought. Wanton dreams of him, perhaps? He caught himself smiling at the thought and fought down the curiosity.

"I want to go for a walk. Why don't you go back to bed?"

Yes, Matilda, Bastien urged silently. *Go back to bed.* He wanted to be the one to accompany Isabeau on her walk.

Isabeau stepped from the doorway and turned her face up to the sky. Her hair flowed down her back like a dark river. Bastien wondered what it would be like to gather up the heavy locks in his hands, to push them aside and press his lips to the base of her slender neck. He almost took a step forward when she spoke.

"What a night," she said, almost reverently. "It's so clear here. The air tastes of moonlight and night-blooming flowers."

"The wind's coming from the stable," Matilda answered, and yawned again.

Isabeau laughed, and turned quickly around, her thin linen underdress swirling around her legs. The material clung, outlining her breasts and the length of her thighs. Bastien's body was growing tight with need and he prayed Matilda would go away.

"You have no romance in your soul, Matilda," Isabeau told the girl. "But you do have a pretty good nose. Very well, the night smells of horses and hay. It's not such an unpleasant smell."

"No, my lady," the girl agreed. She sounded distressed by Isabeau's words.

Isabeau must have heard the hurt as well, for she said, "There's nothing wrong with being practical. And

if you think I've insulted you, tell me so. Don't let anyone get away with treating you with less than the
respect you deserve."

"But, my lady—"

"Isabeau. Just Isabeau. We're equals." Isabeau
moved out of the moonlight, so he could no longer see
her, but he could hear her voice. "You have to learn to
stand up for yourself."

"Henry would not like—"

"Especially to Henry. Haven't you seen how his
mother leads Sir Stephan around by his—I mean,
haven't you seen what an equal relationship his parents
have? Henry's used to strong women. But I think his
mother's maybe a little too smart and Henry doesn't
know he's used to strong women. Sibelle is subtle. I'm
not sure Henry understands subtle."

"I am not subtle."

"Me either. I'm more likely to kick a man in the
ball—I mean—"

"Shin?" Matilda supplied with a giggle.

"Yeah, shin. Anyway, I'm more likely to yell at a
man who is acting like an ass than I am to wheedle
what I want out of him."

Bastien listened to this conversation with almost
amused fascination. So, here was what women talked
about when they were alone. And here was what Lady
Isabeau of Lilydrake thought she was about. Was she
really so honest and direct? Or was she lying to herself
as well as Matilda?

"I have seen you raise your voice to Henry," Matilda
conceded. "He liked it."

Isabeau sighed. "I know. Why don't you try it? You
can't let Henry get away with treating you badly."

"He is my lord."

"He's your husband—or will be. Marriage is a part-nership, you have to respect each other."

Bastien found himself nodding agreement at the woman's words. His marriage had been like that. It broke his heart to know that it was gone. He felt the threatened sting of tears behind his eyes and cursed the noblewoman for reminding him of his loss. He damned her even as he found something to admire in her attitude.

"Your words confuse me, Isabeau, but I will think on them," Matilda said softly as the dogs came bound-ing back to the tower. One stopped to sniff at Bastien but he pushed it away before he was noticed.

"All right, you two," Isabeau said to the animals, "let's get back to bed, shall we?"

He would much rather it be him rather than the dogs and the girl who accompanied Lady Isabeau back to her chamber. But he stayed where he was, aware that now was not the time to follow her inside. Though he'd learned something of the woman, acting on hun-gry impulse had been a mistake. She slept with her women and the dogs in the tower, so the tower was no place to confront her. He had to get her alone.

"You kissed me, woman," he whispered into the lonely night. "Soon I'll be kissing you. And more."

"I have got to get the man alone."

"What?" Marj asked.

Libby didn't answer. She shouldn't have spoken aloud, but her belt was sending out short bursts of heat that tingled the spot just above her navel. The belt sensor had not been built to draw attention to its wearer. What it was silently telling her right now was that Bastien of Bale was nearby. She supposed that he was concealed under a hood and a stooped walk amid the group of workmen she, Marj and Matilda were observing. He was probably the one who'd just paused in his work to pet the two no-good watchdogs who'd run off to mingle with the workers as soon as they were let out of the tower.

She didn't know why Bastien was at Lilydrake, but she'd first sensed his presence two days before. Her supposition was that he was spying on the intentions of the sheriff. If she'd been an outlaw based only a few miles from the castle, she'd want to know what Reynard was doing in the neighborhood.

"Trying to get a date with Jones," she muttered, "that's what he's doing."

"What?" Marj asked again. She planted herself firmly in front of Libby. "Lady Isabeau, are you well?"

No, she wasn't all right. She was having headaches and weird dreams that weren't exactly dreams but weren't memories, either. And Bastien of Bale was hiding out in her castle when he was supposed to be running around in the forest where she could study his activities. If the blasted man didn't start cooperating with her research soon she was going to be tempted to turn him in. Maybe then the sheriff would leave, she could find some other outlaw to investigate and she could have a decent night's nightmaring that didn't involve fooling around with the man who'd held a knife to her throat. Last night she'd very nearly gone off to kick him awake for a confrontation that was really more about her over-active, libidinous subconscious than about his proximity. Only Matilda's presence had stopped her from doing something really stupid when she'd taken the dogs out.

"I'm fine," she told Marj.

"Ah, good morrow, ladies," the rich voice of the sheriff rumbled before any more could be said. "What a fine sight to greet the day with." He came striding up to them from the direction of the wall tower. His cheeks looked freshly shaved, his mustache was trimmed, and he had a bright smile turned on Marj. "Lady Marjorie," he said. "Think you your lady might spare you from your duties for the day?"

Marj turned a look on her that was both panic-stricken and hopeful. "I do not think that—"

"Oh, go on," Libby said as an idea occurred to her. While Marj was by her side the sheriff was there as well. Even if Bastien hadn't been in the castle she wouldn't have been able to venture alone into Blean. Reynard of Elansted was always nearby, always vigilant. Maybe if he went off with Marj she could get some work done. "I think you should spend your day with Sir Reynard," Libby told the historian. "It will do you good."

"You see," Reynard said. He momentarily turned his smile on Libby, "Your lady thinks of your welfare, and mine. You have my gratitude, Lady Isabeau."

"But—" Marj said. "I don't think—"

"It'll do you good to stop thinking for a while," Libby said cheerfully. "Won't it, Matilda?"

He held out his hand. Marj looked at it as though she didn't know what hands were for, then she looked up into his smiling face. She took his hand, and was still sputtering that she shouldn't be doing this as he led her off.

Matilda gaped after them until they disappeared from view. When she looked back at Libby the girl was blushing. "What do you think they'll do? Together. Alone?"

"What I think they're going to do," she told Matilda, "is none of our business."

The girl blushed a darker red. "Yes. Of course." She looked at the ground, then at the sky, then at the men working within earshot of their conversation. "Lady Isabeau?"

"Yes, dear?"

"May I talk to you? Alone? About things?" She leaned close and whispered, "About men and women?"

Libby knew that theoretically Isabeau was a maiden herself, and wasn't supposed to know about these *things* either. Obviously Matilda found her far more worldly than she was supposed to be. It was probably those dreams the girl had been overhearing.

She sighed. "We live in an earthy age, child, with little privacy. I'm surprised you don't already know—"

"I do!" Matilda looked around hastily. "I know, basically. But—"

Well, if Lady Sibelle or the girl's mother hadn't explained the finer points, it was about time someone did. All Libby could do was hope that she didn't mess up "the talk" since she wasn't sure if all those heated dreams she'd been having had any basis in her memory. Frankly, she wished she could just hand the girl her romance novel collection and a couple of Harrison Ford movies for an audiovisual explanation of what romance was all about.

She pointed toward the wall tower. "The roof's repaired. Let's go up there and look at the view while we talk."

The warmth from the blinking belt sensor intensified as they moved away. She didn't look back, but apparently Bastien of Bale was following them. She wondered why. She didn't mind, as she was looking for a chance to get him alone. Maybe one would present itself soon. She also wondered if having him listening in was going to interfere with the sex education lecture. For Matilda's sake, it had better not.

"In your sleep you spoke about tongues."

Libby blushed. She looked out on the sight of forest and fields beyond the castle wall. "Did I?"

"What have tongues to do with coupling? What should I do with my tongue to please Henry?"

Bastien was lurking on the walk that led from the tower to the curtain wall. He was hidden from view by the top of the tower wall, deliberately spying on them. How could she talk about tongues—and stuff—with Bastien of Bale not ten feet away?

She looked down at the freshly mended wood, then up at a passing flock of birds. What to say? He was going to laugh at her, wasn't he? She looked back at Matilda.

The girl tucked her hands in her sleeves and said meekly, "Father John said that women's tongues were to be kept behind their teeth, that they should be silent."

Let him laugh.

"Father John's a jer—an ass."

"Henry would agree with him."

"Henry needs training. Now, about tongues." She stepped close to Matilda and began to whisper as softly, but as clearly as she could, into the girl's ear.

Bastien felt like a bloody fool as he knelt behind the tower wall. He was trying to look like a busy servant while he listened in on the women's conversation. The worst part was that all he could hear was an occasional giggle from Lady Matilda. Whatever Isabeau was saying was definitely shocking and amusing the girl by turns. It fed his imagination almost beyond all limits.

It was proof positive that the noblewoman was a wanton who deserved any shame he might bring on her and her house. She was already debauched. Perhaps all he needed to do to punish the owners of Lilydrake was to make a public scandal out of the woman's private vice. The seduction would be as sweet as the revenge. Perhaps that was his real reason for returning to Lilydrake, not to spy on Reynard, but to find a way to pay the owners back for what had happened to him here. Taking the heiress to his bed would make a good beginning to his revenge.

The thought brought Bastien up in shock. Seduction? Was vengeance worth such treachery to all he'd loved and lost? Did he truly mean to take Isabeau of Lilydrake to bed? To commit adultery for the sake of retribution? It wasn't his wife's fault the memory of her was a faded, uncatchable thing. Gone or not, she was his wife, the woman he'd sworn to be faithful to.

He was shaking with disgust, at himself and the Jezebel wiles being taught to the girl on the tower when he forced himself to stand and walk away. He didn't return to the work crew, but walked out the castle gate. He had stayed too long for no good reason. It was time to return to the forest.

Where's he going? Libby wondered as she stood on the tower and watched Bastien of Bale make his exit from Lilydrake. She could tell by his stiff-backed walk that the man was furious about something. The further

Bastien was from the belt sensor the slower and cooler the pulses became. By the time he was out of sight the signal had stopped altogether. Libby touched the numb spot over her stomach. For a moment it seemed that she was missing the thrumming of a second heartbeat that was as necessary to her life as her own.

The momentary loneliness was broken when Matilda tugged on her sleeve. "My lady, look!"

She was looking, but his form had disappeared beyond the thick stone walls of the keep. "He's gone," she told the girl.

"No, he hasn't even arrived yet."

There was fear in Matilda's voice. Fear and excitement. When Libby looked at the girl, she saw hope as well. "Who?"

Matilda pointed toward the road. "Henry."

Oh, God, not Henry too. Libby felt like dropping her face into her hands and crying. She didn't know why they'd bothered to come back to a secret installation that was turning out to be the main tourist attraction in Kent.

"Maybe I should just open up a bed and breakfast," she muttered. Then she gave Matilda a hard perusal. The girl looked like she was getting ready to sniff. "No crying. You haven't cried since you got here and I don't want you starting now. He isn't worth it." No man's worth it, she added to herself, and found that she was thinking of Bastien's abrupt retreat back into Blean Forest.

As Henry and his men rode noisily through the gate she almost wished she'd gone with him.

8

Dining at Lilydrake was alfresco. The household gathered outdoors to eat the main meal at trestle tables set up under large canopies. Libby thought this was a pleasant way to eat while the new hall was under construction, as long as the weather was fair and there weren't too many jellied eels on the menu. This evening, fortunately, the cook had provided them with fish, cheese and fresh-baked bread. The sunset-vivid sky was clear and it was still too early in the warm season for bugs to be a nuisance. Libby thought she could almost have enjoyed dinner, if her latest uninvited guest wasn't seated by her side.

Unfortunately, the era's strict code of precedence dictated that she share her trencher with the highest ranking nobleman at her table, who happened to be Henry. Marj had said so. Then again, Marj was probably just trying to get even for Libby having sent her off to spend the day with Reynard.

Marj was sitting on her other side. Libby leaned close to her and whispered, "So, did you have a good time?"

Before Marj could answer, Henry put his hand on her shoulder, claiming her attention. "You are more lovely than I recalled," he declared. "I've missed you, sweet lady."

Libby glared at him. "I'm sure Matilda missed you, as well. You should look at her when you tell *her* how lovely she is."

"I was not speaking to—"

"Don't get started."

Henry jumped at her sharp tone. "Lady Isabeau?"

She looked past him to the girl seated on Henry's right. Matilda was wide-eyed and pale with misery, but she wasn't crying. That, at least, was an improvement. "Remember what we've been talking about?" Libby asked her. Matilda nodded. "Why don't you discuss it with Henry?"

Matilda made a small, faint, whimpering sound, but she did reach out to put her hand on Henry's sleeve. "My lord?"

Henry jumped again, like he'd been bitten. "You have a voice?"

"Be good," Libby directed him sternly.

Then she deliberately turned away, in hopes that the two would start working out their relationship on their own. What she saw when she looked elsewhere was Marj and Reynard with their heads together, deep in quiet conversation. Oh, hell, she thought, love was in bloom all around her. She bet even Bastien had gone home to one of the women at the outlaw encampment. She didn't like the thought.

Even though her interest in Bastien was supposed to be purely professional, she wasn't feeling at all objective about the man. It was an infatuation that would pass if she'd ever stop dreaming about the man and started remembering just who she'd once been involved with. She was convinced there was someone she had been involved with.

She glanced down the table to where Joe Lario sat. He was talking to Ed. She wondered how old he was, and if he was married. And, if so, was he married to her? She remembered being kissed, and she remembered Joe. She didn't know if the two went together at all. She concentrated on her feelings for Joe Lario, but all she could come up with was that she liked him.

All right, if it hadn't been Joe that had kissed her on that remembered day, who had? She briefly considered Ed. No way. Maybe the only logical explanation was that her memory of being kissed during the Thanksgiving picnic wasn't a memory at all. Maybe it was just wishful thinking, a product of her overactive imagination. Like her hot dreams about the outlaw.

Maybe, she thought as she looked around the gathered household. The sight of the costumed diners under the pretty canopies and servants moving around the torchlit setting would have made her mother's medievalist heart sing. It was all so perfectly period. Somebody was even tuning a lute in preparation for entertaining the company. Libby didn't want to hear it. She didn't want these people here. If she was going to be anywhere in the Middle Ages she wanted it to be on the windswept, barren, vast, *empty* Asian steppes, not in the crowded English countryside.

She wanted desperately to be alone.

She stood up. And all the noise immediately stopped. Every gaze turned her way. She pushed back her chair and a servant hurried forward to offer her help. Henry sprang up to offer his hand. Marj and Matilda moved to join her.

She was the bloody Lady of Lilydrake and these people were taking the Middle Ages too damn seriously. They believed in this aristocratic hierarchy. This was her fief and she was complete ruler of it. They lived to serve her.

"Like a bloody queen bee," she muttered.

"My lady," Marj said, warningly.

Libby gave her an annoyed look and waved her back to the table, back to the waiting Reynard. "I want to be alone." She motioned Matilda away as well. "Entertain Henry," she ordered. "I'm going for a walk."

Before anyone could stop her she stomped away and headed for the castle gate. The dogs bounded along at her heels. Maybe they served her because they loved her, not because she was the highest ranking officer in the place.

There was one other possibility.

She didn't want to think about it, so she walked on along the moonlit path and just concentrated on finding her way. She didn't hear anyone but the dogs following her from the castle. All she wanted was to be left alone, and as long as she was left alone there wouldn't be any trouble.

She didn't want to think about that other possibility, but she did. She couldn't stop the progression of her troubled thoughts, as hard as she tried. She knew there had been five people involved in the time machine accident, but only three had gotten back to the future. No one knew what had happened to the other two. Missing, presumed dead. Probably dead. She didn't know their names, hadn't yet remembered their faces. Nobody, not even her mother or father, had told her more than the bare facts of what had happened. If she'd had some romantic connection to one of the missing people the information certainly hadn't been included in her briefing for this mission.

Then again, maybe nobody back at Time Search knew she'd been involved with anyone. More importantly, maybe she hadn't been and her memory of being kissed during the picnic was false. Maybe she'd gotten her impulsive kissing of Bastien mixed into her recovering memories. She hoped and prayed that was the truth, because the thought of having to mourn a love she didn't yet know she'd lost was too hard to contemplate.

"The Bastien theory makes more sense," she said as she entered the ruins where Lilydrake village had once stood. Not only would it make more sense, but dealing with her impractical attraction to the outlaw would be far less painful than the alternative of coping with the loss that she feared. Bastien was here and now, something tangible she could cope with. She hated the thought of having had a part of her life ripped away. How did one cope with that kind of pain?

The track widened into a square, and Libby looked around, recognizing her surroundings even though they were moon-frosted and weather-damaged. There wasn't much left of the few village buildings. Much of what had been left had been scavenged by the workmen as material for repairing the castle. The only standing structure she could make out was the hulking stones of the Norman church. Of course, it was a Norman church, this was Norman England. It was just that she'd been to this church in her own time. In the twenty-first century it was a tiny restored gem of the period's religious architecture. In the present period it was a temporarily abandoned hulk, home to rats, bats, and outlaws if the sudden pulsing from her belt sensor was any indication.

"Well, well, well," she murmured, and reached down to scratch the head of one of the suddenly alert dogs. "It looks like he didn't go very far."

So Bastien was still spying on Lilydrake. The thought brought on a rush of pleasure. Libby couldn't help but smile in the direction of the church. It was ridiculous, she knew it was, to have this tingling of anticipation just because Bastien was nearby. She smiled up at the moon. "Maybe the tingle's a sensor malfunction."

She doubted it. Unreasonably, stupidly, against all the rules, she was attracted to the man. It was dangerous not to admit it. Having admitted it, she could ignore it and get on with the job. All right, so she'd seen him naked, and he'd held her in his arms, and when she'd kissed him he'd kissed back.

Never mind what had happened, the context had been all wrong. He was interested in watching the sheriff. She was interested in studying outlaw behavior. Neither of them had any personal reason for being near each other.

Still, he hadn't gone far, and she was here, alone as she so rarely was. She should grab the chance to do some research while she had it.

"I think it's time Bastien of Bale and I had a little talk," she murmured as she moved toward the church door.

"I was married here." He spoke without turning around.

He knew she was standing behind him. It was as though he'd felt her approach. He hated his almost tangible awareness of her presence. She was nothing to him. She was the enemy. He turned toward where she stood framed in the doorway, beautiful as a ghost in moonlight.

"Married?"

Her voice held colors and shades of meaning. The one word held more questions than he was prepared to answer. She took a step forward, into shadow, out of light, closer to him. He could almost feel the warmth of her nearness in the cold emptiness of the church. He took a step back, toward the altar, the place where he'd spoken his wedding vows. Isabeau followed like a temptress from the devil. He wondered if holy water would drive her away. He wondered if he'd use it if he had any to hand.

"What are you doing here?" he demanded, as if he didn't know why a woman would be alone in the dark with a man.

"I want to talk to you."

He laughed.

"You needn't take that tone," she said, voice as chill as a winter wind.

"I'm not the one who did the kissing."

She cleared her throat. "Point taken. But I'm here to talk, that's all."

"You're a fool."

Instead of reacting with indignation that a peasant should speak so to her, she laughed. A soft, self-mocking laugh. "Possibly," she agreed.

"I'm a dangerous man," he reminded the Lady of Lilydrake. "You should run in terror at the sight of me."

"Well, if I could see you in this gloom maybe I would."

The dogs were with her. They padded forward silently to sniff him. It took some effort to push their heads away.

"I think they like you," she said. She didn't sound intimidated in the least. "But then, you've worked hard on gaining their trust."

So, she knew he'd been in her castle. "You should have told the sheriff."

"Yes, I should have."

Bastien sneered at the woman. She no doubt expected him to be grateful for keeping his presence at the castle secret. "What are you trying to purchase from me with your silence?"

"Purchase?" she sounded puzzled. "Why do you use that term? I thought this society worked mostly on a barter system, along with vows of obligation between lord and vassal."

"I'm neither lord nor vassal," he reminded her. "I live outside the law."

"I know. That's what I'd like to talk to you about. I'm going about this all wrong, I know, but I don't know when I'll get another chance to speak with you."

"You're insane," he told her. "Moon mad."

"I know. But I still want to talk to you."

"Why?"

"I want to know about your life. How you came to be outlawed, what you're doing in Blean."

"It's none of your business." Besides, he didn't know. Trying to think about it made his head hurt. "Cynric found me," he heard himself say, answering her despite himself.

"When?"

"It doesn't matter."

He didn't know why he was listening to the woman. He should take her jewels and run. But this was a church, somehow it would be wrong to rob her in the church. He'd come here to pray for his wife's soul, not to commit another sin, no matter how much the woman deserved it.

"It matters to me."

"Go away," he told her. "Go while you can."

Libby heard the man's rough tone and thought that perhaps she was making a big mistake. He was right, she should go. This was no way to conduct research. She wasn't observing, she was interacting, and she couldn't help herself despite the stupid Time Search rules. The urgency, the pain, even the anger in the man's voice drew her to him. She had an almost overwhelming urge to take him in her arms and comfort him. Something he probably didn't need or want.

There was another, far more primal drive that urged her into his embrace. Desire for him had haunted her dreams, and as she confronted him it raced through all her senses, making her distrust all her reactions. She would not allow dreams to control her actions.

She did take another step closer. He flinched as she moved, his fingers going up to his temples. "Does your head hurt?" she asked.

Libby knew about headaches and had an intimate hatred of them. She sympathized with anyone who suffered from them, even bloodthirsty outlaws. She wanted to stroke the pain away, but she carefully kept her hands at her sides instead. She was not going to touch the man. She couldn't trust herself to touch the man.

"Yes," he snarled eventually. "My head hurts. Go away."

Not tonight, I've got a headache. She just barely stopped herself from muttering the words out loud. She didn't want the man to think she was mocking him. He wouldn't understand the joke, or that she used sarcasm to cope with her own mixed-up, pain-laden life.

"Do you get them often? The headaches?" she asked, relentless even though she knew it would be wiser to take his advice and leave.

He sank to sit cross-legged on the floor. "There's no getting away from you, is there?"

"Well, you could leave."

"I was here first."

"It's my property."

"You would remind me of that."

This bickering seemed familiar, and far more good-natured than the tense situation should warrant. Badgering Bastien of Bale came easily. She'd noticed that even while he was holding a knife to her throat.

She sat down in front of him. She could barely make out his features in the gloom, just a sketch of sharp cheekbones, a hint of his wide mouth and narrow eyes. Enough to know he was there. Enough to talk to. Enough to tantalize her imagination. "How long have you been an outlaw?"

"Will you leave me alone?"

"No. How long?"

"I thought you were sympathizing with my headache."

"I am. I get them too. Talking helps."

"Liar."

"It *might* help. Have you tried it?"

"Wine helps, and sleep. No. Not sleep."

"Sleep doesn't help," she agreed. "When you sleep, you dream."

"Everyone dreams, or so Cynric tells me."

"How long have you been an outlaw?" she repeated.

He sighed, and capitulated. "Six months with Cynric's band. My band."

"How were you outlawed? Why?"

"It doesn't matter. Men hunted me. I ran. I didn't get caught."

Something he'd said was setting off warning alarms in her head. People had come to the gates just before the accident. Had Bastien—Bastien the cunning outlaw—come to rob Lilydrake and gotten robbed of his memory instead? No. It couldn't be, she thought. Could it? Could he have been involved—?

"Six months. Headaches. How long have you had the headaches? Where did Cynric find you? You said you're married? There was a woman at—? Do you remember the fire at Lilydrake?"

His head came up sharply, his breath coming out in an angry hiss. He moved swiftly, grabbing her by the shoulders, pulling her close. "What do you know of the fire? What do you know of the woman?" He shook her hard. "My woman."

Bastien's fury sent a shiver of fear through her, his anguish lashed her. She hurt for him, but she controlled her reaction to say calmly, "I wasn't there." She wasn't sure she should lie to him like this. But she wasn't *supposed* to have been there. But if he'd seen her—? If he had information—

"I don't believe you." His voice was calm, the kind of calm found in the eye of a hurricane.

"What do you know?" she demanded, as desperate as he was furious. "Tell me. I need to know."

"You need to know. Always what *you* need."

"You don't even know me!"

"I know your kind, *Lady Isabeau.*"

Lord, but the man knew how to turn a title into an insult. "You don't know me," she insisted. She wanted to tell him that she didn't know herself, either, but this was not the time. She needed to know what he knew about the accident. Perhaps it would help her get her memory back. "What were you doing there? You and your wife?"

He ignored her questions. "What happened to her? How did she die?" He shook her again. "Was it your doing?"

"What were you doing at Lilydrake?" she demanded in turn. "Would you have killed us when you broke into the castle?"

They were talking at cross-purposes, and the situation was definitely out of control. Libby knew that she should calm down, think logically. Most importantly, she should get away from the man before he drew a weapon and she was forced to do something drastic to escape. She should stay in persona, act like a frightened woman, and run away. The frightened part wouldn't be acting. Yet, even through the fear she was drawn to him.

He pulled her closer to him. With his lips close to her ear, his voice as soft as a caress, he said, "Tell me everything, and you may see another sunrise."

The velvet-voiced threat sent cold terror through her, and a hot rush of desire. Her own reaction angered her more than his words. He was large, dangerous and lawless, but she refused to be intimidated, or seduced by power.

"Let go of me."

Bastien laughed. The sound had an insane edge to it. He heard himself as though from a distance, through a haze of confused pain. Control was coming hard. If he let it go he didn't know what he would do to Isabeau, but he knew they would both regret it. He wanted to let her go, to deal with her when he was lucid, but his hands refused to release their grip. His soul screamed for revenge. His body was aware of every warm, inviting curve and hollow of hers, of her heat and vulnerable softness. And some demon of lust was whispering to him that the altar behind them was wide enough for him to lay her down and take her. That would be the beginning of sweet revenge, though he knew that was not the kind he truly wanted.

"I gave you a chance to leave, lady. You should have listened."

"I've decided to leave now. Let go of me."

"I'm not one of your serfs. I give the commands here."

The man's arrogance infuriated her, but not so much that she wasn't aware that he was technically correct in thinking he was in control of the situation. "What if I say please?" she asked.

The dogs had backed away when they'd started arguing. She heard them moving around them. One reacted to the tension with a low, warning growl. She didn't think the threat from the dog was the reason Bastien let her go and took a step back. Then another. He retreated as far as the altar and all she could make out was his darker outline in the heavy darkness of the room. His breathing was loud and ragged, her own echoed his as they both fought to master their emotions.

He didn't know why he'd responded to her sudden humility. It shouldn't have mattered that she asked instead of demanded. It had mattered. It had stopped him from hurting her, at least for the moment. It didn't stop him from wanting her.

She stood before him in a patch of moonlight filtered through a small side window, tall, head lifted proudly as she faced him, hands clasped nervously together, giving the lie to her fearless stance. The stained glass painted her in a patchwork of muted, silver-tinged colors, confusing his perceptions. She looked different, not like the Lady Isabeau he'd held close, twice now, with threats of violence mixed with desire. She looked like someone else, but her name wasn't Isabeau. Pain stabbed through his head when he tried to remember hearing her called by another name.

Perhaps he'd never heard that other name. Perhaps it had been in one of his dreams. "I'm mad, you know," he said. Lights were beginning to burst behind his eyes. He would be blind in a moment.

"I know," she answered, and her voice seemed to come from very far away. "It's not your fault. It's mine."

He wanted to ask what she meant, but words would no longer come. All his senses were concentrated on the pain. Slowly, he sank to his knees. Humiliation burned through him at his weakness. If she touched him now, he would kill her. Then the dogs started barking and the sound drove into his head like hot nails.

When the deerhounds headed noisily toward the door Libby realized someone was coming. "Damn," she muttered. This was no time for an interruption. She glanced to where Bastien huddled, barely visible by the altar. She understood exactly what the man was going through; she'd been there herself not so long ago. Only she'd had doctors and painkillers and therapists. Never mind what he'd done, he'd had six months of hell. Something had to be done about it.

"Lady Isabeau?" Reynard called from just outside the door.

But not now.

"Sheriff," she called back loudly, and rushed outside.

"Are you all right, my lady?" he asked as she came tumbling through the door, barely managing not to trip over the dogs who insisted on going through the doorway first. "Blasted spoiled animals," he added as they sniffed at him and jumped up to be petted.

"Bless them," she said, thankful for the distraction Luke and Leia were providing. "What are you doing here?" she asked as she stood firmly in front of the church entrance.

"Looking for you, of course. Lady Marjorie is worried."

She doubted Marj had sent him looking for her. Marj Jones knew that she was armed to the teeth, though all of it was carefully camouflaged and only supposed to be used in emergency situations. Even the garnet-studded hairpins holding on her veil were designed to explode. She was just glad she hadn't been forced to use any of her disguised armory on Bastien of Bale. There'd been a few minutes there when she'd been very tempted.

"What were you doing in the church?"

"Praying."

Reynard moved to step around her. With the help of the dogs she blocked his way. "Alone?" His voice was a deep, suspicious rumble.

"Of course."

"You're sure? I thought I heard voices as I came across the square."

"I pray loudly."

"In a man's voice as well as your own, lady?"

Damn. Reynard of Elansted was far too clever. She was not going to turn Bastien over to him. Maybe the outlaw deserved to be arrested. Not now. Not if she had anything to do with it.

She stepped determinedly forward and took Reynard by the hand. "I think we ought to return to the castle now," she told him.

He chuckled. "I take it you don't want me to see who's in the church? Was it a lover's tryst I interrupted, then?"

"I'm not prepared to answer that," she replied, as prim and proper as she possibly could.

"What would your father say, lady?"

He would say she was a fool to mess with someone like Bastien of Bale, she said to herself. "My father trusts me, Sir Reynard," she said to the sheriff. "As should you. Come along," she said as she tugged on his hand.

Much to her relief all he did was chuckle again, and let her lead him away from the church.

9

The air was damp, *not really cold, but uncomfortably chilling. She shivered and pulled her cape close around her as she stepped outside the hall. Thin wisps of mist curled in the courtyard. Her head ached. She'd probably drunk just a little too much the day before, but she felt like she'd been drugged. Her memory of the party was muzzy, unfocused. That wasn't like her. She shook her head, and wished she hadn't. She'd come outside because she thought she'd heard something, but the bailey was silent, and empty of everything but the ghost-like mist.*

"Must have been my imagination."

"Must have," Ed answered.

She didn't know when she'd stopped being alone. The two of them were standing by the gate, though she hadn't noticed moving.

"I better go check the holoprojector."

She nodded. Someone knocked on the heavy wooden door. A woman called out. Outside the gate, someone screamed. Then the screaming came from inside the gate.

The gate was open without anyone having unlocked it.

A woman ran across the courtyard, skirts and red mane flying. Men poured in. Weapons were raised.

The next scream came from her own throat. Terror shook her. Nowhere was safe. She ran for the tower.

Bastien was there before her. He was wild-eyed, frantic. He fought off a swordsman with his quarter-staff, then turned on her, angry-eyed. He pushed her inside. "You'll be safe here."

"No! There's no safety there! Don't you under-stand? It's going to—"

He grabbed her, and kissed her hard. So hard she felt bruised and branded. He stroked her cheek, ran a finger across her lips. He started to say something.

One of the invaders called out, "That's Bas! Get him!"

He ran away. He left her. Then the darkness came and swallowed her whole.

She woke up in darkness, curled up in a knot and sobbing her heart out. "It was just a dream," she whispered when she finally knew she was awake, but it was a long time before reality settled on her. She realized that she was in the tower room she shared with the other women, lying on the straw-mattress bed Ed had made for her. The room wasn't as grimly dark as she'd thought it was. Maybe the world wasn't either.

Libby sat up and wiped her eyes. "That was a bad one." When she took her hands away from her face she became aware of the two dogs and two women who were all carefully watching her. She looked at Marj. "Tell me I wasn't talking in my sleep?"

"You were talking in your sleep," Marj replied. She

looked significantly at Matilda. "But the words were in your native tongue, Lady Isabeau."

She shook hair out of her face. "What time is it?"

"Just past Prime," Matilda answered.

Which made it sometime in the early morning. She didn't remember going to bed. She only remembered coming back to the castle with Reynard. She'd had a headache by the time they'd come through the gate. After that was all a blank. Too much of her life was a blank and she was getting sick of it. Much of the dream had been real. It had been confusing, disjointed, but full of some painful truths. She just had to organize her thoughts, sort out memory from imagery.

"I can do that," she said.

"Do what, my lady?"

She glanced from one concerned face to the other. "I need to be alone."

As she got out of bed the women and the dogs stepped back. She quickly pulled a silk chemise over her head. She always wore silk next to her skin, it was a habit she'd picked up in Mongolia. Then she put on an overdress Matilda handed her and let Marj lace up the back fastening since it would have taken her longer to do it herself. Once Marj was done fussing with her, she rushed out the door, heedless of her bare feet and uncombed hair.

She went up to the tower roof, where she could look out over the forest as she thought. It was a cloudy day, and the dark green depths of the woods looked mysterious and forbidding. Bastien was somewhere in the forest. Wherever he was, she knew now that he was as lost as she was. For a long time all she could do was wonder where he was and what he was doing.

She knew what Bastien had been going to say, and it

bothered her. Mostly because it couldn't be true. Partially because she wanted it to be true—or her subconscious wouldn't have included it in the dream. Her subconscious was just going to have to get hold of itself. He might haunt her dreams, but Bastien was not the man of her dreams. He couldn't be. They were quite literally from different worlds. Worlds that could collide and clash but never connect. It was against the rules for a very good reason. They were aliens to each other, they could never be together. It was wrong.

"Besides, he's married." No, he was a widower, and he blamed her for his wife's death. Maybe he had good cause.

"You talk to yourself too much, you know that, don't you?"

Libby sighed, and turned to face Marj. "Yeah, I know." She eyed a steaming cup in the woman's hands. "What's that?"

Marj looked into the cup, then said, "I don't know. Matilda made it. She says you've been talking too much and this'll help calm your nerves."

"She's right."

"She's worried about you. So am I. You going to drink this stuff?" Marj held the cup toward her.

Libby sniffed the concoction. "Familiar. Has it got opium in it? Don't tell me Lady Sibelle sent along her recipe book?"

"Matilda says every girl needs to know how to brew a few 'simples.' So, why are we up here?" Marj asked as Libby took the cup from her and dumped it over the side of the tower. "You aren't looking into the woods and pining for your own dear love, are you?"

Libby blushed, and turned quickly away. Marj came

to stand beside her. They leaned on the parapet and didn't say anything for a while. Birds called, and the sun came out from behind a bank of clouds. They could hear Joe and Ed giving orders to the castle workmen. Eventually Libby said, "I need to talk to them. I think I got some memories back last night. We need to compare notes."

"What about Bastien?" Marj asked.

Libby gave the historian a sideways look. "What about him?"

"Reynard said you were with him last night."

Libby straightened abruptly. "What?"

"In the church. Were you?"

"How did he know?"

"You were with him last night." The woman's tone implied that far more than a casual conversation had taken place.

"No. Not like that. I was doing research. He's my research contact, remember?"

Marj leaned forward, resting her arms on the flat stone surface of the wall. "It's hard *not* to interact, Libby. I *know*. You know I know. I didn't come up here to accuse you of inappropriate behavior. My granddaddy would say that was the pot calling the kettle black," she added. "Though since the man never used anything but a microwave I doubt if he knew what he was talking about."

Libby gave a wry laugh. Then she gave Marj a puzzled look. "If Reynard knew it was Bastien why didn't he arrest him?"

"He suspected it was Bastien. An obvious assumption considering the way you two reacted to each other back at Passfair." While Libby winced, Marj went on,

"Reynard figured it was only a matter of time before you two saw each other again."

"It wasn't like that," Libby protested. "At least, I didn't expect to see him. I don't think he was interested in seeing me. He's spying on the sheriff. That's why he was at the church." And praying for his late wife, she reminded herself. Libby wondered what exactly had happened to the red-haired woman.

Marj shook her head. "So Bastien suspects Reynard is setting him up. Meanwhile, Reynard's using Bastien the same way you are. You don't turn him in because he's a research subject. Reynard doesn't arrest him because he wants all the outlaws and is going to use Bastien—your and Bastien's obvious attraction—"

"It isn't that obvious."

"Ha. Reynard's going to use that attraction to trap Bastien, and to track the criminals down."

"Why, that manipulative scumbag!" Libby was angry enough to march down to where Reynard was drilling his men and throw him out of *her* castle.

"He's just doing his job."

"He's using me."

"You're using the people here, why shouldn't they do the same? Our ancestors aren't any less complicated and conniving than we are."

Libby hated to acknowledge the truth of Marj's words. She hated the fact that anyone had to use anyone. She especially hated the fact that Reynard was using her as a tool to trap a wounded man. "When did he tell you all this? Why did he tell you?"

"He is here to protect you, too. He knows that's my primary function. Besides, since you're also obviously using me to distract him for your own purposes and he thinks that's unfair, why shouldn't he and I be allies?"

"Ouch. He's a clever man, isn't he?"

"Yes. I'm not exactly stupid, either."

Libby squirmed guiltily. "I'm sorry, Marj."

"I don't mind spending time with Reynard." She leaned on her arms again and gazed toward the horizon. "I know it's only for a short time. I'm going to enjoy it while it lasts." She looked back at Libby. "Just make sure you feel the same way about Bastien."

"It's not like that," Libby asserted, far too quickly and firmly to sound convincing even to herself. "When did you and Reynard discuss all this plotting and scheming?"

"He told me after we put you to bed last night. You had a nasty headache, you know. We were all worried." Marj put her hand on Libby's sleeve. "Did Bastien do something to cause the headache? Did he trigger the memories?"

"Maybe." Libby sighed. She looked around as she tried to collect her thoughts. "This thing has gotten really complicated, Jones. Some locals seemed to have been involved in what happened." Marj gave her a shocked look, and she explained. "I haven't sorted fact from fantasy yet, but I think outlaws broke into the castle at about the same time the accident happened."

"Locals?" Libby nodded. "Did they cause the accident?"

"I don't know. Maybe. I remember a woman. A red-haired woman at the gate, and some strange men and running, and I almost remember the hall being set on fire. It's all very hazy, but details are starting to come back."

"Bastien was one of the outlaws?"

"I'm not sure. He remembers men chasing him. Maybe he came here for refuge. All I'm sure of is that he and his wife were at Lilydrake." Libby turned to gaze down on the activity in the courtyard. "Look. Henry's actually talking to Matilda." As she spoke, Henry glanced up and waved to her. She stepped quickly back from the wall.

"What about Bastien?" Marj persisted.

She didn't want to talk about Bastien anymore. She didn't want to tell Marj what she planned to do about Bastien because it was definitely against the rules. She owed him for six months of madness and pain and she always paid her debts. "Whatever he did doesn't matter," she said. "Why don't we go down and try to talk Henry into taking Matilda home and marrying her?"

Because, she added to herself as she and Marj started down the tower stairs, the fewer people there were at the castle, the easier it would be for her to run away and find Bastien.

Why did she have to be beautiful? Why did she have to be sympathetic? Why did he have an unreasonable longing to claim her as his own? Most importantly, why hadn't she turned him in to Sir Reynard? Bastien leaned his back against the wide bole of an ancient oak tree with his bow in his hands and tried not to think of Isabeau of Lilydrake. It would be much easier for him to hate her if she didn't keep helping him escape from justice.

"She's playing with me," he said. He glanced at Cynric. The old man was looking at him with a mixture of curiosity and amusement.

"Then why don't you let her?" Cynric questioned.

"What?"

"Play with her, lad. The pair of you would make great sport in bed."

Bastien tried to be offended, the images the old man's words conjured up were distracting. "Don't be ridiculous."

"It would be easy for a handsome swain like you to have the lady. Wait until the sheriff moves out, then move in and warm her bed. Many a man's earned himself a title by possessing a castle and the woman that goes with it. How do you think nobles get to be nobles, lad? They take what's not theirs and hold on against all comers. Isabeau'd be nice and soft to hold onto, I'd wager."

"I don't want a title."

"But you want the woman."

"I do not want the woman." Bastien spoke slowly and very firmly.

Cynric was unimpressed. He spit into the bracken. "Lilydrake's a fine holding. You could do worse."

Bastien decided that watching the road for approaching travelers would be preferable to continuing this conversation. He did not want the woman, he told himself as he moved cautiously forward. He wanted his wife. Only he couldn't remember his wife's face, and Isabeau's haunted his dreams. It had been three days since she'd left him in the abandoned church. Every time he'd closed his eyes in that time he'd dreamed about her. And not every dream had been a nightmare. In most of them he'd touched her, tasted her, claimed her, found peace lying beside her.

It wasn't right. He had no right to find comfort with another woman, even in his dreams.

Cynric followed him. "She's a nice lass. You could do worse."

Bastien rounded on him. "She's a noblewoman!"

"Nothing wrong with marrying above your station. You can move us all into the castle as your servants." Cynric bowed. "I'd be willing to consider the post of guard captain, my lord."

"I'm not going to marry—"

The sounds of approaching horses silenced their argument. Bastien checked quickly to see that his men were in place, then stepped out onto the track with his bow raised. A moment later a pair of riders came into view, one on a warhorse, the other astride a donkey.

"An ass riding an ass," Bastien said, and aimed his bow at the startled rider. "What brings you back to Blean, Father John?" He'd heard about the priest's exile from Passfair.

"You!" The priest's surprise changed to an expression of deep hatred. Bastien smiled, and gestured his men forward. Father John looked at the circle of weapons trained on his party, and snarled, "I should have put an arrow through you when I had the chance."

"You didn't have the chance," Bastien remembered angrily. "You would have killed Lady Isabeau."

It was the other rider who responded with a deep-chested laugh. "That wouldn't have done me much good, priest."

Bastien turned his attention to the horseman. There were other riders, and footsoldiers and servants with a baggage cart in the party, but this man was obviously the leader of the group. "And what is the lady to you?" Bastien asked as a cold, possessive anger began to gnaw inside him. It was none of his business. He was on the road to rob passersby, not to question each and every one who passed about the woman. She was going to ruin his business if he wasn't careful. "Well?" he asked the staring man in a low-voiced threat.

"She's my promised bride," the man finally answered after a good long look at him. "And you're a stinking wolfshead." He put his hand on the pommel of his sword. "Clear out of my way."

Bastien wondered if Lady Isabeau knew she was betrothed, and what she would do about it if the news came as a surprise. All he knew was that the man's words had sent an unpleasant jolt through him. He managed to keep his tone light as he said, "I almost feel sorry for you, friend." The stranger was big, fleshy-featured, his knotted fists reminded Bastien of well-used clubs.

The horseman looked at the priest. "Is this the one?" Father John nodded. "Well, then," the man said, turning his attention back to Bastien, "it's you I feel sorry for." He leaned forward a bit, glaring menacingly at Bastien. "When Lilydrake is mine I'll burn down the forest if I must to clear vermin like you out of it. But you I'll take alive, and hang your guts up before the lady before I let you die."

What a charming man, Bastien thought. He found it difficult not to loose the bowstring he was holding taut. "I doubt the lady has any interest in my guts," he said.

"She lusted after you for all to see," Father John accused. "Now she'll have Rolf of Gesthowe to tame her sinful cravings."

"I wish you luck," he said to Rolf. But he couldn't keep his thoughts away from the man's meaty fists and the knowledge of what they could do to tender flesh. He wondered just what sort of salacious lies the vengeful priest had told this man about Isabeau. "The lady's none of my business," he said, and forced himself to believe it. He shifted his grip on the bow slightly and quickly checked the positions of his men. All was secure. He gave Rolf a dangerous smile. "It's your possessions that I take an interest in. Take your hand off your sword, Rolf. In fact, take off your sword. Get to work," he said to his waiting men. "Once we've relieved you of your valuables," he promised his prey, "you're free to go about troubling Lady Isabeau's life with my blessing."

Libby knew what the phrase "watched like a hawk" meant. She'd grown up with a sharp-eyed father who was aware of every scrape his too-clever children could possibly get into. Sir Reynard reminded her a lot of her father, only she was too old to appreciate his protective impulses now. She'd been trying to get out of the castle for days. Every time she did he was there. It was like the man had a built-in sensor set to her readings. Oh, he would have been perfectly happy to accompany her on any trip into Blean Forest, but since she had no intention of leading him to Bastien she always had to decline his kind offers.

So she stayed home and fumed, watched the progress of the rebuilding, lectured Matilda on self-esteem and feminism, and tried to avoid Henry's inexpert advances. Actually, Henry's seduction attempts were becoming less frequent, but he was still keeping up a token effort while Matilda was making advances in holding his attention.

"Aren't those kids ever going to go home?" she wondered sourly as she glanced at the young couple.

"More importantly," Marj answered as she leaned close to her, "are we ever going to go home?"

"Are you saying this mission isn't exactly a success?" Okay, so the presence of locals was preventing Joe and Ed from setting up the timegate equipment, Sir Reynard was blocking access to the outlaws she needed for her research, and her and the men's memories were still leaky as sieves, but that didn't mean they should just pack up and go home. Did it? Yeah, it probably did. So what?

"It's not my place to say what you should do, my lady," Marj said with humility that was belied by the sparkle in her blue eyes.

Libby didn't answer. There was nothing to discuss. She had no intention of leaving the past just yet. Not until she found a way to help Bastien.

She turned her attention back to her embroidery while Marj continued to whirl a top-shaped spindle, transforming clumps of undyed wool into coarse thread. This domestic scene was taking place while they shared a bench underneath the shelter of the eating pavilion's awning. Matilda and Henry sat nearby playing a game of draughts while Sir Reynard looked on and offered them advice. Around them buildings were going up and people were busy with daily chores. There were chickens and geese in the bailey and the dogs were getting plenty of exercise chasing the cackling birds. Libby was considering getting up and chasing the dogs, just to have some physical outlet for her restless spirit. Being a medieval lady entailed far more sitting around than she was used to.

She pushed away the embroidery stand and stood up. "I'm going for a walk."

Sir Reynard was at her side almost instantly. "Lady Marjorie and I will accompany you."

"And I," Henry declared.

"As will I," Matilda added.

Libby fought her exasperation and gave the lot of them a wan smile. "Of course," she said unenthusiastically. "I wouldn't think of going anywhere without all of you."

She was going to have to kill all of them, Libby thought as the group trooped out into the courtyard. It was the only way. Or maybe she could borrow a large supply of opium from her godmother and brew up a giant-sized sleeping potion.

She was smiling at this thought as she went through the outer bailey. She looked toward the open gate and the false promise of freedom in the forest beyond, just as a group of riders rode through the castle entrance. The newcomers were immediately surrounded by Sir Reynard's guards. The sheriff hurried forward, Libby came with him. At least it was something to do.

"Stay clear, my lady," he warned.

She ignored him, and wished she hadn't when a burly man jumped down from a very big horse and strode purposefully up to her. "So, you're Isabeau," he declared and grabbed her before anyone could stop him. "I'm told you're a whore. Good. I like my women lusty."

The next thing she knew she was being kissed. The experience was far from pleasant.

He should never have let Rolf and Father John go. Bastien paced the length of the camp, then back, all the time his thoughts worried at the mistake he'd made. His initial impulse had been to chase them out of the forest. He should have acted on it. Instead he'd left them with their clothes and their mounts and sent them off to harass the woman he knew to be his enemy.

But it wasn't their job to torment Isabeau, it was his. He wanted revenge, but what good was revenge if he didn't inflict it?

"She deserves better than Rolf," Cynric said as Bastien passed his hut, though Bastien hadn't said a word to him about what was bothering him.

Bastien halted. "She deserves no better than any other noblewoman."

Cynric shook his head at Bastien's attitude. "A husband who beats her and breeds on her and beds the servants in front of her? I've seen it break many a gently reared lady. My quarrels with the nobles have never been with their women. The women I pity."

"Putting up with the men is the price they pay for their soft lives. I'm not worried about Lady Isabeau being broken." Though if she was broken, he thought, he ought to be the one to do it. He was the one she owed.

Then again, what exactly did she owe him? Something deep inside him screamed that he'd lost everything that meant anything to him at Lilydrake, but could he really hold Isabeau responsible? She'd done him no harm, give or take a shove off a castle wall.

In fact, he owed her. She could have easily turned him over to Reynard while he'd been lying helpless with pain inside the church. She hadn't.

He wanted to know why she hadn't.

"I still say the girl deserves better," Cynric said. "She's not like other nobles. She helped us back at Passfair."

He didn't want to be reminded of her virtues again. "Enough." He ran his hands through his hair. "This Rolf worries me. I should never have let him go."

"He means trouble for us," Cynric agreed. "More than Reynard of Elansted."

"Elansted's too clever for his own good. He lurks and waits like a spider. But this Rolf looks to be a typical knight. He may well mean to burn the forest just to have things his own way. Damn." Bastien shook his head. "I want word sent to Sikes. We may need his help."

"That's a hard thing to admit."

"That it is," Bastien agreed. He put his hand on the old man's shoulder. "Move the camp again. Further into the forest. Then move it again every few days. I don't want this Rolf to be able to track us down. Keep away from the forest villages. If the peasants don't know where we are, they can't tell him."

"That won't stop him from pillaging them when they don't give him answers," Cynric pointed out.

"Maybe it won't come to that," Bastien answered, but he had no hope that Rolf would leave innocent people to go about their business.

"Maybe he'll be too busy playing the besotted bridegroom to worry about us for a bit," Cynric suggested.

Fury shot through Bastien like a bolt of lightning. Never mind that it was none of his business, the thought of Isabeau wed to another did not sit well with him at all. He remembered Rolf's arrogance, the cruel look in his eyes, his thick features and ham-sized hands. Bastien wanted Isabeau of Lilydrake, and he'd be damned if any man would have her before he took both pleasure and revenge by making her love him.

"No," he answered Cynric, voice cold when all the rest of him was burning with fury. "I don't think so."

Cynric was unruffled by his temper. "You think not? A woman like Isabeau could make any man forget himself for a while. That is if the man has sense enough to see that she has more to offer than a place to plant his—"

"I don't want to hear it," Bastien cut him off. "I've had enough of forgetfulness. It's some memories I want."

Memories to match the dreams that haunted and aroused him. He craved them like life-giving water, like food and fire and shelter. He was sick of dark dreams, of phantom lovers. He wanted a real life. He wanted the reality of the woman's touch. He wanted to run his hands through her dark hair and down her body, he wanted to see her eyes lit with passion, her mouth open for his kiss. He wanted to make her his and not forget the experience when he awoke at the break of day.

New memories for old, he thought. Perhaps that was what he needed, perhaps that was what the heiress of Lilydrake owed him. She could never replace what he'd lost, but perhaps she could fill up some of the emptiness inside him. "See to moving the camp," he told Cynric. "I'm going to Lilydrake."

The old man cackled. "I thought you might be."

He didn't care what Cynric thought, nor did he care about the man's schemes to make him lord of Lilydrake. He had his own plans for Isabeau, and marrying her wasn't one of them. But for many, many reasons he owed her a visit.

10

"Thanks."

"My pleasure," Reynard said, and rubbed his knuckles. He looked down at the prone man. "I assume you're ready to apologize to Lady Isabeau now."

Libby touched her swollen lips. She was almost numb with surprise at what had just happened. At the same time she was nauseated and bruised from the way the man had handled her before Reynard pulled him away and hit him hard enough to knock him to the ground. She seriously considered adding a few well-placed kicks to Sir Reynard's handiwork, but managed to refrain from such unladylike behavior for the moment.

She looked around to see that Henry had his sword out, as did all of the sheriff's men, and that Ed and Joe had their staffs in their hands. Marj, and even shy Matilda, stood protectively at her side. The castle servants were gathered around the other men who'd arrived with the intruder. She was surrounded by a crowd, all willing to defend her. She felt a warm glow of appreciation for these people, then the glow went cold as Father John pushed his way through the crowd.

"What are you doing here?" she demanded. "Get out of my castle."

He ignored her as he helped her assailant to his feet. "Leave the man be, Elansted," the priest ordered the sheriff. "He's here at the king's command. As am I."

"I'm Rolf of Gesthowe." The man spoke to Reynard rather than to her. He pointed at her. "I've come to marry the whore of Lilydrake."

Sir Reynard hit him again. The man staggered, but didn't go down. "I thought I told you to apologize," Reynard said.

Rolf rubbed his jaw. "For what?"

"For mistreating Lady Isabeau."

"I'll treat my wife any way I choose."

Rolf looked at her, the same way a very hungry man looked at a very large plate of food. It made her want to run for the gate despite the numerous folk standing around willing to support her. She fought the urge to panic and glared back at the man.

"I'm not your wife," she pointed out. "And neither you nor the priest is welcome at my castle."

"My castle," Rolf corrected her. He looked back at Reynard. "Who are you? If you're another one of her lovers I suppose I'll have to kill you."

"Another one of my—" Libby sputtered. Fury replaced her alarm at the man's attitude. She took an angry step forward, but was stopped by a stern look from Reynard.

"I am not the lady's lover," Reynard told Rolf firmly. "Nor is any man. I don't know what the priest told you, but Lady Isabeau is beyond reproach."

Rolf rubbed his bruised jaw. He eyed the sheriff with a certain amount of respectful caution. "You'll swear to that?"

"I will."

"As will I," Henry piped up. "Lady Isabeau is all that is modest and chaste."

Libby wouldn't have sworn to that herself, but she was glad the men rushed to assert her honor. "Thank you."

Rolf glanced from Father John to Reynard to her, then back at Reynard. He looked confused, but about half convinced. "What about the outlaw?"

"What about him?" Libby asked, belligerent despite Reynard's warning frown.

"The wolfshead held her prisoner before all our eyes," Henry asserted. "There was no chance for him to sully her purity in any way. We would have hunted him down like a dog by now if he'd raped her."

Father John laughed. "She would have welcomed—"

"Quiet, priest," Rolf ordered. He rounded on Father John. "If you've made a fool of me before my betrothed I'll have you beaten."

"Remember who talked the king into giving you Lilydrake," the priest snarled back. "I can find another to take your place easily enough."

"I'm here and I'll—"

"You've already let the wolfshead take your sword. Will you let the Welshwoman take your ba—"

Libby put her fingers to her lips and whistled loudly. "Excuse me!" she shouted. When she had their attention she demanded, "Just what the devil is going on here?"

Rolf went down on one knee before her. "Lady Isabeau," he proclaimed, "the king has seen fit to reward my service to him with the fief of Lilydrake and your hand in marriage." He snatched her hand from her side and kissed it.

She snatched it back. "What?"

"I can only apologize for my rude words and actions." He gave Father John a dirty look. "I was led to believe false charges against you."

"What has the king got to do with this?" Marj asked as she stepped quickly forward. "Daffyd ap Bleddyn is master of Lilydrake."

"The king's father gave Lilydrake to the Welsh mercenary," Father John answered. "Since the Welshman does not hold the fief himself and his heir is unwed, the king claims the right to take the woman in ward and gift her to the man of his choice."

Libby gaped at Marj. "Can he do that?"

The historian licked her lips nervously. She nodded. "He can do it, my lady. It is a great honor, actually," she added.

Libby remembered Lady Sibelle saying something like this could happen. She just hadn't paid any attention at the time. That was before she'd realized how much the locals could influence her life. As if having Bastien's amnesia to deal with wasn't bad enough, now she was being given away to a stranger by the king. So much for observing rather than impacting on the local culture. It looked like she was the one having to absorb the impact.

"Ouch," she said, and tried to think rather than follow the impulse to either laugh or cry hysterically. She noticed that Father John was looking smug. She looked at Rolf of Gesthowe and knew why. He didn't look like a Rolf. A Rolf should look like a wisecracking, piano-playing Muppet, not an ugly imitation of Meatloaf.

Father John, who hated her for no good reason, was delighted to have found the nastiest lout he could hunt up for her future husband.

Rolf, however, was also looking at her with a puppy-dog adoration that was as surprising as it was sudden. Now that he'd been assured of her chastity, he was gallantly on his knees to his lady fair. Maybe he wasn't as bad as he seemed. Maybe he believed in this chivalric ideal stuff. Maybe she could work with this.

She steeled her nerves and queasy stomach and dropped a light kiss on the man's sweaty forehead. "Welcome, my lord," she proclaimed as sweetly as possible. "Now that I know your errand I can but humbly thank you for your earlier greeting, shocking though your kiss was to my untried senses." She looked at the priest and was pleased to see that he was frowning. Then she batted her eyelashes at Rolf. "Please rise, good sir."

"You're laying it on a little thick, aren't you?" Marj whispered to her in English.

She glanced at the worried historian. "Trust me."

"You've got a plan?"

"A cunning plan," she answered, though it was just barely forming in the back of her mind. "Cunning plans run in my family." And running was just what she had in mind, but she had to make a few arrangements first.

She noticed that both Reynard and Henry were staring at her. She turned a persuasive smile on both of them while Rolf lumbered to his feet. "Our guest is tired and in need of refreshment," she said. "And no doubt he has brought news from court. Why don't you men join him for a hot bath in the laundry shed?" Henry gave her a skeptical look, but she shooed her erstwhile suitor forward. "Please. And you too, Sir Reynard."

"I could use a bath. And a new sword," Rolf added. "We were attacked by robbers in the forest."

Reynard stepped forward. "Bastien's men?" He took Rolf's arm and directed him toward the wash house. "Come, friend, we have much to talk about."

Libby sighed with relief when Henry and Father John followed after the other two. She hoped they'd have a nice long soak and a nice long talk. She needed some time. She turned to the two women who were staring at her. "I think we need to prepare a feast for our guests."

"A feast?" Marj asked.

Libby nodded. "With lots of wine. What's the flavored stuff called? That wine mixed with herbs drink?"

"Hippocras," Matilda answered.

"Right. Hippocras. Matilda, dear," she said sweetly, "you did bring a box of herbs from Passfair, didn't you?" The girl nodded. "Good. Let's go have a look at your supply, shall we? I think I want to brew a little something special for my *dear* betrothed." A little something the Wicked Witch of the West would be proud of, she thought as she lead Matilda back toward the tower.

"I don't think poppy is one of the ingredients in the mixture, my lady."

"This is how we do it in Wales, dear," Libby replied as she stirred the large pot of warmed wine. "It's very soothing. Pour a little more in, why don't you?" The girl looked dubious, but complied. "That should do it." Libby carefully removed the pot from the brazier.

While Matilda watched she poured the mixture into several stoneware beakers, then called a servant in to take them away. "Make sure these are only served to high table," she ordered. "Is the evening meal being served?"

"Yes, my lady," the woman answered, then left the tower room quickly to serve the hippocras before it got cold.

"You better go down and join Henry," Libby told Matilda. "I'll be down after I've made myself beautiful for my lord."

"Shouldn't I help you change?"

"No, no. I'll be fine." Libby wondered why her voice was so calm. If this didn't work she didn't know how she'd escape from the castle without resorting to pyrotechnics and possibly small arms fire. She didn't want that. She didn't want to have to make a run for the timegate where they'd arrived. She wanted to escape into the forest, not go back to her own century to evade marriage to Rolf of Gesthowe. She had other plans, plans that had nothing to do with Time Search's rules and regulations, or even her own desperate needs. She had a mission, and his name was Bastien of Bale. "Go along, dear," she urged Matilda. "Henry will miss you."

Put that way, Matilda was eager enough to leave her alone. Libby sighed with relief when the girl was gone. She was also delighted that Marj Jones was already outside keeping an eye on Father John as Libby had asked her to do. Being alone gave Libby a chance to make up a small bundle of necessary supplies.

After she locked the dogs in the tower she took her stuff downstairs with her and managed to hide it inside the horse paddock without anyone noticing her presence in the bailey. Once satisfied with her preparations she made her way to the eating pavilion and took her seat beside Rolf. His cheeks were flushed as though he'd drunk quite a bit already.

He grasped her hand the moment she sat down, and gave her fingers a rough squeeze. His gaze on her was ardent and hopeful. She made herself smile winningly at this evidence of his affection.

"Come, share the wine with me, my lady," he urged and held out the silver cup they were supposed to share.

"But one sip, my lord," she answered, with her eyes modestly downcast. "To pledge my troth." She took the cup and tipped it to her lips, but was careful not to drink.

He sighed loudly. "Prettily done."

She noticed that Henry's head was already resting on the table. Matilda was looking concerned, but the girl wasn't crying as she took a sip of the wine. Sir Reynard was turning his cup round and round in his hands. He looked thoughtful. Libby did not take that as a good sign. Father John was drinking his wine. For once he was quiet, his attention on the refreshment rather than on preaching the evils of the female sex.

"What cheerful company," Libby said, and got a warning look from Marj. "A toast," she added, and took a cup of ale from a server as she stood. She turned an adoring gaze on Rolf. "Drink deeply, good people," she said to the company, "in celebration of my good fortune." You too, Reynard, she added to herself, as a few cheers and shouts of congratulations went up in answer to her words.

Rolf staggered up, put his arm around her waist and quickly downed the drugged wine in his cup. The other men followed his example, even Sir Reynard. Rolf sat down quickly when he was finished. Within moments Father John had tipped backward off his bench. He was snoring almost before he curled up under the table.

"I think there was too much poppy, my lady," Matilda ventured. And yawned.

"Yes, it would seem so," Libby agreed. "Oh, dear." She put her hand on Rolf's shoulder. "I'm so sorry." Rolf slumped forward, face down in the food-laden trencher. Libby patted him on the head.

"Poppy?" Reynard asked, voice heavy and slow.

"I must have made a terrible mistake."

"I'll say you have." He raised a reproachful finger, or tried to. His hand fell heavily back into his lap before he could repeat the gesture, then his eyes closed and he joined the other sleeping men, with his head resting on Marj's shoulder.

Libby noticed that Joe and Ed were also dozing and Marj was very, very woozy. She'd be out any moment now. Good. She didn't want to incriminate anyone else from Time Search in the trouble she was going to get involved in.

She rubbed her hands together with satisfaction. "I thought they'd never go to sleep." She looked at the servants and soldiers who were staring at the odd goings-on at the head table. "These people need to be put to bed," she ordered, thinking for once that there were advantages to being obeyed without question. "See to it. I'm going down to the church to pray," she added as an excuse to leave the castle. "I expect to find my lord comfortably settled by the time I return."

Which will be about the same time hell freezes over, she added to herself as she headed swiftly for the stable.

* * *

When he tried to think about it logically, Bastien didn't know why he was doing this. He'd made his way to the shelter of the abandoned church without thinking. After pausing in the sanctuary to wait for darkness before making his next move, he stopped running on instinct and began to use his brain. Or, he tried, but thinking about Isabeau didn't come as easily as reacting to her.

Logic had nothing to do with his response to Isabeau, it never had. He kept wanting to protect her, then he thrust her into danger, which was no more than she deserved, but that wasn't true either. All he knew was that he dreamed about her when he slept, and thought about her when he was awake. His reaction to her beauty was simple enough, plain, basic lust. His reaction to her personality was complicated, unpredictable, maddening. Adding more madness to his already addled senses was the last thing he needed.

He sat on the low step below the altar, rested his hands on his knees and murmured, "But here I am." What he needed, he thought, was less of a reason for his being at Lilydrake than a plan of what he was going to do next. Then he heard the thud of a horse's hooves as a rider crossed the square. He wondered if he was about to face Rolf, or Sir Reynard, and made ready to fight.

The last thing he expected was for Isabeau to walk in the door and say, "If I told you my belt was throbbing for you I don't suppose you'd understand what I meant, would you?"

He relaxed tensed muscles and looked down at her waist. He had noticed her belt before. What thief would not take note of such a finely jeweled piece of goldsmith's work? He stood up and came slowly toward her. "It must be worth a hundred marks," he said.

"A great deal more than that, actually."

"You have too much wealth, lady."

"Don't make it sound like an insult, Bas. I have to appear wealthy or this whole thing doesn't work."

He looked her over carefully, both below and above her belt. Her overdress was forest green, embroidered in brown and yellow bands, her dark hair was worn beneath a fresh linen veil. She wore rings and a necklace and he thought he caught the glint of a gold bracelet below the edge of her long sleeve. This was no appearance of wealth. Her abundant riches reminded him of why he hated her kind.

He stood slowly as he said, "Most women own a single dress in their whole lives. I've never seen you wear the same kirtle twice. Your wealth is an insult to every woman who has to toil for her livelihood."

Libby wished she'd kept her mouth shut about the belt. She knew this was no time to get into an argument about social injustice. "You're right," she told him. "I have absolutely no business living in luxury while the poor starve."

His hands landed heavily on her shoulders. "Don't," he said, voice low and menacing, "patronize me."

Libby had had quite enough of men grabbing her, but for some reason she didn't find Bastien's touch threatening. Annoyingly possessive, perhaps, but nothing to be frightened of. He was a dangerous man and the threat was real, but she still wasn't frightened. She had a bone-deep confidence that the man wouldn't hurt her. A confidence she had to admit was probably sheer wishful thinking on her part. Besides, they didn't have time for her to be afraid.

She was too annoyed at his bad attitude to try to convince him that she actually did agree with him. "Let go of me."

He smiled at the threat in her voice. "Or what?" The heat of her skin radiated warmth to his hands, warmth that spread the heat of desire through him. She smelled of crushed herbs and clean linen, heady and rich and inaccessible. But he was holding her between his hands, with her face defiantly turned up toward his. Temper lit her dark brown eyes, temper mixed with humor. He ran his thumbs along the line of her collarbone and he knew that her slight reaction was because she was ticklish, not because she was repulsed by his touch. He wondered how she'd react if he scrabbled his fingers down the length of her rib cage. Would she squirm and giggle and beg for mercy? Not that he had time for that sort of teasing play. He told himself he had no interest in it, either. Besides, how could he know if delicate Lady Isabeau was really ticklish?

Delicate Lady Isabeau brought her hands up and pushed hard against his chest. "We don't have time for this," she said as Bastien stumbled back a step. "We have to go now."

He regained his balance and crossed his arms. "We? Where do you plan to go, lady?" Had she come to the church to pray and found him by accident? Or was she here with him by design? And what did her belt have to do with it? She had said something about her belt throbbing for him, hadn't she? He blinked as a twinge of pain pulsed in his temples. Perhaps it was better not to try to think about her odd words. "Well?" he demanded. "Where would you go but back to Lilydrake—and your betrothed's arms?"

"My betrothed's arms are presently asleep, along with the rest of him. And I'm getting out of here while the getting's good."

She didn't suppose telling the outlaw that she had specifically planned to find him when she left Lilydrake would make any sense to him. She was supposed to be a demure and dutiful medieval lady. It was probably better to let him think he'd captured her so he could drag her off and hold her for ransom or something. Of course, there was the possibility that he would knock her over the head, strip her of all her valuables and escape into the forest. He was no Robin Hood. She was taking a big gamble assuming that the man possessed an innate gallantry. Still, he had risked his life to rescue his imprisoned men, and he hadn't harmed her the other times she'd encountered him, except for the matter of a small knife cut which really hadn't been his fault. Besides, if she was going to live up to her responsibility to help him she had to take the risk. She was just going to have to convince him that he wanted to take the risk of taking her with him. Perhaps playing to his pride would provoke the right response.

"I only stopped to say a quick prayer before I ride back for Wales," she told Bastien. "I'm running away," she confided. "I won't marry Rolf. You'd better run yourself. Say your prayers for your wife elsewhere, wolfshead, for you won't be safe here anymore. You can't defend yourself against a warrior like him. Surely Rolf will come looking for you if you lurk around Lilydrake looking for scraps from his midden."

She hoped she'd laid it on thick enough, though she thought she sounded stupid and insensitive. She needed the taunts about his wife and his ability to fight Rolf of Gesthowe to goad him into retaliating by taking her prisoner. She'd apologize later, after she'd helped him get his memory back. Right now they needed to get away from Lilydrake before the narcotics wore off her dinner guests.

"Run, wolfshead," she advised, and wondered what Bastien was doing in the church in the first place.

So, she was trying to escape from Rolf of Gesthowe. He didn't blame her, but the fool woman would never make it far on her own. Rolf would find her, drag her back and then there'd be hell to pay. He had come to help her, but the impulse was trampled by her harsh words. She probably deserved whatever Gesthowe did to her, but he knew he couldn't allow anyone to mistreat her. Unless, of course, he was the one who did the mistreating. He smiled coldly at that thought. Let her fear him. She deserved to learn a few lessons in humility.

And while she learned, he could get her safely away from the real danger that threatened her. Not that he would let her know he was helping her. She'd think she had some power over him then. She'd try to use him, and he wouldn't allow that. No, he would take her into the forest, keep her for himself, and somehow she would repay him for all he'd lost at Lilydrake. She'd be his and no one else's. Again, it would not do to tell her so.

He grabbed her by the arms again. "I'll go," he told her, "and you'll come with me." He held her fast when she tried to pull away this time. "No more games, no weakness. You're my prisoner, Isabeau of Lilydrake, until I ransom you back to your rightful lord."

11

"*We could have* taken the horse," Libby complained as she walked along the track in front of Bastien. The bundle she carried wrapped in her cloak was heavy.

"Horses are too easy to track," he answered. "Too noisy, and too expensive to keep. They're rather like a noblewoman, that way."

"Thank you." Why had she wanted to help him? she wondered. Responsibility, she reminded herself. She wondered how she should start, what the best tactic for treatment was. She knew that very little except returning to this time period had worked on her, and she still only had a few tantalizing bits of her past back. A few memories were better than none. If Bastien only recalled part of his missing life at least he might be able to come to peace with himself. She suspected from the restless anger that seemed to consume him that he desperately needed some peace.

She didn't know how much time they'd have together, so she might as well make a start. She kept walking, not turning to look at him as she said, "You have to forgive yourself. That's the first thing they told me. It wasn't your fault."

Bastien had no idea what the woman was talking about. Her words, coming out of the quiet darkness of the forest, were like the voice of his own conscience. They'd walked in silence while the night darkened around them. He'd grown comfortable with no more than the sound of her footsteps, with watching the outline of her shape before him and the contact of his hand on her shoulder to guide her. Her words effectively shook him out of his complacent mood.

"I'm not a priest," he told her. "Granting forgiveness isn't my occupation."

"You aren't listening to me, Bastien." She stopped, and he bumped into her.

His arms went around her waist. He pulled her close without thinking. He felt a shiver run through her as he leaned his head down to whisper close to her ear. "I don't want to listen. I'd rather do this." He kissed the side of her neck.

"Don't," she said, but her breath came quicker and she tilted her head so his lips could explore her throat more easily. She didn't object when his hand cupped her breast.

The forest enveloped them like a black cloak. There was only the sound of their breathing and the heat of their bodies in all the world. Bastien was aware of the distant call of a nightbird and the thin trickling of a nearby rill, but nothing was real to him but the woman he held. She felt like salvation and forgiveness, for nothing had been real to him for a long time. He let time stand still, hot velvet darkness envelop them. He didn't move. He barely touched her, his hand hovered, his lips brushed her skin, desire built, and he just drank in the reality of the moment.

Then she stomped on his foot, and that was real, too.

"Ow!"

She whirled away from him. "I said don't, and I meant don't."

"You didn't mean it very much."

Since it was the truth, Libby decided not to argue with him about it. She picked up the bundle she didn't remember having dropped. "Don't you want to make camp, or something? It's dark out here."

"And the spoiled lady is tired, no doubt," was his sarcastic reply.

She didn't argue about that comment, either. "Yes. And hungry."

And not just for dinner. Her skin was still sensitized with arousal where he'd been touching it. The warmth of his body had permeated through her clothes and into her nerve endings. She was almost painfully aware of his presence. She'd very nearly not been able to pull away from him. This was not a good beginning if she was going to be running around in the woods with him for the next few days. She couldn't let herself get physically involved with this man.

"Get moving."

His gruff command helped steel her resolve against wanting him, a little. She would have to keep reminding herself that he hated all she supposedly stood for. Instead of obeying, she looked around, not that there was much to see. They were near a stream, but the ground was thick with trees and low bushes. "We need to find a clearing."

"No."

"Why not? Aren't you tired and hungry? Why don't you go shoot a rabbit or something while I—"

"I'm not your servant, woman."

The man was *so* class-conscious. "Bas—"

"Keep walking. There's an abandoned hut not far from here," he added before she could argue any more. "We'll sleep there."

"Fine," she grumbled.

She settled her bundle over her shoulder and moved forward. They continued on in a silence that grew more tense by the moment, until he finally took her arm and led her toward what she at first thought was an overgrown mound of earth. It turned out to be a low hut. He pushed her inside, where it was completely dark and something squeaked in protest at the human intrusion.

She turned around to leave and slammed squarely into his chest. He blocked her exit. "There are rats in here."

"They'll get used to you."

She was not amused by his sarcasm. The darkness was worse than the rodent company. And being in such a confined space with Bastien brought home to her that he was a large and basically unpredictable male presence. She tried to get around him again, but any movement while standing was awkward. They were both tall, and neither could stand upright in the little building. Bastien went to his knees, and pulled her down with him. She landed hard and found herself in his embrace.

"I do not like this place," she told him. "I want out."

"Too late now, my lady," he said. His voice contained far more sensual promise than it did sarcasm. Before she could react, he snatched her belongings from between them and tossed the bundle aside. "Lady, I think we are going to spend a great deal of time here."

Libby was at a loss how to react. Her instincts were behaving in one fashion, eliciting a particularly female response to his actions. But her common sense shouted a warning that this was no time to let her mating instinct, or his, do anything stupid.

While she thought, and fought her own reactions, Bastien's hands began to roam in slow, sensual caresses over her back and buttocks and thighs. His lips found her throat, the top of her breast, then moved further down. She stopped thinking as his mouth found her cloth-covered nipple. In fact, the world, the tiny hut, all their problems went up in a blaze of heat. She could barely fight her way to sanity through the need that was building between them.

This was ridiculous. She had to stop. She couldn't keep acting on impulse with this man. He pulled her hips closer to his, bringing her in contact with masculine heat and hardness that sent her senses spinning.

"Oh, dear."

It took her a long time to find her voice again. "This is all a power play on your part," she told him. She was breathless and aching, but she'd fought back from the edge of abandon. "It has nothing to do with how we feel about each other. As people." Her fingers were working at the lacing of his tunic of their own will. Beneath his coarsely woven shirt she found he wore a softer shirt. A smooth layer of silk intruded between her skin and his. She forced her hands to stop what they were doing.

"I like how you feel." He rubbed his hands up and down her hips and the back of her thighs and cupped her rear in his hands. Then he tickled her ribs.

"Bas, no!" As she squirmed and giggled he laughed. There was something endearing about hearing the brooding outlaw laugh. He kept tickling her, mercilessly tormenting her until she lost control. "Stop! Please!" she begged. "Bas, you know I hate this! You asked for it!"

It was as much desperation as anything else that caused her to fling all her weight against him and flip him down on his back. She landed hard on his chest. Then she used the only distraction possible to keep his torturing fingers away from her ribs. She covered his mouth with hers.

Bastien knew he'd lost control of the situation when he realized she was kissing him again. It had been going on for some time. Their tongues were twined together with his enthusiastic cooperation when it finally occurred to him that his plans had gone all wrong. He was the one on his back and she was having her way with him. It didn't matter that he was enjoying it, this wasn't the way it was supposed to be.

He sat up and pushed her angrily away. He wiped his hand across his mouth, but he could still taste her. He could just make out her shadowed form sprawled at the back of the hut. "You're right," he told her, "This is about power."

Bastien's voice shook with emotion. Libby knew that beneath the anger was hard, controlled passion.

She appreciated his control, and fought for her own. There were far too many emotions flying around this tiny, enclosed space. Things could not be allowed to get out of hand again.

She got slowly to her feet though she had to bend over to move. She inched toward the doorway. His hand shot out to stop her.

"Where do you think you're going?"

She swore tiredly, realizing that she was his prisoner whether she'd volunteered for the job or not. There was nothing caressing about the hand holding her arm, it had more of the feel of a shackle. The problem was that her body was still aching with awareness of every spot he'd touched and tickled and suckled. She stood perfectly still and waited for whatever he would do next.

He released his hold and got up. "Time you earned your keep, Lady Isabeau."

He pushed her before him out of the hut. The moonlight was faded from its full glory of a few days before, but the faint light it shed was welcome after the hut's blackness. She turned her face gratefully up to it. Lord, but she was tired, and being here with this man was probably sheerest folly. He needed her, she reminded herself. *You don't need him to care for you,* she lectured herself. *And he hasn't got any reason to trust you.* It was foolish to want anything from him. She should just try to help him get back as many memories as she could and call things even between them. They had no future other than that. Just get on with it, she commanded herself.

"Fetch some firewood."

She could tell that he expected her to argue with him. He expected her to sulk and complain as though she was used to having servants anticipate her every wish. Libby smiled to herself. He was going to just hate it when he found out she had nothing against doing her share of the work. Oh, yes, Bastien of Bale was going to be quite a challenge on many levels.

"Sure," she answered agreeably. "What are we having for dinner, rat stew?"

He didn't say anything, just stood by the hut with his arms crossed and watched as she wandered around the clearing picking up dry sticks. She came back to him when she had an armful and he directed her back into the tiny building. She found a depression in the floor she guessed must be a firepit, so she dumped the wood into it. Bastien knelt and began working with flint and tinder. She sat down and pulled her bundle into her lap. By the time he had a small blaze going she'd found some dried fruit and a flat loaf of coarse bread.

"I didn't run away completely unprepared," she told him as she held out some of the food to him. "Here. Only owls go hunting at this time of night."

"You don't know much about poachers, then."

She chuckled. "I suppose that's true. Take the food, Bas. Please."

Bastien hesitated to take Lady Isabeau's offering for a moment. It made him feel beholden to her even though she presented it with gentle words. Since he was hungry and he'd too often gone to bed with an empty stomach since joining the outlaw band, he didn't hesitate long. He took her food. He settled back to look into the fire rather than at her while he ate his meal.

Libby scooted closer to the firepit. She liked the light even though she found the smoky heat uncomfortable. "Light without heat would be useful," she said.

"Doesn't work that way," he answered, with his gaze fixed on the dancing flames. "One gives birth to the other."

Libby smiled, impressed by the man's observation of physical laws. "Remind me to introduce you to my father."

He glared, his green eyes catching the reflection of the flames. "The last thing I want is to meet your father."

This probably wasn't a good time to explain that her father was a physicist, and not the famed and ruthless warrior people in this period thought he was. Instead she said, "You're not the first man to tell me that." Getting dates as David Wolfe's daughter had never been easy. "Maybe he is a ruthless warrior after all. My grandmother's meaner," she added.

"And how many men have you had?" he asked before she could launch into a description of her family tree.

"I don't know," she answered. "How about you? Women, I mean?"

Bastien sprang to his feet, hit his head on the roof and sat back down. "It's none of your business!"

"And my sex life is your business?"

"A woman should be chaste until she's wed."

"And a man shouldn't? I hate double standards. Besides," she added, "I'm not sure I've ever been with anyone."

Bastien touched fingers to his lips, as though he was recalling their last kiss. "You've been with a man. Don't pretend otherwise."

"I'm not pretending," she admitted. "I lost part of my memory. There are a lot of things I do not know about my own past." She took a deep breath and held it for a heartbeat or two before finishing, "Just like you."

Suddenly he was across the fire and holding her shoulders. His expression was one of wild fury. "You were at Lilydrake?"

She gulped. "Yes."

He shook her. "What happened to my wife?"

"I don't know."

"What happened to me?"

Her head began to hurt. She began to grow dizzy. She hadn't expected to fall prey to the physical symptoms of her memory loss just from talking about it to Bastien. She was tempted to use her combat training to break his hold on her, but getting into a fight with him just now wouldn't help him trust her. "The same thing that happened to me," she told him. "We have to try to remember together."

He shook her hard. It did not help her headache. "I can't remember her face. Do you know how that feels? To lose everything and not know what you've lost?" He kept shaking her. "Damn it, woman, it hurts!"

She hurt. And she was getting dizzy. She shouldn't have told him. For the first time she was truly afraid of Bastien. "Don't," she said weakly. "Please." She squeezed her eyes shut against the firelight and his furious face. "The pain. In my head. It—" She couldn't speak anymore as a wave of nausea hit her.

Bastien gathered Isabeau into his arms when her eyes closed. He recognized her pain, knew it was real. "I'm sorry," he whispered. His own anger turned into an overwhelming need to comfort. "It's my fault. I didn't mean to hurt you." He held her head over his heart and rubbed her temple with his thumb. He knew too well what was happening to her. He didn't wish this punishment on his worst enemy. He'd reacted to her words without thought, and that cruel thoughtlessness had brought this suffering on her. "I'm sorry," he murmured again. "I'm sorry."

He stretched out as best he could in the small space available and kept his arms around her. He used his body to shield her, knowing how lonely the night could be with only the pain as company. "Rest," he whispered though he thought she was in a place where words made no sense. "It will be all right. Tonight I'll keep you company. Rest easy, Olivia, tomorrow we'll be enemies again."

"Her father is going to kill me."

"Her mother is going to skin me alive."

Marj sat up slowly. Beside her, Reynard did the same. They looked at each other. If her eyes were half as bloodshot as his she looked terrible. Her head ached, her muscles were cramped from lying twisted on the ground, and she was aware of a deep sense of panic. She didn't know the details yet, but she was certain deep in her bones that Libby had done something terribly, terribly stupid.

"What?" she asked Reynard, "do you know about her father?"

Reynard ran his fingers through his graying hair, then across his thick mustache. "Her father," he finally answered, "is one tough, bad-tempered, dangerous whoreson. Or so local legend says."

"You have no idea how accurate legend is." Libby's mother, on the other hand, was Marj's immediate superior and had given her the assignment to make sure her daughter did nothing to inadvertently interfere with history. She hadn't said anything about Libby's overtly interfering with history, but Marj knew that was worse.

Reynard helped her to her feet. Around them a crowd of servants looked nervously on while the drugged people at the high table stirred back to consciousness. The first hint of dawn was lighting up the morning sky. Reynard pulled her away from the pavilion so they could continue their conversation in private.

"There will be hell to pay if that Welsh warlord gets wind of what I think his daughter's done. He'll lay waste to the shire to get revenge on the outlaw. I can't let that happen."

"Never mind Daffyd, Rolf will be hard enough to deal with."

"That's a fact, my dear." He shook his head, and looked like he wished he hadn't.

Marj cupped his cheek in her palm. "Just what do you think she's done?" Marj had her own theory but she wanted the shrewd sheriff's opinion of the situation.

"She ran off to be with the outlaw." He glanced toward the pavilion. "Better than Rolf, or so she's mad enough to think."

Marj nodded, but anything she might have said was drowned out by Rolf shouting, "Where is my woman?"

Marj hurried back to the pavilion, the sheriff right behind her. "Lord Rolf—" she began.

"I told her the recipe was wrong," Matilda interrupted. The girl spoke apologetically to Rolf. "Lady Isabeau was trying to please you, my lord, but she has little knowledge of simples."

Rolf ignored the girl. "Where is she?"

"I am sure she's somewhere—" Marj began.

"She would have woken in my arms if she was in the castle." Rolf seemed very sure of this fact. "She was hot for me and eager for bed."

"He seems rather sure of himself," the sheriff murmured, low enough that only she heard.

Rolf grabbed a servant by the front of his tunic. "Where's my woman, churl?"

"At the church," the man answered hastily. He pointed toward the gate. "She rode down to the church."

"To pray for your swift recovery," one of the other servants said. "But she didn't return."

Rolf flung the first man away and rounded on the other one. "Did you look for her?"

The man flinched at the harsh words. "No, my lord. She said —"

"No one went with her? No one followed to see to her safety?" Rolf struck the servant.

Reynard stepped in front of Rolf. "Keep your hands off Lady Isabeau's people. Let me deal with this. You," he pointed at one of his watching men. "See if Lady Isabeau is keeping vigil in the church."

While they waited for the soldier to return from the church Marj washed her face, had a cup of ale to clear the horrid taste from her mouth and made a thorough check of Libby's tower room. Many of Libby's things were missing, and the restless dogs she'd left behind had torn up much of the rest. The dogs loped down the stairs in front of Marj when she went back outside. The swift, sleek animals headed out the gate while she went to join the others in the pavilion.

Reynard was in the center of the pavilion, watching the others with his arms crossed, a faint smile half hidden by his mustache. Rolf and Henry were pacing, Matilda was sitting on a bench, wringing her hands nervously, Father John was bent over, his head resting in his hands. It pleased her to see that the trouble-making cleric was still miserable from being drugged. He shouldn't have drunk so much, she thought as she came to stand next to Reynard.

"Any news?" she asked the sheriff.

"Lady Isabeau was not at the church."

"The outlaw has her," Rolf declared.

"We have no proof of that," Reynard said.

"He carried her off, I'm certain of it. Carried her off to ravish her to spite me."

If she doesn't ravish him first, Marj thought. "There is no need to make such a frightening assumption," she told the men. "Perhaps she's visiting the sick, or some other necessary task. She could be home any moment."

"There is a fever in one of the nearby villages," Matilda offered helpfully. "Someone might have—"

"Abducted her," Rolf interrupted loudly. "The filthy churl's probably raping her while we wring our hands and talk. The poor girl was snatched from the church while praying for my recovery. I have to save her."

Henry stepped in front of Rolf. The young man had his hand on his sword and fire in his eyes. "Go back where you came from, Gesthowe. I'll save her," he declared.

Rolf gave the younger man a fierce glare. "The woman's mine, pup. Go home before I take your head off."

"She is kindred to my family, or may as well be," Henry answered. "My parents and hers have sworn mighty oaths of friendship. It is my duty to defend her honor."

"You want to bed her, you mean," Rolf told Henry. "She's mine, do you hear?"

Henry's face went bright red, but Matilda spoke up before he could answer. "Yes, Henry, she is."

Henry swung around to face his betrothed. "What?"

Matilda flinched, but she stood her ground. She looked Henry in the eye, tears brimmed in her own, but she didn't cry. She said, "You are my betrothed. Leave Isabeau to Rolf and take me home to be your woman."

Henry's head darted forward as he looked Matilda up and down. He acted as though he'd never seen her before. "What?"

She lifted her chin proudly. "Take me home," she said to him. "Marry me."

He pointed at her. "Matilda? Is that you?"

"Of course it is. We've been betrothed for ten years, Henry DuVrai, it's time we made good on our parents' promises to one another. Honor demands it, does it not?" He gave a slow, thoughtful, nod. "You want someone who will care for you, do you not?" He nodded again. "Someone to warm your bed and give you sons? I can do all those things."

"But—you cry."

"I'm not crying now. You have to promise not to make me cry anymore. No true and chivalrous knight makes a lady cry."

Henry hung his head. "I'm sorry."

"I know you will be kind and loving to your own good and obedient wife." Her voice took on a sultry promise Marj hadn't believed the girl was capable of. "I'm very obedient, my lord." She stepped close to him. "As I'll gladly show you."

Henry gulped. "I—see." He brightened. "You will?"

"You want a wife, well, here I am." She held out her hand to Henry, and gave him a seductive smile. "I will make you a good wife, my lord."

"I—uh—Yes, Matilda." Henry took her by the hand. He looked as stunned as if he'd been hit over the head as she led him away from the pavilion.

Reynard chuckled. "Well, that's one rescuer taken care of." He walked up to Rolf.

He towered over the thickset man, Marj realized. It was like watching a wolfhound next to a bulldog. Both dogs were tough, but she didn't have any doubt which one would win a confrontation.

"We don't know Lady Isabeau's in any danger," Reynard informed Rolf, "but I'll have a look around the countryside to see if I can find her."

"She belongs to me," Rolf answered belligerently.

"That she does," Reynard agreed, "and you're welcome to her. That's not what I said. I said I'd find her for you."

"You?" Rolf sneered. "I—"

"You don't know the area," Reynard pointed out. "I do. You're not properly armed. It's not your duty."

"She's my—"

"Me sheriff." Reynard pointed at Rolf and spoke very slowly. "You wait here. I go into forest. Come back with woman for you. My job. Me sheriff," he repeated slowly. "Bring this man ale," Reynard added to a servant. "Lots of ale."

Rolf looked unhappy at the sheriff's words, but he did accept a large cup and drank down the contents quickly. After he wiped his mouth on his sleeve, he gave Reynard a grudging nod. "Do your job, man. And bring back the bastard alive." He gave an ugly laugh.

Marj tried not to listen to the things he threatened to do to Bastien once he had the outlaw in his power.

She followed Reynard out of the pavilion. "Do you think Rolf will stay here while you search for my lady?"

"For a while, perhaps," Reynard answered. "He'll get drunk, and then he'll get restless, but we've bought some time. There'll be hell to pay in the local villages if he decides to hunt for her himself."

"Then we'd better find her quickly," Marj told him.

He nodded. "Let's get to the horses and get out of here."

They were riding through Lilydrake village before it occurred to her that Reynard hadn't disputed her going with him.

12

Bastien woke before dawn, but was too comfortable to move for a very long time. Isabeau's head was on his chest, soft strands of her hair blanketed his shoulder and brushed his cheek. She was lying more than half on top of him and his arms were around her, holding her in place. Their embracing each other felt right, smelled right, warm and intimate and comfortable. Her presence had brought no nightmares, he realized, but instead the kind of peaceful sleep he hadn't known for months.

The birds were beginning to sing when Isabeau lifted her head and looked at him. Their gazes met in the faint, pre-dawn light that filtered in through the doorway. Her eyes were dark, dark brown, their expression solemn and still a bit sleep-drugged. Her hair was as dark as her eyes, darker, nearly black, a fine frame for her strong, beautiful features. He found himself wanting to trace the stubborn line of her jaw, the slightly cleft chin, the delicate curve of cheek. He found himself wanting to wake up with her sprawled across his chest for a thousand mornings, and maybe a thousand or two after that. He had no idea why that should be so, only that she made him feel as if he wasn't alone anymore. He couldn't quite remember the foolish reasons he'd made off into the forest with the Lady of Lilydrake when just being with her seemed like reason enough. Maybe that was all the reason he'd really needed.

He hadn't known he'd been holding his breath until he let it out in a long, slow sigh. "I'm dreaming," he said aloud. "I must be. I can't be. My dreams are never the happy kind."

"Neither are mine."

Her voice was so low he barely heard her words, but it didn't seem like he had to hear her to know her meaning. They were linked, somehow, for now, in the dawn of an early summer day in a hut no one wanted in a land neither of them called home.

His gaze slid away from hers. He couldn't say the thoughts that came to him while he looked into her eyes. "Am I—in your dreams sometimes?" When she didn't answer him for a long time he made himself look back.

"Yes," she answered when their gazes met. "When I dream," she went on, "I try to find someone I think I loved. But I can't see past you."

He held his breath as something hard loosened from around his heart. The pain was the only armor he had and he didn't want it to go away, but he couldn't keep from asking, "In your dreams do you love me?" Maybe she would say no and he could keep on hating her.

Instead she closed her eyes, turned her head so that

he saw only her fine-etched profile and answered, "Yes. Sometimes. In my dre—memories—I have you scrambled up with someone else, I think."

"Someone you should know but don't remember." It wasn't a question, for he was certain that whatever madness had descended on him had engulfed her as well. He touched her hair, ran the back of his hand across the softness of her cheek. Her head moved beneath his touch like a cat being stroked by a gentle hand.

Daughter of the devil she might be, but it wasn't her fault. He didn't want to punish her. In fact, he suspected he'd been trying to rescue her since the first moment he'd seen her. Rescue her from what? Wicked knights? Or lonely nights? Or was he looking for her to rescue him?

He was thinking too much, but his thoughts ended when she turned back toward him and settled her mouth against his. This time he didn't care that she was the one kissing him. He just accepted the sweet heat of the moment and the moment drew out until he was lost in it.

It ended with a sigh as she lifted her head. He didn't have to open his eyes to know she was crying. He could feel her tears on his face. "Bastien," she said, her voice full of uncertainty. This was madness, he could tell that she knew it as well. She sat up. When she was no longer touching him the world went cold.

Bastien moved to kneel beside her. There was nowhere for her to retreat in the tiny hut. She looked trapped, not by him but by her own demons. The look she gave him was one of entreaty. It told him how tired she was of always being in control of herself, of the situation. It begged him to make the choice for them both. He moved closer, so that the heat of their bodies met and mingled though they didn't quite touch.

"There is no right or wrong here," he told her. "There is just us." He knew what she needed, so he held her face between his hands as they looked deeply into each other's eyes. "It is time," he said, "to let the madness rule." This time he did the kissing.

Libby put her arms around Bastien's hard, slender body and drew him to her. She clung to him fiercely as the kiss deepened. This was wrong, stupid, against the rules. She couldn't stop it and didn't want to. He was right. They couldn't not make love now if they tried. Let the madness rule, she agreed, and God help us both when this is over.

His kiss, his touch, became demanding and she answered in kind, losing herself in ardent need. She flung away reason and lived only in sensation. She stripped off her jewelry and unbound her hair while he watched her deliberately provocative movements with a hungry, scorching gaze. She touched the silk of his undertunic and her chemise, bunching and pulling it away. Then the silk disappeared and they were flesh to flesh, fitting perfectly together. Their bodies twined, her dark skin against his pale, forming seductive sinuous shadowed patterns as they moved and twisted across the tiny room.

They shared kisses that were the deep joining of souls sort, and then there were kisses that explored each other's bodies in intimate, lingering detail. They touched, hands and mouths working over hard muscle and deep into soft, hidden places. They fought a long, pleasurable game with sweet invasions and gentle forays, each more arousing than the next. Each touch grew more urgent, more demanding, as they strained closer to completion.

They shared sounds, sobs and moans, gasps of delight mixed with cries of pleasure so intense it was near pain, and, occasionally, laughter that was nearly silent but full of shared secrets and discoveries. No words passed between them, there was no need, their communication was flawless. They answered each other's needs so perfectly it was as if they'd never made love to anyone else.

Her blood had long since turned to molten fire before he entered her. Yet she was still so full of need for this man that she was lost in a fresh storm of sensation as he filled her. The storm built out of control. It flooded through them, swirled around them, dragged them under its relentless currents. Time stopped as he moved inside her and brought her to completion once more. Or it stretched out to forever as the tempest took her again. They weren't alone, they weren't lost and nothing existed but this long, delicious moment of consummation.

Bastien held her close as the world came back into focus. His body was covered in sweat, and with the memory of her kisses, of her caressing hands. The memories were fresh, and burned into him. She was the only woman in his world. He couldn't remember how any other woman had ever felt. The musky scent in his nostrils was hers alone. The taste on his tongue was uniquely her own, sweet, delicious and his. Her breasts were pressed against his chest, soft, round and heavy to the touch.

"Mine," he whispered, without rancor or regret. "You are mine. All of you." And he lay his head on those soft breasts and fell into sated, exhausted, peaceful sleep.

"Yeah, well, I wouldn't get all possessive if I were you," Libby answered, but there was no seriousness in the softly spoken words. She didn't think he'd heard her anyway. Besides, she kind of liked the thought of belonging to someone. No, she liked the thought of belonging to Bastien. "I'm as crazy as you are," she concluded, and fell asleep with her arms around his shoulders.

She woke up laughing, happy for the first time in a long time. She was also alone, but she didn't mind that for the moment. "It's going to be all right," she said to the flimsy walls as she sat up. "Really. I think I'm beginning to figure this whole thing out. Maybe. At least I was dreaming some lovely dreams." Her memories were stirring. Though she couldn't call them up at will, she could feel things bubbling close to the surface of her mind, almost ready to burst into the light. Somehow the touch of Bastien's hands, the feel of his body covering hers had stimulated more than just her senses and emotions. Something was definitely going on in her head. "Sex as therapy," she said with a satisfied smirk. "Why didn't the shrinks think of that? Of course, they couldn't have provided Bastien back at Time Search headquarters." She didn't think anyone less than Bastien would do. She stretched and yawned. "I wonder how long I've been asleep?"

It was dark in the windowless hut, with more rain than light coming in through the narrow door. She was naked, but Bastien had left her covered with her cloak when he'd left. Not only was she naked but she could still feel the imprint of his hands where he'd touched her. Claimed her. That's what he'd done.

She couldn't help but smile, wondering if he felt as possessed by her as she did by him. If he didn't, she thought she just might have to work on him a little more as she relished the thought of making love to him again. Not that she should, of course. Not that she ought to. Not until they'd gotten their memories completely back at least. It really wasn't therapy, she told herself sternly, just self-indulgence, but she didn't believe that. He didn't deserve to be used by her.

But she didn't feel like that was what had happened. They'd made love because it didn't seem like they could do anything else. She hadn't been able to stop it, and didn't think she could wait for some more suitable, appropriate time. Because, if she was honest with herself, she'd have to admit that no time was suitable. It nearly tore her heart out to be honest with herself, so she pushed honesty from her thoughts for a while longer. She felt like she'd been waiting all her life for him as it was. She supposed she should be guilty about what had already gone on between them. Maybe she'd try to be guilty later. Maybe she'd try to be strong later. Right now, she supposed she should find this Bastien of Bale.

She hoped he hadn't gone far and hurried to dress. They had a lot to talk about, a lot to work through. "And maybe we can get some breakfast while we're at it," she added aloud as she finished dressing in just her underdress and kirtle.

She stepped outside into the rain and turned her face up to the sky. Her hair was disheveled, her clothes were wrinkled and her teeth could use brushing, but she felt just fine. The cool water on her skin was invigorating, though she supposed getting soaked through might prove uncomfortable later. She hoped it was drier under the trees as she crossed the clearing.

Even though Bastien had taken her belt from her and draped it over the horse's saddle before he sent it on its way she didn't think she was going to have any trouble finding the outlaw without the sensor tuned to him. She was tuned to him, or at least she felt like she was. She knew this wasn't logical, that the sort of almost telepathic pull she experienced toward him wasn't possible, but she followed her instincts anyway.

Her sense of where he was took her through the undergrowth and scrambling down a stream bank. Her soft leather shoes slipped in the mud but she managed to keep her balance as she reached the edge of the bubbling water. She found Bastien concealed behind a gigantic rotting log on the edge of an iris-filled pool. He held his bow and an arrow in his hands. His attention was focused on the trees on the far side of the pool. She hesitated for a moment before approaching him, just taking in the sight of him. His hair was tied back with a leather thong and a dark band of beard shadow accentuated the narrow lines of his face. His profile was very much that of the hunting hawk, all dangerous, steely concentration. Even soaked with rain and wearing stained homespun and deerskin he was the most fascinating and handsome man Libby had ever seen. She had to swallow hard and put a tight rein on kindling desire before she could move toward him again.

He gave her a disgruntled look as she settled down beside him. "I could hear you coming for half a mile. The deer probably could as well."

So, he was waiting here to bag them breakfast. She

concentrated on mundane necessity and refused the temptation to run her fingers up the length of his arm. "Sorry I interrupted you," she whispered. She glanced toward the woods, where the only movement was the dripping of fat raindrops from leaf to leaf. "Deer generally don't come down to water this time of day."

"It's dark and rainy, they might not be so shy on a day like today."

She nodded. "That's true."

His green eyes narrowed beneath the heavy arch of his brows. "And what does a fine lady know of deer stalking?"

She told him the truth. "My father taught me bowhunting."

His expression lightened somewhat. There was a hint of humor in his voice when he asked, "So you poach the king's deer in Wales, do you?"

"Nope. Northern Michigan, we've got a cabin on the Upper Peninsula. And I've never poached, I always have a hunting license."

The woman made no sense. Bastien wasn't surprised by that. What surprised him was the effect she had on him. He'd felt her watching him though he hadn't turned to look, her gaze had been like a caress along his skin, invisible but very real. He'd made himself ignore it and concentrate on the necessities of survival. His mind was filled with vivid images of what had happened between them, which he tried to ignore, but a part of him was certain she was necessary for his survival. He tried to block such foolish sentiment with the knowledge of how angry he was at himself for using Isabeau. Not at using her beautiful body. Their lovemaking had been a willingly shared experience though he feared she might try to deny that in the light of day. He wouldn't blame her if she did, if that was the defense she used against their growing, impossible feelings toward each other. He was angry for grasping onto the pleasure she'd given him to replace the emptiness inside. At the time he'd thought it was right, now he wasn't so sure.

He'd stiffened inside with tension when she came to stretch out beside him by the old log though he didn't move a muscle to give away his misgivings. He hadn't been able to do more than speak gruffly to her and was grateful she answered in kind even though her words were somehow disturbing.

He concentrated hard to answer her. "Then your father truly must be favored by the king if he has leave to hunt the royal deer."

She got to her knees. Her movement stirred up the scent of the decaying wood and crushed wet leaves. He looked up at her when he should have continued to scan the woods for signs of game. Her dark brown eyes were hidden by half-lowered lids, and there were bright spots of color in her cheeks. "I don't think I want to talk about my father right now," she said.

Bastien gave up the idea of hunting for the moment. He sat up and leaned his back against the log. He continued watching Isabeau. "What do you want to talk about?" It was a dangerous question. It would be better for him if he stayed silent, aloof. He couldn't manage it.

She looked at him, squarely meeting his gaze. "We need to talk about Lilydrake." She crossed her arms under her breasts, bunching the fabric of her dress tightly across her bosom. Her nipples stood out against the wet cloth.

Bastien couldn't help but look. He licked his lips while his hands remembered how those breasts felt, cupped in his palms. Remembering what had happened at Lilydrake was more important, he reminded himself harshly. He made himself meet her gaze again, and nodded as he acknowledged the flicker of humor at where he'd been looking shining in her eyes. "I'm a man. You're a beautiful woman. Some things can't be helped." Her blush deepened, but she didn't look away. "You have no modesty."

"None," she agreed. "Thanks for the compliment."

"It is the truth. Tell me what you know of that day at Lilydrake, Isabeau."

It seemed to be a hard decision for her, but she made it and said, "Very well. Tell me if you remember any of this. There were five people at Lilydrake that day. Only five. Myself, Joseph, Edward and two others."

"Who were the others?"

She shook her head. "I don't remember their names, and I don't see anything but shadows when I try to remember their faces. But those shadows are getting clearer. There were two men. I think I was involved with one of them."

"Involved? Do you mean married?" The words came out as a jealous snarl that surprised him. He could tell by the way her eyes widened that it surprised her as well. It shouldn't matter to him that she had been married. It should only matter to him that he had been married.

She nodded, very slowly as her tawny skin went sickeningly pale. "I think—maybe I was. I get all dizzy and disconcerted when I try to think about it."

"I know how you feel."

She rubbed her hands nervously along her upper

arms. "You'd think somebody would have mentioned to me that I was married, though, wouldn't you? The trouble is, no one will tell us anything."

"You and Joseph and Edward?" She nodded. He said, "Edward looks familiar to me. When I competed with him at the May Day fair it seemed as though I'd fought with him before. When I saw the boy start to strike you it was as though I had seen something like that happen before. This time I stopped it." Bastien's voice trailed off. He put the bow aside and closed his eyes. Images moved through darkness behind his closed lids while cool rain washed across his upturned face. As always, the images refused to make clear pictures in his mind.

Confusion threatened to overtake him, but Isabeau went on before the pain could start. "I got dizzy the first time I saw you. That should have been a clue, but I didn't make any connection. You see, what happened to us—how do I explain this to someone from the Middle Ages? What happened to make us lose our memories involved a kind of magic. There was a—wizard. Yeah, a wizard." He looked at her when he heard the pleased recognition in her voice. "He's some wizard," she told Bastien with a wide grin. "A physicist, really, but with the stuff this man does there's not much difference between science and magic."

Bastien tilted his head thoughtfully to one side. This talk of magic sounded somehow right, familiar. Hadn't Warin of Flaye once spoken of magic performed at Lilydrake? No. Warin had spoken of the magic more than once, when they'd shared a bottle and got maudlin drunk while Warin tried to get him to throw in his lot with Old Sikes. "What sort of magic?" he asked Isabeau.

She cupped her hands in front of her, as though she might conjure fire out of the raindrops. "He was manipulating time. Trying to make it stretch and bend and do things my father has never managed. A powerful Jedi is my father but—never mind, I get pop culture quotes mixed up with reality sometimes, and this is no time to confuse you more than I already have."

She made a habit of confusing him with her version of reality, he knew that much about her. Bastien did his best to concentrate on the least improbable of the things she'd said. "Your father is a wizard?"

"Oh, yeah. But—" She gave Bastien a long, hard, scrutinizing look before she went on. "The wizard at Lilydrake was very close to building a machine that would go anywhere in time, that's why it was so secret. My father's time machine will only travel from—well, never mind that part. Let's just say that some people— you and your wife, and some outlaws decided to raid Lilydrake at the exact same moment the time experiment got out of control."

Bastien leaned forward. He was intensely interested in this talk of wizards and time out of control. He darted forward to grab Isabeau by the shoulders and pull her close. "A wizard's spell killed my wife? Left me mad?" He shook her. "Where is this wizard?"

"I don't know."

That was not the answer he needed to hear. He told her, "I'm going to kill him."

"I think he's dead already." She blinked and shook her head in confusion. "Maybe. I don't know. I don't remember. Not yet," she added as she twisted away from him. She got to her feet. "I'm going to remember, Bastien. So are you. We're going to help each other remember what our lives were like before the accident." She hesitated for a long time before she added in a tightly controlled voice, "Then we're going to go on with our lives from this point on."

She sounded very certain. So, all she wanted him for was to help get her memory back. After that he was free to go back to the woods, and she back to her castle. Maybe that would be for the best. Maybe, but he wanted to make sure she never forgot him.

Bastien got to his feet and faced her. "I want to know that this wizard is dead. I want to make sure with my own two hands." He had never felt such loathing before. It felt good, gave him something to concentrate on. Something besides the driving need for Isabeau that clouded his already fogged mind. He wondered what Warin knew of the wizard of Lilydrake. "Why were you with this wizard, Isabeau?"

She ran her fingers along her jaw. "That," she said, "is a very good question. They should have sent Marjorie on this assignment, she's the specialist in this place and period, not me. My specialty is Asian history. We weren't expecting visitors. We were using Lilydrake because it was isolated." She gave him a bitter look. "How did the outlaws know we were there?"

Was she suggesting that he'd invaded her castle? Had he? "I don't know."

"You do. You just don't remember that you do. I remember a woman coming to the gate. She's older than you, isn't she? With red hair? What's her name?"

"I don't know."

She'd hoped the sudden question would shake the memory loose. He'd spoken each word with sharp annoyance instead. Libby went on anyway. "I remember her screaming, but I don't think there was anything wrong with her. I think it was a diversion, that she tricked us into letting her into the castle. I think the outlaws followed her in. I think she must have been your wife." She pointed at him. "You probably were the leader of the outlaws."

Her tale made sense, but he didn't believe it. He took a step closer to her. "I would not marry a treacherous woman."

Isabeau retreated a step. The back of her legs encountered the log, and she sat down on it. As she looked up at him she said, "Considering how badly you hate the nobles I don't see how you could call it treachery. Aren't they your enemies?"

He found that he was looming over her. "Aren't you my enemy, you mean, my lady?"

Libby could only assume that he was annoyed because she'd just accused him of being an outlaw, a rather clever outlaw, actually. "The diversion was a good plan."

"It wasn't mine."

He sounded certain, and looked furious. Libby refused to be intimidated. "Then what were you doing at Lilydrake?"

His expression clouded for an instant. He shook his head. "Outlaws came to the castle. I'll grant that. I can almost remember that. I wasn't one of them. Nor was my wife."

She appreciated his defending the woman's honesty, but Libby also remembered the red-haired woman who'd come to the gate. Her own explanation was the only one that made sense, even if she didn't remember anything more than that the woman had come to the gate. "Why were you at the castle?"

He shook his head. She could tell by the slight pinching of the skin between his heavy brows that he was getting a headache. She reached out, took his hand, and gently pulled him down beside her. Bastien sat down heavily on the log, his arm went around her shoulders. She felt the wiry strength of his muscles against her back. His closeness spread warmth through her. "I am not your enemy," she told him. "We'll figure out what happened together."

He looked at her, green eyes clouded with pain. "Why do you want to help me? Why help me if I attacked your castle? Why not just let the sheriff hang me? It would be better than never knowing," he added softly as he looked away.

Libby turned in his embrace. She cupped his cheek in her palm and forced him to look at her again. Their gazes met and locked, both searching for and offering comfort that was beyond words. His beard stubble scratched her hand, the masculine abrasion sent a pleasant shiver through her. This is no time to get physical, she thought, and an instant later was kissing him anyway as his mouth descended to cover hers. The heat that flared inside her then was enough to burn away good intentions and logical explanations. All that mattered from the instant their lips met was the demanding need that she had to answer. Even rain and wet earth meant nothing as they eased onto the crushed grass before the log.

The pain stopped when he held her in his arms, when he claimed her mouth. It wasn't just the pain and confusion in his head that ended, but the pain that engulfed his heart. He hadn't meant to kiss her, but once he started, once he held her body close, he didn't want to go back to a conversation that did nothing but leave him blind and hurting. All he needed was her hands splayed against his back, pulling him tightly against her soft, hot body. Her lips found the base of his throat while he ran his hands through her tangled hair and brushed her cheeks and eyelids with quick kisses. She tasted of fresh rainwater, her scent was her own, familiar and arousing.

"Olivia," he whispered against her temple, "I need you so badly."

She stiffened against him. She would have pulled away, but he let her go as he heard the rustling sound of something large moving through the trees on the other side of the stream.

"Stay here," he ordered.

Libby sat up as he moved swiftly away, his dagger drawn. She grabbed the bow and arrow he'd left behind and looked around for his quiver. She armed herself without thinking. She was having enough trouble controlling her breathing and getting her emotions under control. She didn't want to complicate a potentially dangerous situation by thinking about what he'd called her. She blocked the name away for now. She'd bring it out and consider what it meant later.

The log was large, offering her plenty of cover for the moment. She peered over the top of it to watch Bastien move forward with a combination of graceful speed and caution. He was like a hunting cat, poised and deadly. Not a hawk, she thought, a panther, Bagheera himself. But even a panther could use a little help sometimes, so she watched carefully, in case he needed backup.

Then a man stepped out from behind a bush and waved. "Bastien," he called. "Well met, friend."

Bastien's stance straightened, but he didn't put his dagger away. "Warin," he said. The word wasn't a greeting. "Do you come searching for me?"

Warin jumped across the stream. "I do. Sikes sent me to find you. It seems there are men in the forest looking for you."

As the newcomer moved closer Libby got a better look at him, though not without difficulty. She could make out that he was thin. Lank, blond hair peeked out from beneath the gray hood of his cape. Bastien was carefully keeping himself between the man and her position. There was something familiar about the way Warin moved. Libby's temples began to twinge with pain.

"Sikes sent me to offer you the safety of our camp," Warin went on.

His voice was more familiar than his movements. It sent a shock of pain through her, followed closely by the disorienting dizziness. *Hey,* she thought before she passed out, *I know that guy.*

13

Bastien did not want Sikes's man to see Isabeau. The old outlaw would try to take the Lady of Lilydrake as his own prisoner if he knew Bastien had her. Sikes was as likely to turn Bastien in to Reynard or Rolf and collect gold for Isabeau's return as well. Her ransom would make her captor very rich. Or the clever old man might find some other use for her. Nothing Isabeau would find pleasant, of that Bastien was sure. It was said her father had hunted down Sikes's first outlaw band, and had nearly caught Sikes himself. The old man might be one to hold a grudge.

"There are always men hunting us," Bastien reminded the other outlaw. He recalled that he had sent to ask Sikes for help. He had more than himself to think about, being with Isabeau had almost made him forget the people who depended on his protection. "My men can take care of themselves," he told Warin. "But if Sikes will take in the women and children I'd appreciated it."

"Sikes won't like granting such charity." Warin laughed. "But that termagant wife of his will make him. She's been trying to save his soul, she says, since he abducted her from a village fair when they were both young." Warin clapped a hand on Bastien's shoulder. "But I came looking for you, friend. To warn you that there are horsemen in the forest, and not that far behind me."

Damn. He needed to get Isabeau to safety. He needed to get rid of Warin of Flaye first. "Then you'd best seek your own safety, friend."

"Come with me, Bastien."

That he would not do. He shook his head. "I mean to hide myself in Blackchurch." The people in the village he'd named were known to be suffering from a catching fever. He had no intention of going there, but hoped to frighten Warin off.

Warin nodded. He looked as if Bastien's decision was one of the wisest things he'd ever heard. "I— what's that?" Warin whirled at the sound of a distant shout. "They're coming this way."

Bastien listened carefully, recognizing the sound of many men making their way as carefully as they could through the woods. "Horses," he said, "as well as foot-soldiers. Damn." He grabbed Warin's shoulder and pointed. "You go south, I'll head east." A look of indecision flashed across the other outlaw's face. "It'll be safer if we split up," Bastien told him. "Do it. Meet me at Maiden Well at moonrise."

Warin gave a sharp nod. "I'll take you to Sikes then."

"Yes," Bastien lied. "Go."

Warin turned and ran. He soon disappeared into the gloom of the forest. Bastien sprinted back to Isabeau's hiding place. She was sitting with her head braced against her drawn up knees. She groaned as he pulled her to her feet.

"Men are coming. This is no time for a headache, woman."

"Men? Who was that man? I know—"

"Horsemen. Your betrothed, I'd wager. Come on." He scooped up his bow and quiver, then grabbed her hand and hurried her around the iris pool. He picked out the tallest of the nearby oaks and pointed into the branches. "Up. Hide yourself in the canopy. Hunters from outside the forest often forget to look over their heads."

"Two-dimensional thinking," Libby agreed as she shook her head to clear it.

"Just so. Can you climb?"

She looked at the weathered, lichen-covered trunk. "This thing's been here since the druids."

"No doubt. Hurry. Or do you want to lie in Rolf's arms tonight?"

"No way."

"Then get up that tree."

She heard the urgency in his voice. More importantly, she heard people coming. She hoisted her skirts up and scrambled for a foothold on the wet wood. The climb wasn't easy, but she managed. Halfway up, she looked back to see if Bastien was following her. He was nowhere in sight. Her heart stopped for a moment, then fear for him rushed through her as a shout went up in the distance. She heard men and horses crashing through the underbrush.

"Wolfshead!" someone cried. "There he goes!"

Libby almost jumped down to rush toward the shouting men. They had come looking for her. Bastien was

creating a diversion to keep her from being caught by
Rolf. She didn't have any weapons on her, she'd left all
her supplies in the hut. She didn't know the forest the
way her outlaw did. He was probably safer with her out
of sight up in the tree. So, shaken with worry and frustration, she found herself a wide branch and settled down in
the concealment of the thick layers of oak leaves. After
a while the noise of the chase passed her by.

The arrow had been nearly spent when it hit him. There
wasn't much blood, not with the arrowpoint still buried
in the wound, but it hurt. It had hit him in the back of his
arm, the position awkward and hard to get at. The shaft
had broken off when he'd tried to pull the barb out.
Bastien ignored the pain as he made his way carefully
back to where he'd left Isabeau. It was near dark. The
rain had stopped, but clouds still hung low and heavy
above the treetops. He'd long since lost the men who'd
been chasing them. In fact, he'd watched them ride away
along the Canterbury road while he bled in the shadow of
a tree and no one noticed. It had been Rolf and his men,
ill-armed and ignorant of the tricks and hiding places of
Blean Forest. They'd be back, he thought, but he and
Isabeau would be long gone before they returned. If he
could remember in just which tree he'd left her, that is.

She was waiting for him at the base of an oak as he
approached the iris pool. She leaned against the wide
trunk with her arms crossed and a stern expression on
her face.

"You've been practicing that pose for hours, haven't
you?" he said as he approached. He straightened his
spine as he walked forward, and tried to look as

though he didn't care that there was an arrow sticking out of his arm. She noticed anyway.

"You're hurt," she said as she rushed forward.

He didn't try to deny it. There was, after all, an arrow sticking out of his arm. He let her help him sit on the ground. He couldn't see what she did as her fingers examined the wound, but they were firm and confident, hardly adding to his discomfort at all.

"We've got to get the point out."

"Yes. Not here," he said.

"Of course not. I've got a first aid kit back at the hut. Let's get you back there so I can build a fire and—"

"No fire," he said. "We shouldn't stay in the same place two nights running," he added. "Blackchurch."

He hadn't planned on going there, but it was nearby. They could find shelter in the village long enough to deal with the wound. Then he remembered that there was sickness in Blackchurch. He wasn't afraid of the fever raging there for himself, but what about Isabeau? It had been foolish to consider the place even for a moment. It would be too dangerous to take her there. He could not expose her to the contagion.

"No," he said on a gasp of pain. The wound throbbed as she tied a bit of her torn-off underskirt around his upper arm.

"Blackchurch. Old Osbeorn's keep. I remember where that is."

"Have to stay away." He put his head back against the tree. He was beginning to get light-headed even though he hadn't thought he'd lost that much blood. "Not the keep, the village. We can't go—"

"I'll get the stuff from the hut and be right back," she told him.

"Fever," he said, but she was already hurrying away.

"You won't get a fever if I can help it," she called back. "Rest. Everything's going to be fine."

Bastien closed his eyes. Maybe with Isabeau in charge for the moment everything would be fine. At least he could pretend it would be for now. Being back with her and knowing she was safe, he could rest, just for a little while.

By the time Libby returned from the hut with her hastily gathered stuff, Bastien was propped against the tree. He was asleep. He woke the moment she knelt beside him. His eyes were a bit glazed, his skin a bit waxy. "Can you walk?"

He didn't answer, but he didn't resist when she helped him to his feet. His eyes might be unfocused, but there was a grim, determined set to his jaw. He wobbled a bit unsteadily and leaned heavily on her after a while, but he walked. For as long and as far as she needed him to go.

Marj looked from the horse to Reynard to the ornate belt he was holding in his hands. She could see that many of the jewels had already been picked out of their filigree settings. The young man who'd been riding the appropriated horse sat in the mud on the edge of the road, a hand cupped around his sore jaw. He hadn't wanted to get off the horse when they'd stopped him, or hand over his loot. So Reynard had knocked him off the animal and taken the belt and a jewel-filled pouch from him. Marj thought she should have been shocked at the sheriff's violent action. Instead she agreed that it was the only sensible thing Reynard could have done, short of drawing his sword. She wasn't feeling particularly civilized at the moment.

She was feeling extremely frustrated, however. They'd been following the belt, which had stopped transmitting a few minutes before they'd actually captured the thief. Of course, Reynard did not know that they'd been following a signal. He had decided to follow the horse's tracks away from Lilydrake at her insistence. So she couldn't explain about sensors and tracking devices. Before meeting Reynard it hadn't bothered her that she couldn't explain anything to the people she encountered. She tried not to be bothered now.

It was nearly dark, and the forest seemed to be closing in as night approached. It had rained all day, which hadn't helped with tracking the animal. It was starting to rain again. The trees were still dripping with water from the last downpour, and the rutted track was more like a small stream than a roadway. Of course, it hadn't been much like a road to begin with. Since the road led to Canterbury, Marj had been half tempted to quote Chaucer all day. But the author of *The Canterbury Tales* wouldn't be born for quite a while yet and Reynard wouldn't understand if she started speaking Middle English. There was so much he wouldn't understand, even if she tried to explain in Norman French. She had no words for things like miniature electronics and brain wave pulses and the fact that being alone with him was not good for her at all. No, she had words for that, but she wasn't up to trying to explain. Despite the fact that they'd spent the day riding through the countryside on a fruitless quest, she'd had a wonderful time.

She sighed, and tried to stick to business. "I'm sorry," she apologized. "I was so certain the horse would lead us to Isabeau. I can't think why she abandoned it."

Reynard held up the belt. "Your lady had nothing to do with abandoning the horse. Bastien did this to show his contempt for her wealth. It seems it's the lady herself he wants."

Or Libby did it to throw me off her trail, Marj thought. To Reynard she said, "I think that they are a pair of fools."

Reynard nodded. "Blind with lust, you think?"

Works for me, she thought, and tried not to concentrate on his craggy features and knowing smile as he looked up at her. "It's not just lust," she said. "She isn't just running from Rolf, either. Isabeau wants to help Bastien."

Here was something else she couldn't explain. She was getting sick of this role playing no matter how necessary it was. Libby seemed to have forgotten the necessity in her zeal to fix the mental damage the time accident had inflicted on the outlaw. Maybe Libby was just reacting this way because she couldn't fix herself and thought she could do better with Bastien. Libby was not a person who dealt well with being thwarted.

Or maybe it was just lust.

"Help the outlaw?" Reynard asked. "How?"

Marj sighed, and went on with telling half-truths. "Apparently he's a grieving widower."

Reynard tilted his head to one side. He looked skeptical. No, he looked amused. The expression was gone in a moment, and with the light fading Marj really couldn't tell if Reynard had been close to laughing or not. She still said, "This isn't funny."

He wiped the back of his hand across his mouth. "Of course not, my lady." He turned to the horse thief sitting by the road. "Where did you find the animal?"

The boy got slowly to his feet. He looked frightened, but eager to explain himself to the big, deep-voiced man. He pointed back toward the direction of Lilydrake. "I found it just outside the village, my lord. I was bringing it back, but I got lost."

"Please spare us that tale," Reynard said. "Did you see Lady Isabeau, or the wolfshead called Bastien?"

"No, my lord. I saw no one."

"Just found the horse wandering down the road?"

"Yes, my lord. I swear by Saint Thomas!"

Reynard rubbed a finger across his mustache. "I wish I didn't believe you." He looked back at Marj. "Lady Isabeau's more than a little trouble, isn't she?"

She nodded. "I'm sorry to bring you into this."

He smiled. "It's an excuse to spend time with you, my dear."

While she blushed with pleasure the boy backed up a few steps, toward the nearby trees. It looked like he was going to run for it. Reynard did not look like he was interested in stopping him. Marj was relieved. They needed to continue the search, not worry about arresting a horse thief. Besides, she had no urge to see the man lose his hands, or suffer worse punishment, for taking Libby's abandoned horse.

Neither she or Reynard made any comment when the thief turned and ran. She got down from her own mount and stood in the middle of the road next to Reynard.

"What do we do now?" she asked him.

"Make camp. We'll continue searching for your lady after we've gotten some rest."

There was nothing else they could do in the dark, with no tracking device to follow. So Marj looked around and said pragmatically, "I just hope we can get a fire going."

He put a hand on her shoulder. His voice was a deep, rumbling, suggestive purr. "I don't think we'll have any trouble with kindling a fire, Marjorie."

She was suddenly having trouble breathing as she grew warm from the inside out. Just before he kissed her, she said, "I meant with wet wood, good sir."

Then, standing in the middle of the Canterbury Road, in the pouring rain, she put her arms around Reynard of Elansted and forgot about everything but loving him for a while.

It was well after dark before they finished the silent trip to the outskirts of Blackchurch. A big, thatch-roofed barn loomed out of the darkness on the edge of a field. By the size of it Libby thought that it might be a tithe barn, used for storage except during harvest time. Libby left Bastien long enough to reconnoiter the building. When she found it empty she guided Bastien inside and helped him to sit, propped against a thick, wooden post. Then she closed the barn door and sat down beside him in the dark. The barn was dry and smelled comfortingly of fresh hay. She searched through her bundle by feel and brought out a tiny round box. It looked like a piece of delicately carved ivory, suitable for holding needles, perhaps. It could be used for that. She flipped back the lid of the box, pressed a switch, and light filled the area around them. She glanced at Bastien, to see his reaction to this bit of magic. His eyes were closed, his wide mouth slack. Asleep. She brushed her fingers affectionately across his cheek, and found it cool to the touch. No fever, yet. Good.

She set the light on the barn floor and continued her search through her belongings. Her first aid kit was as well disguised as her flashlight. A native of the thirteenth century would have thought the object she placed beside the light was a reliquary, made to hold some saint's bones or ashes. She did say a prayer when she opened it, praying that she retained the memory of how to field dress a wound. Even if she didn't, she was going to have to do something for Bastien before infection set in. Libby took a deep breath, gathered the supplies she needed and got to work.

The first thing she did was cut Bastien's homespun tunic sleeve away from the broken shaft of the arrow. Beneath the tunic he wore a silk shirt. She'd forgotten about that, but smiled when she saw the bloodstained material. It was not too bloodstained. Silk was a very strong fabric. Instead of the threads breaking, the silk had probably been gathered around the twisting arrowhead as it drove into flesh and muscle. The silk shielded Bastien's flesh from actual contact with the arrowpoint. It helped protect him from the damage that could have happened when sharp metal pierces human skin.

"Well, I'll be," she murmured. She ruffled fingers through his hair. "What a clever fellow you are, and you don't even know it."

He made a small sound, a cross between a moan and a question. She wanted to hold him and make comforting noises, but that wouldn't get the arrow out. "Just hold still, and we'll get this over with, babe."

Babe. Now who was it she used to call babe? Never mind. She didn't have time to do the amnesiac routine right now.

She applied a tiny shot of anesthetic to his arm, and talked while she waited for it to work. "Now the Mongols," she told the mostly unconscious man, "the Mongols know about silk. And they know about archery. They are a bunch of warrior tribes off on the Asian plains. That's what I do. I study the Devil's Horsemen. That's what the West will be calling the Mongols in a few years, after Temujin—that's Genghis Khan to you—consolidates his power and gets the conquests started. Anyway, the Mongol army has this very sensible rule, which brings me back to silk. Every soldier has to wear a silk shirt under his armor as a protection against arrow wounds."

Bastien groaned again. She began to work the silk-wrapped arrowpoint out of his arm. Carefully, very carefully. With the help of the silk it came out easily enough. She hurried to apply disinfectant, and then bandaged it. She finished with another concentrated shot, an emergency combination of antibiotic and painkiller.

When she was done she eased Bastien down to lie on the barn floor, and stuffed hay under his head until he looked comfortable. Then she got up, brushed her sweaty hands against her still damp skirts and walked out of the barn. She'd done a fast, efficient job of dressing the wound, and thought she had earned the right to go outside and throw up.

"I was never meant to be a medic," she confided to the night when she stepped out the door. She didn't throw up, but she did lean against the wall, close her eyes, and breathe in large gulps of cool, evening air. She looked up at the sky. The clouds were clearing, leaving open great patches of starry sky. She smiled up at them while something nagged at the back of her mind. It was something about silk.

She always wore silk next to her skin. It had to do with hard lessons learned while working in Asia, sometimes within an arrow's flight of bands of Mongol warriors.

"So many stars here," she murmured as questions rolled around in her mind. "Not like at home with all the light pollution. Not as many stars here as the night sky over the steppes, though, where there's hardly any people. It's not as lonely here." A smile came to her lips as she thought of Bastien. She hadn't been lonely at all since she'd met the outlaw. Frustrated, furious, intrigued, tempted—more than tempted—but not lonely.

Why did Bastien wear silk next to his skin?

She remembered the smooth, rich feel of it as her hands moved across his chest and back. She remembered it against her cheek, the slippery sound of the cloth mixed with the steady thrum of his heartbeat as she cradled her head upon his chest to sleep.

Her head was beginning to hurt.

Why did Bastien wear silk like a Mongol warrior?

Where had an English outlaw learned that trick?

Her head felt like an egg someone was trying to crack from the inside.

She felt like a jigsaw puzzle that was assembling itself at light speed. She couldn't catch the pattern yet because she was the pattern and the pattern was coming at her at a thousand miles an hour. It was going to hurt like hell when it hit.

Libby slipped to her knees, and the darkness of the English countryside exploded around her. The present escaped her attention as her past rushed in to drown her in minute, intricate, impossible detail.

She bent forward until her forehead touched the cool, wet ground. It felt good. It felt real. She pressed her hands into thick clumps of grass. That was real, too. She was real. She was dizzy, light-headed, but her head didn't hurt anymore. She knew it would never hurt like that again. She didn't know how long she'd been kneeling in the grass, but the pain was finally, permanently, gone.

All because Bastien wore silk.

Because he'd been wounded by an arrow.

She knew why she'd kept having dreams about Mongolia.

She knew everything, remembered every detail of the four missing years of her life. She knew how the time accident had happened, and why, and who was responsible.

She straightened to look at the stars once more. For some reason she started to laugh. After a while she began to cry. With grief and anger at first, but then her tears changed to those of relief. She had her memory back. She decided to just be grateful for that for a while. She stood up and went to check on Bastien.

"Bastien." The word was a cross between a curse and a question.

This wasn't over yet, and it was more complicated than she had imagined it could be. Bastien was very much a part of it.

"He better live," she murmured. "So I can kill him with my own two hands."

14

    "Where am I?"

    "1227."

There was something about the caustic tone of Isabeau's voice that made Bastien regret having woken up. She prodded him in the side, with her foot, he thought. He wasn't sure he wanted to open his eyes and find out. He could feel her annoyance, it covered him like an invisible blanket. What had he done to make her so angry? Other than abducting her, holding her prisoner and forcing his will on her? Was she regretting having willingly gone along with all of it?

    "Wake up."

It was a cold anger, he judged by the frosty sound of her words. So whatever was bothering her was something she'd had time to think about through the hours he'd slept. Slept. Bastien wondered why his arm didn't hurt. And why he felt so well rested. And where they were. He sat up slowly, before he opened his eyes. He carefully moved his arm, as he concentrated on how it felt.

"It'll be sore for a few days, but it isn't bad."

His senses agreed with her judgment of the injury. He was going to be all right. How? Had the noblewoman taken time to nurse the outlawed peasant? Was that why she was annoyed, because she'd been forced to perform such a humble task? Perhaps that was the cause of her anger, but he doubted it. She could have left him to die, but he remembered her determinedly helping him to safety instead. Maybe he'd better try to find out what was really wrong instead of making up excuses for her behavior.

He nodded, and opened his eyes. They were in a large structure, with sunlight filtering in from the open door. Isabeau was standing in the patch of sunlight, glaring down at him with her arms crossed under her bosom. She looked tired and bedraggled, and wonderful. He smiled.

"What are you looking at?"

Smiling obviously wasn't the proper response this morning. "You're beautiful," he told her as he got to his feet as quickly as he could.

She looked him over from head to foot, eyes blazing. He stood still and let her, and he kept smiling because he couldn't help it. He was happy to be alive, happy to be with her.

In love.

The knowledge hit him like a lightning bolt and he immediately pushed it away. "What's wrong with you, hellcat?" he asked, instead of telling her what he felt for her.

Abruptly, her evil glower turned into a bright smile. She put her hands on her hips. "You really don't know do—"

Her words broke off as she snatched up his bow and whirled toward the door.

He'd heard the noise too. As he drew his dagger he was grateful the arrow had hit his left arm. He might be hurt, but at least he could still fight. "Stay back," he whispered to her, but she was already at the door. Damn. He followed quickly, meaning to push her behind him.

Instead she relaxed as he reached her and murmured a disgusted, "Oh, for God's sake."

Her two wretched deerhounds came bounding in the door as she spoke.

Libby gave a breathy laugh and went down on her knees. She rubbed the enthusiastic animals' sleek fur from ears to tail as they wove and squirmed around her. She wasn't sure if she was happy to see Luke and Leia or if she was just so relieved that they weren't a group of sword-wielding warriors that she needed to hug something.

She wanted to hug the man standing so nearby, but didn't think that would be such a good idea at the moment. They had to work some things out first. For once she wished she had a therapist with her, someone who'd know the right questions to ask, how to direct conversation to get at information. Well, she didn't have a therapist with her.

Besides, it hadn't been the shrinks at Time Search who'd helped her get her memory back. Bastien had been her trigger. She would be his. That was why she'd run away to find him. She certainly couldn't back out of that commitment now. And she would try not to be furious until he fully understood what she had to be angry about.

She pushed the dogs away and got to her feet. They turned their attention to Bastien. So did she. "They like you." *I like you, you bastard. More than like you.*

"They followed us," he answered. He looked worried even as he scratched Luke's and Leia's ears. "I hope no one followed them."

"Me too. The village is really quiet," she told Bastien. She picked up the bow and slipped the strap of the quiver over her shoulder.

"What are you doing?" he asked.

"Going hunting."

"You're doing no such thing."

She couldn't help but smile at the combination of protectiveness and machismo radiating from him. It made her feel all warm and wanted. Not that she was going to let him have his way, of course. "You've lost blood, you could use a high-protein meal. I won't be long. These are hunting dogs, time they did some work."

He stepped in front of her. "I forbid you to leave this—" He looked around. "Where are we?"

"Blackchurch," she answered. "The parish tithe barn, I think. I had a look around before you woke up."

"You did what?"

"I wasn't seen. No one is in the fields this morning. I heard church bells, so maybe it's some important saint's day and everyone's worshipping."

Blackchurch. The knowledge seeped through him as dark fear. Not for himself, but for Isabeau. He took her by the arm. "We have to get out of here. Those bells," he told her before she could argue, "were calls to a funeral Mass. There's a plague here. We have to get out."

"An epidemic?" she asked. "What is it?"

"A fever," he said. Her intense question told him she was more tempted to nurse the sick than to sensibly run away. He wished there was something they could do to help, but knew it was useless. He cursed the helplessness, but wouldn't expose her to danger. "I never get ill, but I won't take you near the sickness."

"Damn it, Bas, I've got medicine! Maybe I could—"

He pointed toward her small bundle of possessions. "Could you dose a whole village?"

Libby hated knowing he was right. She couldn't help everyone. Besides, it was against the rules. Time Search personnel were immunized against every possible ancient disease, but it wasn't possible to extend that protection to the entire population of the Middle Ages. Maybe they'd better get out of town before her conscience got the better of her and she threw even more rules out the window.

"You can't stop people from dying."

Bastien spoke her thought aloud, and she nodded in acknowledgment. "I hate this."

"I know." He urged her out the door. "So do I. We better go."

"Yes." She slipped out of his grip and gathered up her things while he waited by the door. He held out his hand to take the bundle when she came back to him. "No thanks."

"It's not chivalry," he told her with a smile. "I'm wounded, and you're better with a bow than I am."

"Not much." She realized that she was defending his masculine pride for him, and could tell by the laughter in his green eyes that he didn't feel the need for any defense. He was secure in his abilities, and confident of hers. She started melting inside all over again. The last thing she needed right now was sloppy sentiment over the man, but she couldn't seem to help it. "All right," she agreed, and passed the bundle to him. "Let's get moving." She let him lead the way, taking point. She and the dogs followed as they headed back into the woods.

"Who was that man?"

Bastien glanced over his shoulder at Isabeau. It was past midday, and they'd walked for hours without exchanging a word. "What man?"

"The one you were talking to yesterday. Before Rolf's men arrived."

He wasn't sure it was any concern of hers. He continued walking, keeping his eyes on the narrow trail that followed the bank of the Stour River. The forest was thick and silent on either side of the brisk current. The water was high from yesterday's rains, and the trail was sometimes covered in shallow water. They'd taken off their shoes, and Isabeau had tucked up her skirts to keep from dragging them in water and mud. He wished she was walking ahead of him so he'd have the chance to appreciate her long, shapely legs.

"Who was that man?" she repeated after a while.

"An outlaw," he answered.

"One of your men?"

"No."

"What's he called?"

Persistent woman. "Warin."

"Warin?"

She sounded like she didn't believe him. Bastien stopped and turned around. Her expression was as skeptical as her voice had been. "Warin of Flaye," he told her. "Satisfied?"

"Where's that?"

"I don't know."

"If he isn't one of your men, who does he work for?"

"Why do you care?"

"Why don't you want to tell me? What do you have to hide?"

"I am an outlaw," he reminded her. "A brigand, a wolfshead. I have a great deal to hide."

She smiled sweetly. "Not from me."

His arm was hurting, he wasn't quite sure where they were going, and he was hungry. He didn't need any more irritation. "Why should I tell you anything?" Her answer was a maddening, enigmatic smile. He'd seen it many times before. There was no escaping when she was like this. "Warin is one of Sikes's men."

She tilted her head to one side. "Is that so?"

"You've heard of Old Sikes?"

"Yes. What were you and Warin talking about?"

"About Sikes's band giving my people shelter."

She glanced at the river for a while. He watched thoughts flow across her expression faster than the rushing water. When she looked back at him she said, "It might be a good idea. I'd like to meet this Sikes." She looked like a wolf eager to meet its dinner.

"Why?"

She shook her head. "There's a clearing up ahead. Why don't we rest for a while?"

He decided that he didn't want to continue the discussion about Sikes, so he accepted her diversion. "Fine."

They made their way along the bank a little way, then climbed a small hill just beyond a stand of willows.

The hillside was covered in bright wildflowers, and they settled down side by side in the fragrant blossoms. The dogs spotted a rabbit and took off after it through the undergrowth.

"Hope they catch dinner," Libby said as she watched the sleek hounds race away. "I think Luke and Leia are pretty good at taking care of themselves."

She wrapped her arms around her drawn-up knees. Her impulse was to wrap her arms around the tired man beside her, but she kept her distance for now. He stared off into the distance, silent and moody. Because she wasn't quite sure how to proceed, she let the silence draw out. Eventually a pair of gray herons landed on the edge of the river and began to strut cautiously through the shallows, fishing for their own dinner. She watched the big, graceful birds for a while before looking at her companion once more. He looked more sad than tired, the expression in his eyes darkly despondent. She still didn't reach out to him, though she longed to.

"What are you thinking about?" she asked.

He didn't take his eyes off the fishing herons. "Are they mates, do you think?"

"Yes," she said. "Probably."

"Mates for life?"

"I'm no expert on birds, Bas."

He turned his anguished stare on her. "People should mate for life. It was all I ever wanted."

Libby's throat tightened with pain. Her heart ached for him, and for herself. She fought hard not to cry. She held her hand toward him, but he moved away.

"We should go to Sikes," he went on before she could find any words. He got to his feet.

She was confused by this abrupt change of subject. She leaned back on her elbows to look up at him. She didn't like being loomed over, but Bastien looked like hell, tired and defeated, so she didn't complain. "Why do you want to go to Sikes?" she asked.

"I left her at Lilydrake," was all he said before he turned and walked away.

Yeah, she thought, as she glared at his retreating back, *you did.* Her irrational bitterness lasted only a moment. Still confused, she hurried to catch up with him.

"What's leaving your wife have to do with Sikes?" She suspected she knew the answer to this much better than he did, but she wanted his explanation just the same.

He continued along the river path. "There's a ford near here," he said. "We'll have to cross the river to get to Maiden Well. Maybe Warin will still be there. I told him that's where I'd meet him last night. Sikes's camp must be on the other side of the river, as well."

"And Warin will take us to Sikes?"

"You'll be safe enough there while I'm with you," he answered.

She'd been right, he was guilty because he'd left his wife and didn't want to make the same mistake with her. He blamed himself for what had happened. Libby put her hand on his arm, grasped his tunic and forced him to stop. "I can take care of myself, you know. You know that better than anybody." She wasn't boasting, or arguing. She was trying to be reassuring.

"Can you fight off all of Rolf's men?" He shook her off. "I'm going to see that you stay safe."

His expression was closed, he was locked in with old pain and Libby didn't know what to do about it. He'd had no help dealing with six months' worth of physical and emotional trauma. She couldn't afford to make a wrong step or he might never recover. She knew she had to do something, but she wasn't sure what would help. So she decided not to push him right now. Besides, she very much wanted to have a talk with Warin.

So she let him lead the way to the ford. She even let him guide her across the river with his good arm around her waist. The bottom was slippery and the current fast. She was appreciative of his support. When they reached the other side and she kissed his cheek in thanks he pulled away as if he'd been burned.

Bastien walked almost blindly away from Isabeau, not because he hadn't wanted her touch, but because he wanted it too much. Wanted it, and didn't deserve it. He set off through the woods again, carefully listening to make sure she followed, but not taking the risk of looking at her. He'd lost the one woman he'd loved. He wouldn't lose this woman, but he wouldn't let himself love her. The irony of the situation was a scalding ache. He'd wanted to make the Lady of Lilydrake love him as punishment for the loss of his wife. He hadn't gotten what he wanted.

As the dark, secret pool known as Maiden Well came into sight, he couldn't stop himself from saying, "I should never have made love to you."

"Yes, you should have." Her words were full of serene assurance. She had no doubts, no regrets. Had it meant anything to her? He turned to face her. She was smiling at him, a tentative, concerned smile. She took a step toward him. He backed away. "Bas?"

"It was nothing to you, was it? Just a way to pass the time with a peasant." He was trying to convince himself more than hurt her with his accusations. "Did my body please you, my lady?"

"Completely," she answered. "And I pleased you." She pointed a finger at his chest. "I'm not going to let you get away with this, you know."

"Get away with what? Making you my prisoner? Having sex with you? You manipulated this entire situation." She didn't deny it. "Who had who?" he demanded.

"Isn't that an old Aretha Franklin song? Or maybe it's AC/DC? My mother collects antique CD's, I'm into old movies." She swept a hand through the air, as if brushing away her own strange words. She was very serious when she spoke again. "Stop trying to punish yourself by hurting me, Bas. You're not going to get rid of me that easily. I'm tough, remember? Tough enough to love you."

"I don't want your love."

"Oh yes, you do."

He didn't know if it was her words or her refusal to acknowledge that he didn't mean anything to her that was giving him a headache. He gave her a mocking bow. "You want my body, you mean. Shall I perform for your pleasure again, Lady Isabeau?"

"Don't call me that."

"That's who you are, isn't it?"

"No."

"You are a great man's daughter, I'm a peasant."

"Let's not bring my father into this."

He stepped closer, trying to use his size to intimidate her. But he came close enough to feel the heat of her body, and the longing to touch her drove him back a step. All he wanted was to take her in his arms, to be with her forever. That would be wrong, a final betrayal.

He lashed out at her instead. "My life is forfeit if I'm captured. Will you betray me when you're done with this adventure? Will you laugh when they hang me, my lady? Will you marry Rolf of Gesthowe and remember our night together sometimes from the safety of your strong, warm castle? Will you take other villeins as lovers? Will any peasant do? Or just outlaws?"

Her fists went to her hips, her chin rose to a combative angle. "Bas, where do you get these—medieval—ideas from?"

"From Cynric," he answered without thinking. "Cynric taught me how treacherous nobles are."

"Good for Cynric. Have you got any thoughts of your own?"

"None that I want to share with your kind."

"Who do you want to share your thoughts with, then? Your wife?"

Her voice was soft as silk, and as strong. The words went into him like an arrow. The pain in his heart was far worse than that from the barb that had pierced his arm. She'd pulled that arrow out only to drive this one into him now. His breath came in a gasp of agony. "I don't want to talk about my wife. Not to you." He wanted to turn from her, but he was trapped by her angry gaze.

She came to him and clutched his arms in a taloned grip. She ignored his wound to inflict her words on him. "We're going to talk about her."

He shook his head. "No."

"You don't remember her, but I do."

His temples were beginning to pound. "I left her," he said. He hadn't wanted to talk about it, but the words came of their own will. "I ran away and left her.

I can't remember her face or her name. I only remember that I had a wife. I remember I lost her."

"That's a place to start," she said.

Her voice was gentle and understanding. It was oh, so seductive to listen to that voice, to accept her touch, her company. She didn't understand. She couldn't. So he told her.

"When I look at you I don't want to remember her. You fill the place where she should be. You take the pain away."

"You think you need the pain to keep her with you?"

He nodded. "You make me—happy. Angry. Exasperated. You make me feel like a man again, not just a walking shell."

"You do the same for me. Don't you know that you're what makes me whole?"

She sounded as desperate as he felt. He hated hurting her, but he had no choice. "When I'm with you I don't hear her laughter, or the sound of her voice in my memory," he explained.

"Could you remember her before you saw me?"

"No."

"Then what makes you think—"

"I tried to remember her. I've almost stopped trying since I first saw you. It's your laughter, your temper, the feel of your skin, the taste of you that fills me. You're becoming all I know."

"Oh, Bas." She touched his cheek. He pulled sharply away. He felt her sympathy, her caring. He wanted her to hold him.

"No. I need to remember my wife. I have to hold on to whatever I can of her. I can't let myself love anyone else. I have to remember her. I owe her."

"Because you love her?" Her tone was bleached of all color. He looked back at her. She was as pale as her voice had been. Her dark eyes looked enormous, full of anguish, and something he couldn't read. "Is it love, Bas, or is it just guilt?"

He flinched inwardly. "I love her." He wanted it to be the whole truth, but he wasn't sure. "I can't love you and love my wife."

"God damn it, Sebastian, I AM YOUR WIFE!"

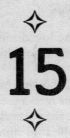

15

"Oops."

But for the drip of water from the spring into the pool the clearing was utterly soundless. No birds called. There was only silence for a long time after she spoke that one last word, acknowledgment that she'd said exactly the wrong thing at the wrong time.

"Oops," she said again, into that dark, deep silence.

He just stared at her, eyes wide and as green as the moss and ferns that filled the clearing. Eyes that were empty of every emotion but confusion. His lean muscles were bunched and corded with tension, his stance wide as though he were trying not to fall to his knees.

She had told herself she couldn't make any wrong steps, and then she'd trampled all over every good intention with only a few words. And she'd done that trampling because she was used to cajoling, teasing and arguing him out of his brooding, moody depressions anyway. He'd always been a royal pain in the butt when the melancholy struck him, but she loved him anyway. So, she'd reacted out of habit, and risked his sanity in the process.

"Sebastian?" He turned his head away, showing his sharp profile. She could tell that he neither recognized the name, or her. She felt more annoyance than sympathy. "Your name is Sebastian Bailey," she told him. "And you're a wizard."

"You're not my wife." The words came out as a parched whisper.

"The hell I'm not."

She couldn't stop herself. She knew telling him the truth wasn't going to help him remember it. Hadn't the shrinks tried to convince her that memories had to come back on their own or the patient might never believe they were real?

It was more important to help him than to try to ease her own sense of loss. She couldn't just grab him and shake the memories loose—not physically, not verbally—no matter how much she needed to. She had to stop herself from saying anything more.

"Making love to you once doesn't make us married."

He turned to face the pool. She wondered what he saw in its reflecting depths. She wondered if he'd heard her call him Sebastian. She wondered how he'd come to be called Bastien, how he'd survived six months on his own. She wondered how he'd clung to the mangled memory of having a wife when she hadn't retained any memory of the last few years at all. She wondered if maybe it was better if he'd blocked out the painful information she'd told him. She wondered what he would do if she tried to touch him right now.

She didn't think she wanted to risk finding out.

Bastien ground the heels of his hands into his temples as he tried to deny the growing pain. He stared into the water, his face showed up as a pale image in the center of the pool. He had no idea what he should look like, the reflection wore the face of a stranger, as it had for far too long.

Who was Sebastian?

He was Bastien of Bale—Cynric had told him that was what he'd called himself when he was found wandering the forest. Had Cynric heard him wrong? Was he someone called—

Torment stabbed through his head before he could finish the thought. In the distance he heard someone swear, then hands were on his arms.

A voice said, "Bas, there's someone coming. I think it's trouble. Let me help you into hiding."

Trouble. She needed him. He forced his eyes open, only to find that he couldn't see beyond the lights exploding behind his eyes. He had to help her.

Fingers brushed his temples. "It's okay. You get migraines—that's besides the injuries from the accident. I'm sorry I didn't bring any of your medication with me, but, babe, I thought you were dead. Actually, I didn't know you even existed."

He heard a chuckle. He was barely aware of her helping him walk, but the velvety sound of her laughter was as comforting as a soft blanket. "Isabeau?"

"Call me Libby. No one will see you here. Yeah, that's Rolf and his boys. We can't run. I'll try to talk our way out of it. Stay here."

She helped him to sit. The ground was cool, damp. He reached out a hand, it encountered moss-covered rock on one side, a thick tree trunk on the other. "Where?"

"Don't move." Her voice had become an urgent whisper. "Let me have your knife." He should be the one protecting her. He tried to bat her hand away when he felt it fumbling at his dagger sheath. He was distracted when her lips brushed his in a quick kiss. She took the dagger. "Don't make a sound," she warned, and was gone.

He didn't see her go, but he felt her absence instantly. Into the empty space left by her leaving came the sound of horses and men's voices. Someone said, "The outlaw we captured spoke true. Look there, my lord."

"Isabeau!" Rolf's voice, loud and demanding.

"My lord," she called back. Even through his pain, Bastien heard the relief, the joy she expressed in seeing her betrothed. "You've found me at last. I prayed to Saint George you would come."

"Were you harmed? Did the churl dishonor you?"

"How could he, my lord? When you wounded him badly when you almost rescued me. You saved me from that horror."

Liar, Bastien thought. Pain drove nails into his head, but the anguish of Isabeau's denial was worse still. He crouched in his hiding place, blind, helpless, and forced to listen to the noblewoman trying to save her own skin. If he'd been able to he would have stepped out of hiding and somehow managed to kill the lord and the lady both.

"Where's the wolfshead?"

"Dead," Isabeau answered. "I finished the job you'd started with his own blade. Then I wandered the forest until I found the pool. I prayed you'd find me here."

Dead. So, she would protect him from Rolf's vengeance. How kind of her. It was just as he'd suspected, no more than a fling for her.

"Come up behind me, sweeting. The dark draws down, we'll pass the night at Blackchurch Keep, then return to Lilydrake tomorrow."

"Blackchurch, my lord? What of the fever?"

"I'm told the bodies are buried, and it has run its course. Never fear, my lady, you'll be safe with me."

"I doubt it not, my lord. Then let us hurry from this place. I so wish to be with you and you alone."

Bastien could almost feel the fluttering of her eyelashes as she cajoled Rolf of Gesthowe. How easily the fool was led by her sweet words. How easily he'd been led. Rolf wasn't the only fool. He didn't want to hear any more of her treacherous words, and the pain obliged. It filled his senses and crushed him down into black, cherished oblivion.

When he woke up the headache was gone and Isabeau was gone and he wished he was dead. He stumbled out of hiding and to his knees before the pool. He plunged his head in and came out to shake like a dog, then he brushed dripping hair back off his face. She was gone, back to safety, back to Rolf of Gesthowe. Rolf thought he was dead. Perhaps the forest would be safe for himself and his people for a while. Perhaps he could go back to his outlaw band and pretend Isabeau had never entered his life. Perhaps, but she'd taken his soul with her when she'd fled back to her castle. He felt used, dirtied. He didn't want to face anyone who might have a concerned question, or a snickering joke about his bout of lust for the noblewoman.

There had never been much for him among the outlaws, it had just been a place to be. He still knew nothing about his past, but he did know that his future was bleak, empty. It always had been, Isabeau had just stripped the pretense that he might find his way home from it. He might as well be dead. He wanted nothing more to do with the Blean Forest or Lilydrake Castle. He didn't know where he was going to go, but he stood up and began to make his way toward the nearest road.

As he walked he tried not to think, but he was alone on a quiet, empty night. He was surrounded only by trees and patches of moonlight. No nightbirds called, no wolves howled in the distance. He had only himself to pay attention to. After a while Isabeau's words began to bubble to the surface of his thoughts no matter how hard he tried to push them away. He was tired, he was hungry, his healing wound throbbed, he tried to concentrate on pure discomfort, but Isabeau's words kept knocking every other concern aside.

Call me Libby. That wasn't her true name, either, he was certain of that. Nor was she Isabeau. Who the devil was she, then?

I'll see if I can talk our way out of it.

I prayed to Saint George.

He gave a soundless laugh at the memory of those words. The only George she revered was named Lucas. How well he knew that particular obsession of hers. She'd even named those foolish deerhounds Luke and Leia.

"As the princess said to the Jedi," he murmured, as he remembered that first surprising kiss on Passfair's battlements.

It was like remembering something that had happened a thousand times before but was new and exciting every time. He touched his lips and couldn't stop the laughter that breathed new life into his soul. He could almost feel her there with him, her lips soft and demanding at once. Bastien stopped walking, his legs felt like they'd suddenly grown roots. His head spun, but not in pain. He looked around, hopelessly confused, almost happy. The memory of a kiss made him giddy.

He reached out, though there was no one there for him to touch. "On our first date," he said to the ghost figure that was just out of his sight, "you took me to a Star Wars film festival. All eighteen hours. I married you anyway."

He had no idea what he was talking about, he only knew that he spoke the truth. For true love, he thought, you made sacrifices. Like going to stupid science fiction movies.

Or like her turning herself over to Rolf rather than letting him be captured.

"Oh, my God," he whispered, and the almost-joy was gone on a rush of fear. "She was trying to save me." He was certain she hadn't meant a word she'd said to Rolf of Gesthowe. How could he have believed she'd betrayed him when she'd only been trying to protect him? How could he have been such a fool?

More importantly, how did he get her out of Blackchurch Keep before Rolf harmed her?

Mark Warin was dead. Libby thought about that as she paced the rush-covered floor in Lady Cicely's bower. Lady Cicely was a youngish widow who held Blackchurch for her young son. The attractive woman was working at a loom in one corner of the keep's only bedroom while Libby paced. Lady Cicely's serving women were preparing a bath for her in another corner of the room. Libby ignored all of them while she tried to get her emotions under control.

She'd left Sebastian lost in pain and the disorientation she knew too well. She was trapped in someone else's castle with the prospect of a wedding night with the wrong man a very strong possibility. She had a lot of troubles, but the thought sickeningly at the front of her mind was that Mark Warin was dead. He'd died after Rolf had caught and questioned him about her whereabouts. Rolf had been quite pleased with having gotten the location of Maiden Well out of the cowardly outlaw he'd then executed.

Mark probably deserved some sort of trouble, but he hadn't deserved to be run casually through with a sword and left to rot where he fell. She was responsible. If Rolf hadn't been looking for her, a man wouldn't have been tortured and killed with no chance to defend himself.

What had Mark Warin been doing in the company of outlaws anyway? What had he been doing with Old Sikes's band? What had he wanted with Sebastian? Those were questions she felt she had the answers to. She concentrated on them rather than the horrific images Rolf had conjured up for her of how he'd treated Warin on the ride to Blackchurch Keep.

Mark Warin was one of the two missing Time Search people the accident had supposedly killed. When she'd first gotten her memory back, she'd realized that it wasn't any accident, but a deliberate act of sabotage and Mark Warin had been involved. In fact, she was certain he was a traitor who'd arranged for the outlaws to attack Lilydrake. She remembered a woman pounding on the gate, begging to be let in because outlaws were chasing her. It had been a ploy to get the gates open for the attackers.

She didn't know why Mark hadn't just let them in himself, but she'd figure it out. Maybe the outlaws had been a cover for some other activity. She remembered how awful she'd felt when she'd woken up. He must have drugged the wine the night before the attack. They'd all passed out after the party, she and Sebastian and Joe and Ed. None of them had been in very good shape the next morning. All but Mark Warin, she bet.

He must have used the time they were unconscious to do something with Sebastian's prototype. He'd been trying to steal it, she supposed, even though Bas hadn't yet gotten the damned thing to work. It had possibilities, infinite possibilities. Mark had talked about the profit and power that could be had from Sebastian's work. Sebastian hadn't agreed with a word he'd said. Mark Warin had probably figured he could work out the bugs in the design himself. Somebody had probably paid him a fortune for the prototype and his own expertise. Maybe the outlaws had been let in to kill the rest of them, make it look like they'd destroyed the prototype and provide Mark with an alibi.

It hadn't worked out like that. She still didn't know what had happened to cause the prototype to malfunction and nearly kill them, or how Mark and Bas had gotten trapped in the past instead of transferred back to Time Search headquarters. She and Ed and Joe had all been wearing subcutaneous medical sensors that had triggered the automatic recall through the timegate. The timegate had been destroyed when the outlaws burned down the hall, but not before the three of them were yanked to safety. She didn't know why the sensor hadn't worked for Sebastian and Mark. Well, the sensor only worked within a certain distance from the timegate. She did remember Bas running away from Lilydrake. Away from her. She still didn't know why. She only knew that his leaving her hurt and angered her, but she didn't want to think about it. If he hadn't left her then—No. No recriminations allowed until all the circumstances were explained.

She didn't want to think about Warin either, or how he'd been killed, but she couldn't get Rolf's lurid images out of her mind.

"Your bath is ready, my lady," someone said.

Libby looked at the servant who waited anxiously beside her, and realized she'd paced a path through the floor covering. How long had she been pacing? How long had she been here? Where was Bas and how was he? How was she going to get out to help him?

"Bath?"

Lady Cicely got up from her loom and took her by the hand. "Come, my dear, and refresh yourself. Lord Rolf would have you beautiful for him tonight." Cicely sounded almost wistful when she said Rolf's name.

Libby remembered that Cicely had given Rolf an enthusiastic welcome to her hall, and hadn't looked too happy when he'd introduced her as his betrothed. She'd been coolly polite to Libby, but happy to attend to Rolf's needs for food and ale and a place to stay. While Libby had tried to shrink into the shadows of the hall, Cicely had talked to Rolf. She'd gone on about her lonely widowhood and the need for a strong right arm to protect her and how she ached for strong loins as well. Rolf had paid attention while he downed a few cups of ale. He'd remembered his fair Lady Isabeau at the mention of loins and ordered her upstairs to prepare for a proper bedding. Lady Cicely had come along to see to her comfort rather reluctantly.

You want him, Libby thought as she looked at the woman. *You can have him. Loins and all.*

She glanced at the large tub filled with scented, steaming water. She could use a bath. She was plastered with dirt and sweat, her muscles ached and she itched from scratches and bug bites. She suspected she smelled rather badly. She wanted just to immerse herself in the hot water and forget about her troubles for a while.

Unfortunately, she didn't have time for that sort of indulgence. Sebastian was alone and in pain in the woods, and Rolf was downstairs waiting to pounce on her. Her bundle full of modern equipment and exploding jewelry had been left behind at Maiden Well. All she had to work with were her wits. She sighed, because she did not feel particularly witty at the moment. Cicely was all she had to work with, so she'd better get on with it.

"Bathe with me, Lady Cicely," she suggested. "And let us discuss Lord Rolf's many fine accomplishments." *I can lie about anything*, Libby thought as Lady Cicely nodded her agreement to share hot water and a little girl talk.

"What ails your heart, my son?"

Bastien looked up, and into the face of a rather wicked looking nun. It was the humorous, wise twinkle in her eye, he decided, that made her look less than saintly. It was only after she smiled at him for a few moments longer that he noticed the other holy sisters standing in the road behind her.

"Who are you?" he asked. At the same time he was wondering how long he'd been sitting on the side of the road staring at nothing. "You should be careful," he told the nuns. "It would be better if you were safe behind doors after nightfall, sisters. There's robbers in this forest."

"There are robbers in every forest," one of the holy women said. She stepped up beside the first nun. She was an attractive woman, with a brisk and efficient air to her. "I'm Sister Susan," she told him. "This is Sister Anne. We are on pilgrimage to Canterbury, but were delayed from reaching the city before nightfall by our sick donkey and the rain. You looked as though you'd been robbed, beaten, had your heart broken, and been excommunicated all at once."

Bastien ran his hand through the long tangles of his hair. His left arm ached when he raised it, but not so badly that he couldn't use it. It was stiff, but healing. Even the discomfort reminded him of Isabeau and how she'd tended his wound. He laughed silently at himself, aware that he must be badly in love with the woman if pain could make him sloppily sentimental over her.

He smiled, and spoke to the nuns. "I don't know about excommunicated, sister, but I've had most everything but lightning strike me the last few days."

"Including Cupid's arrow from the look on your face," one of the robed women said.

He rubbed his stubbled jaw. "There was an arrow involved," he admitted as he stood.

"How can we help you?" Sister Anne asked while the other nuns congregated around him.

There was something about the women, perhaps the speculative way they looked him over as he stood among them, that told him they hadn't always been locked in the innocent cloisters of an abbey. He wondered just what they'd done before they'd become nuns.

In answer to the question he hadn't asked, Sister Anne told him, "Once we followed the wicked calling of Jezebel, but now we seek salvation by pilgrimage, and in helping others."

"What good work can we do for you?" Sister Susan asked. "You certainly look like you can use some— comforting."

"Or a shave and a bath," one of the other sisters added, almost under her breath.

"And a proper night of frolic," one of the others said, equally quietly. They still received stern looks from Sisters Susan and Anne.

Bastien knew he looked awful and felt worse. Rescuing Isabeau was more important than his needs. All he required, really, was to have her safe. "I need help," he told the women.

"Tell us and we'll do what we can," Sister Anne replied. "We have only our donkey, and the good sense God grants us, but that should be enough."

He shrugged. These women weren't sensibly offering to pray for his soul and then go on their way, but to actively do what they could for him. What could holy women do against Rolf of Gesthowe and his men? He didn't want to put them in danger, but their caring curiosity led him to confide in them. "I don't know how you can help me, but I need to find a woman." He'd never heard nuns giggle salaciously before. It was a rather disconcerting sound. "Lady Isabeau of Lilydrake," he hurried to tell them. "She was kidnapped and carried off to Blackchurch Keep."

"Blackchurch is but a few minutes walk from here," Sister Anne said. "We were on our way there to ask for shelter for the night."

"Isabeau is being held there. I have to get her out. She's my wife," he added, sure it was the truth even though he was still uncertain of how and why he'd come to believe this. After he saved her from Rolf he had quite a few questions he needed to ask her.

Sister Susan crossed her arms. "Some evil knight carried your wife off against her will? To ravish her?" Bastien nodded.

There were murmurings of sympathy and outrage. The women gathered in a group in the middle of the road to discuss his problems in a whispering huddle. As he watched the dark-robed figures consulting by moonlight, Bastien was reminded of a scene from a play involving witches that hadn't been written yet. Only he didn't know how he could remember something that hadn't been written. He didn't even know if he could read. The subject of literacy had never come up while living hand to mouth in the forest.

He had a lot to talk about with Isabeau. Which meant getting on with the rescue quickly, before Rolf forced himself on her and she drove a dagger into Rolf's vitals in retaliation. He couldn't let that happen—he wanted the pleasure of gutting Rolf of Gesthowe himself.

As he started to turn away from the women, to go off on his own rather than involve innocents in his troubles, they turned back to him.

"I believe we have a plan," Sister Anne said.

"One that will at least get you into Blackchurch Keep," Sister Susan added, and began to explain.

＊　　　＊　　　＊

All cats are gray in the dark. Libby had heard that saying somewhere, now she just hoped that there was some truth to it. Meanwhile, she had to get through dinner. She'd put this off as long as she could, but after hours of hiding in Cicely's room she'd finally steeled herself to put the night's plan into action.

The carousing had been going on for quite a while by the time she accompanied Lady Cicely and her women to the stairs that led to the hall. Libby paused on the staircase for a moment to observe the activity below her. The place was full of smoke, as well as laughter and shouting; someone was singing, off-key and bawdy. Rolf's men mingled amiably with Cicely's people. Serving women were being molested without too much protest, and a noisy brawl was taking up one corner of the room. Ale and mead were flowing freely. The men were having a great time. Libby could practically taste the testosterone oozing from their pores. It reminded her a lot of some parties she'd gone to in college.

The only pool of quiet in the hall seemed to be the spot where a group of black-robed nuns sat in the very back of the room. She remembered that a servant had announced their arrival while she and Cicely were having their long talk. The Lady of Blackchurch Keep had sighed at the announcement that she had yet more uninvited guests to feed, but she hadn't turned the holy women away.

Libby saw that their presence in the keep was certainly unobtrusive. Only one of the robed figures even stood out from the others at all. Even though the nun was silently bent over her meal like the other women, head modestly lowered, her face obscured by white wimple and heavy black veil, it was obvious that the good sister was a big woman. She was probably at least six feet tall when she stood, Libby guessed, and broad-shouldered. Libby wondered if the poor woman had ended up in the convent because her ungainly size brought her no suitors or if she had a true vocation. Not that the woman's situation mattered, really. Libby knew that thinking about the nun was keeping her from facing the man who waited below for her. She stopped looking at the nun, and made herself search out her ostensible betrothed.

Rolf was seated at the largest table. A tall branched candlestand was placed behind his chair. The light from many tallow candles showed him off in all his broad-featured, heavy-limbed, barbaric glory. She thought it was enough to turn a girl's stomach, but Cicely seemed to have eyes only for him. He looked up, caught Libby gazing at him and leered. He stood and waved her forward. Libby sighed. She supposed it was time she made an entrance.

Lady Cicely reached the table before she did. Their hostess took a seat on Rolf's left. Libby would have sat down on his right, but his arms went around her before she could take her place. His fleshy lips slanted across hers before she could stop him. She wanted to gag, but she obediently opened her mouth for his intrusive tongue instead. She let him paw her as well. Instead of clenching her fists at her side and enduring his touch, she leaned in to him and clutched eagerly at his back. She had to get back to her husband, and the only way that was possible was to pretend lust for Rolf for a while longer.

There were cheers of approval and lewd calls from the other tables. She concentrated on the noise around her rather than on Rolf. She heard a distant crash of crockery from the rear of the hall. There was a loud scrape of heavy wood, a roar of possessive anger and the anxious voices of several women. It sounded as though the nuns were holding their own private riot, but Libby didn't have time to pay attention to what the good sisters were doing. She had a horny bear to contend with.

Rolf grabbed her by the shoulders and held her out to look her over. "Let's go to bed."

Her lips were bruised from his mauling kiss. She managed to pull them into some sort of smile anyway. "So soon, my lord?" She made it sound like she was coyly teasing. Inwardly, she was very close to panicking. She glanced anxiously at Lady Cicely. "So soon?" The Lady of Blackchurch gave her a smile and a nod.

Cicely rose and touched Rolf's sleeve. "I'm having my chamber prepared for your nuptial night."

Rolf's thick brows furrowed. "Nuptials?"

Cicely gave him a sweet smile. "A betrothal is as good as a wedding, is it not? What need you of a priest when both are willing?" she added. "Let us make a celebration of it, my lord. Was that not what you wanted when you came here?"

"Aye. I wanted your priest."

"Send for the priest tomorrow." She pointed at Libby. "Your bride is bathed and scented and anxious for you to come to her."

"I can tell."

Libby fluttered her eyelashes and tried to look lustful. The sound of Rolf's crude laughter echoed loudly around the watching room.

There was another crash from the nuns' table. Libby
gave a quick glance that way, and got the impression
that there was a pile of penguins holding the big one
down. Whatever was going on with the good sisters
wasn't something she could deal with just now. She
had to get back to Sebastian, and that meant concentrating on Rolf and Cicely to do it.

She took Rolf's hand. "I will await your coming, my
lord," she whispered to him. "Naked. In the curtained
dark."

"My bed I offer you for this first night together,"
Cicely hurried to tell him while his eyes glazed over at
Libby's words. Come," she said to Libby, "let us retire
while your lord drinks toasts to your night together."
She gestured her steward forward to pour Rolf a fresh
cup of mead. "Drink deep," she told her guest. "Drink
deep and often to strengthen you for the night ahead."
He gave her a nod, then downed the cup. The steward
filled it the moment he was done.

Libby cupped his cheek. "I'll send for you soon, my
love." Then she hurried to follow Cicely back up the
stairs.

There was no tower in this keep. The living quarters
at Blackchurch consisted of the hall on the first floor
where most activities took place. The main floor was
where soldiers and servants slept after the trestle tables
were cleared away. The bower bedroom on the second
floor was connected to the staircase by a long gallery
that overlooked the hall. There were several curtained
sleeping alcoves along the gallery, occupied at night by
guests and Lady Cicely's women. Lady Cicely had
planned to turn over one of the alcoves to Libby and
Rolf, but Libby had persuaded her to accept a different

plan while they bathed. Now it was time to set that plan in motion.

Libby followed Cicely into the bower and they began the preparations for the night. The large bed was hung with heavy curtains. Eventually all was ready, the heavy bedcurtains were drawn, enveloping the woman lying on the mattress in thick darkness. Only one candle still glowed in the room. A servant went to fetch Rolf. Libby pulled the veil she wore across her face and blended into the shadows.

Rolf was already waiting outside the door. He staggered into the bower, and the servant led him forward. Libby didn't watch him strip off his clothing and climb into Cicely's bed, where Cicely eagerly waited. She couldn't help but hear the other women joking and congratulating him, and his lewd replies. *There but for the grace of a lonely widow, go I*, she thought, and was very grateful for Lady Cicely's help.

Once the bedcurtains were drawn Libby took a large stack of linens from a serving woman. She held them before her as she made her way out the door, just one of a group of anonymous women. From the sounds already coming from the bed Rolf wasn't going to notice anyone leaving.

She didn't breath until she'd concealed herself in one of the alcoves along the gallery. She was supposed to wait here until everyone in the hall was sleeping before sneaking out into the night. Libby sat down with her back to the wall, and waited nervously for time to pass.

She hoped Cicely got what she wanted from Rolf. She hoped Rolf accepted what Cicely had to offer. It seemed like she'd been playing matchmaker a lot lately, which was very odd considering how weird her own marriage had turned out to be. Actually, she and Sebastian had had a lovely wedding, in the restored church at Lilydrake. Only the wedding had been over eight hundred years in the future.

"Bas remembers the wedding," she whispered as she listened to the noise from the hall growing quieter and quieter.

Knowing he remembered at least that much, muddled though the memory was, was both pleasant and painful to her. For she feared he would never remember that she was the one he'd grieved so deeply for. She was almost afraid that he'd reject her even if he did remember, that his having held desperately on to those few shreds of memory would prove to be too painful for him.

Maybe he'd want to start his life over when he returned to the future. But would it be with her? And would it matter, as long as she got him back safe and alive? His well-being was what was important right now.

It would matter. It would kill her if he stopped loving her.

She still wasn't going to think about it right now.

What she was going to concern herself with was the fact that someone was sneaking up the stairs. The intruder moved very cautiously, but the old wooden stairs creaked. She wondered if anyone else heard, or was concerned. She barely heard him move, but she knew the man was there by the faint sound of cloth rubbing against cloth. Was it one of Rolf's men? Had one of the serving women turned her in?

As she got slowly to her feet, her hand went to the dagger she'd gotten from Bas. If the man that now moved very quietly along the gallery was coming for her, she wasn't about to go without a fight.

She heard him stop nearby, in front of the bedroom door. She held her breath and waited. Then, curiosity got the better of her and she parted the alcove curtain just enough to see the gallery. It was faintly lit by dying rushlights in the hall below. What she saw in the dim light was a tall figure dressed head to foot in heavy black, a pilgrim's staff in one hand.

Though she could have sworn she'd made no sound, the black-robed figure swung around to face her. She jumped back, but was grabbed in a hard grip before she could hide herself. The dagger was knocked out of her hand. It hit the wall with a metallic clatter. She was pushed back into the alcove. Air left her lungs in a painful whoosh as her back hit hard against the wall.

"God, Bas," she said on a gasp as she looked up into the man's angry face, "you make one ugly nun."

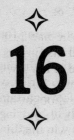

16

"*You're getting rescued* whether you want it or not," Bastien whispered to the wide-eyed woman. He leaned heavily against her, trapping her against the wall. Her body was as soft and yielding next to his as it had looked as she clung to Rolf of Gesthowe. He felt like a fool, and not just because he was wearing the garb of a holy sister. "You let the man paw you. In public. If the sisters hadn't convinced me to wait, I would have killed you both in the hall."

"You're jealous."

He didn't know why she sounded so pleased about it. "I'm jealous."

Her teeth showed in a fierce smile. "Good."

A moment later he was kissing her, all his anger translated into reckless need. By the time he lifted his lips from hers they were both panting. His anger was spent, translated into longing he had no time to satisfy. She leaned her head back against the wall and ran her tongue slowly over her lips, as though she had just tasted something very sweet. He brushed his fingers across her lips, then slowly traced the line of her jaw. There was a languorous look on her face, but her shoulders shook with silent laughter. He thought he should understand the joke, but didn't quite yet.

He put his lips close to her ear and whispered, "What?" She didn't have to answer, because he suddenly recalled what he was wearing. "And you were just kissed by an ugly nun at that," he agreed with her unspoken estimation. "But it is a good disguise."

"A wolf among the penguins," she agreed. "How did you—?"

"I'll explain later." He stepped back and quickly took off the wimple and the black robe he'd worn over his clothes. Once he'd discarded the disguise he held his hand out to her. "Hurry." Only when they were ready to step out onto the gallery did the obvious question occur to him. "Why aren't you in bed with Rolf?"

"I declined the honor," she replied.

He gave her a curious look, but the bedroom door was thrown open before he could say anymore. Rolf stood in the doorway. Naked. Holding a sword. Neither was a pretty sight. Rolf's eyes widened at the sight of Isabeau. He raised the blade menacingly, pointing it at her. Bastien quickly stepped between them. He couldn't remember his objections to learning to use a sword as Rolf snarled and stepped forward.

Bastien hit him in the groin with his quarterstaff. When the man doubled over in pain, Bas punched the end of the pole hard into Rolf's side. His jaw, his spine. There wasn't much room for him to swing or spin the weapon in the narrow gallery, but he did the best he

could. Though his arm protested he put all the strength
he could into each blow. Isabeau stood well back and
gave him room to work. The damage he did brought
grunts from Rolf, but fortunately the man didn't cry
out. No soldiers came charging up the stairs to their
lord's aid. Eventually Rolf dropped the sword and followed it down, falling heavily to the floor.

A woman appeared in the doorway as he went
down. She wore only a blanket wrapped around her
shoulders. She dropped to her knees beside Rolf. Her
face shone as a frightened, pale oval in the faint light.

Isabeau stepped forward. "Cicely?"

"Go," the woman said as she gathered the unconscious Rolf into her arms. "I'll keep him in my care, but
you must go."

"We're not arguing the point," Isabeau told the
woman. She snatched up the fallen dagger, then took
Bastien's hand.

"What about the guards?" Bastien asked. He looked
past the gallery rail to the hall below. No one stirred.
Behind them, people peered out from behind alcove
curtains. No one moved or made a sound.

Isabeau squeezed his fingers. "It's safe for us to go.
Cicely wants Rolf. She's on our side."

He was glad of that. He knew he'd do anything he
had to to keep Isabeau from harm, but it would be better if they didn't have to fight their way out of the keep.
The wound in his upper arm burned like fire from the
brief encounter with Rolf.

"All right," he said as they backed toward the stairs.

After they'd carefully maneuvered their way around
many sleeping bodies to reach the hall door she asked,
"Where do we go now? Back to Lilydrake?"

He grabbed hard onto her wrist to keep her from fleeing. "We return to the forest. Where I can keep you."

Marj and Reynard rode through Blackchurch village a little after dawn. It was a small place, just a knot of wattle and daub huts set between a church and a timber-walled manor house. The place had a look of desertion and death about it. They didn't pause to ask questions in the village, but rode on to Blackchurch Keep. A group of nuns, one leading a donkey, came through the open gate as they approached. The women passed them without a glance. The sisters walked in an orderly row, heads bowed. Pilgrims on their way to Canterbury, Marj assumed, and turned her attention back to Reynard.

"Think we'll learn anything here?"

"I have no idea. Hopefully we'll find out that the fool girl went back to Lilydrake."

They had heard from a passing pilgrim that Rolf's hunt for his betrothed was the talk of the forest. Apparently, Rolf had not had sense enough to leave the search to her and Reynard, and Libby had led him a merry chase.

She gave a sardonic laugh at Reynard's comment. "We aren't going to be that lucky."

Reynard laughed as well. He looked down at the guard by the gate. "Lady Isabeau of Lilydrake?" he asked.

The man, a grizzled warrior, blanched at the name. "By the saints, not another one looking for the wench?"

Reynard leaned forward slightly to rest his forearm on his saddlebow. "Another one?"

The guard looked the lean and dangerous Reynard over from the iron-shod hooves of his mount to the graying hair on his head. The man was in a state of near panic. "I know not how they came to escape, my lord. I was not involved."

Reynard looked at her. "It seems she was here, Lady Marjorie. Come and gone and left chaos in her wake."

Which sounded just like Libby Wolfe, Marj thought. "Was she with Bastien of Bale?" she asked the guard. He gave a nervous nod. "Which way did they go?"

"I know not. It was night. I wasn't on the gate. Don't tell Lord Rolf!"

Reynard frowned in annoyance. "Is Lord Rolf within?"

"Aye. Though they say he'll recover."

Reynard glanced at her again. "Do we really want to know?"

She shook her head. "I don't see any reason why we should talk to Rolf."

"I think we better continue to follow the trail of damage elsewhere."

As they turned their horses a pair of dogs came running up the road. The animals bounded enthusiastically forward, tongues lolling. They looked for all the world as if they were having a wonderful time at whatever they were doing. Before riding on, Marj paused to watch the hounds as they sniffed the ground around the gate. The large brown, black and white deerhounds were familiar.

"Luke and Leia," she said.

"Lady Isabeau's pets," Reynard said. "Do you think they're looking for her?"

The hounds circled the area around the gate for a few moments, then they looked at each other and took off once more. Marj watched the dogs head across a nearby field as they ran away from Blackchurch.

They'd almost disappeared into Blean Forest when Reynard said, "I think we'd better follow the dogs."

They'd walked hand in hand in silence for a very long time. Long enough for the sun to rise at their backs. The path they took wound deeper and deeper into the forest. The day was growing hot, and a great many bugs had been born since she'd first run off into the forest with Sebastian. They had discovered that she tasted delicious. Libby wasn't sure what time it was but weariness was about to overcome her. She stopped abruptly. He glared from under his heavy brows at her, but he didn't object when she sat down in the bracken. He stood over her and looked around restlessly.

She knew that Sebastian didn't want to stop, that he didn't want to talk. She didn't know what he did want. Just to be free of danger, maybe. She didn't blame him. They needed peace and privacy. They needed to break the silence.

The first words she said were, "He killed Mark."

His frown deepened. "Who?"

"Mark Warin." She waved her hand. "Warin of someplace, you called him."

"Warin of Flaye. Who killed him?"

Bastien tried not to show shock that his link to Old Sikes was dead. His plan had been to find Sikes's encampment. It would have been easier with Warin as a guide. He and Isabeau had been heading west. Warin had always come from the west on his visits, and he'd always eluded Bastien's best tracker when he left.

"Rolf killed him." She sighed. "Maybe I shouldn't judge him too harshly. He thought he was executing a robber, someone who had no protection under the law. No, any bully with a sword and a title is the law in this place."

Bastien dropped down to sit beside her. "At least we agree on that point, lady."

She took his hand, twining their fingers together, brown and pale. She had large hands, strong hands. His flesh remembered the feel of them as they'd nursed him, caressed him, pushed him off a wall. He turned her palm up and kissed it.

"I'm no lady, Sebastian," she said on a caught breath as his lips brushed across her skin. "Stop that. We have to talk."

"You touched me first."

"I wasn't trying to seduce you."

He raised his eyebrows. "No?"

"No."

"Pity."

"Well, maybe. A little."

"Thought so." He reached for her.

She wagged a finger under his nose before he could take her in his arms. "Stay." He licked her finger, and she laughed. It sounded delightful.

He wondered why he had a constant urge to tease her. Not just to tease her, but to trade banter that would sound like a bickering argument to anyone listening to them. Why did it seem so right? So familiar?

After a few moments of silence she grew serious again. "I'm sorry about Warin."

"So am I. I needed him."

"We needed him. We needed to know what he knew."

"That's so. Sikes's camp is well hidden."

"I wasn't talking about Sikes. Or maybe I was." Libby took her hand out of Bas's grip. His dark expression told her he expected an explanation. She didn't know how to start. Or if she even should. The logical thing to do was to get him back to Lilydrake and from there to the Downs timegate. She needed to get him home and to proper treatment.

The trouble was, she wasn't sure helping the man she loved was the top priority right now. She didn't know if they could just pack up and leave. Leaving might be more dangerous than breaking all the rules about not interacting with the locals. There were so many unanswered questions about the accident—no, the sabotage. Questions Warin might have answered. Questions Sebastian might even have answers to. She was scared his answers might be ones she didn't want to hear. She felt compelled to find out what she could.

"Why was Warin with Sikes? Why weren't you with Sikes?"

He supposed he should be getting used to her odd questions and disturbing statements. He didn't mind answering these questions. If only to show her that perhaps he wasn't as bad as some of the other wolvesheads in Blean. "How would I know why the man threw in his lot with the murderous old brigand? I only know that I wanted no part of the other band and their black deeds. I trusted Cynric's warning never to trust Sikes, no matter how much wine Warin poured down me on his visits."

"Warin's—visits?" She got to her knees. For a moment he thought she was going to grab him by the shoulders and shake him like a ferret shook a rat.

"What did he want? What did you talk about? Physics? Temporal field theory?"

Bastien grew dizzy at the sound of the words. Familiar words. He knew what they meant, and the disconnected knowledge made his head hurt. Such words were out of place in this primitive time. As out of place as he was. But if he was out of place where—?

He closed his eyes to block out the images of trees and sky that whirled around him. To block out the image of Isabeau's worried face. But with his eyes closed he could still see her, and she looked like his wife.

She wouldn't leave him in his confused world. Her voice was as much a lifeline as it was a goad when she said, "Talk to me about it. Talk to me about Warin. What did he want from you?"

"To join—"

"Yeah, but *why*?"

Bastien opened his eyes. "Numbers. When we drank his wine numbers danced in my mind. Numbers and mad philosophy. He always wanted to talk numbers and—theories." Bastien held his hands to his temples. "So many questions."

Isabeau jumped to her feet, she radiated fury like a fire did heat. "He drugged you, didn't he? I bet the bastard drugged you and then interrogated you about the prototype. He didn't lose his memory at all, did he? But he still didn't know how to get your time machine to work."

"Time machine?" More words that sounded so familiar they hurt. They had something to do with Isabeau's wizard, he thought.

Libby thought maybe she'd gone too far, said too much. Anger frequently made her reckless. "I shouldn't be telling you these things. Not like this."

Bastien was furious at her sudden reluctance, so he grabbed a handful of her heavy skirts and pulled her down beside him. With his face close to hers he said, "You will tell me everything. And you will tell me now."

"I don't want to hurt you."

His head was pounding, but he didn't care. "Stop trying to protect me."

Libby knew she hadn't handled this right from the beginning. From the first all she'd wanted to do was help him. Even when she'd thought he was an outlaw who'd come to rob Lilydrake she'd wanted to help him get his memory back. His welfare had been more important than any rule book even before she remembered who he was. She'd struck out on a reckless quest to save him and hadn't done one thing right. She couldn't be circumspect, she couldn't be subtle.

All she was any good at was telling the truth. She'd never done anything but tell Sebastian the truth. She couldn't stop now. She closed her eyes for a moment and prayed that she wasn't going to completely mess up his head.

When she opened them she met his angry, haunted gaze. "I'll tell you anything you want to know."

What to ask first? He turned away from her for a moment. He looked up at the sky, blue for now but with a cloud bank in the east promising rain later. What should he ask her? About them? About how she came to be his wife? No, he couldn't look at that subject directly. Not yet. He couldn't quite grasp the truth of it. What he could grasp was the instinctive knowledge that Isabeau irrevocably belonged to him. He knew that any effort to look past instinct would bring down a mountain of pain, and past the pain would be a country where he wouldn't want to face himself.

Maybe it would be enough if he lay down with her and took and gave comfort to her with his body. It would be so much easier just to mindlessly claim a mate, do anything to defend her, and leave off thinking forever. Curiosity wouldn't let him take such an easy road, however.

"Tell me about me," he said. He ran a hand down the front of his torn, stained tunic. "How did I come to be like this if I'm such a great wizard?"

She sucked in a great, deep breath between her teeth. "Your name is Sebastian Bailey."

"You've told me that before."

"But do you believe it?"

He shrugged, which reminded him of his injury. "I might as well believe you since you believe it so fervently. Who is Sebastian Bailey?"

Libby could think of a hundred answers to that question, some of them new and startling, for she'd seen some very new sides of him lately. She stuck with the facts. "You'll be born in the early twenty-first century, in Canada, an only child, a child prodigy at that. Everyone calls you Bas, just like almost everyone calls me Libby. You've been working for Time Search for about five years. My dad grabbed you out of a postdoctoral program he was supervising and put you to work. He says—though not in your hearing—that you're smarter than he is." She ducked her head, then smiled up at him from under lowered lashes. "Actually, we Wolfes have made a habit of grabbing you. I knew I wanted you the first moment I saw you."

It wasn't easy, but he waved away the longing to skim his hands down her body while he invited her to go ahead and grab him. He needed to know about himself. But once again curiosity got the better of him, for he needed to know about them more. "When was it, then, and where? This first moment you saw me?"

"In Mongolia," she answered. "I was standing outside a yurt waiting for a repairman. And—"

And the forest was swept from his sight. The imperfect, mangled, imaginary world he'd fought to survive in swirled around him like a cloud of choking smoke. Foul things reared up from the bottom of his mind. And things not so dark as well. Among the murky, frightening things a door opened and spilled out light. He ran toward it. Ran for his life.

If she said more he didn't hear it because of the sudden memory superimposed over everything else.

So that's Wolfe's daughter, he thought as he appeared behind her. The transfer had been a little rough, which didn't add to his annoyance at the Director of Time Search ordering him to personally see to the equipment malfunction. He figured Wolfe was just being overprotective of his little girl.

The landscape was stark, grassland beneath an endless sky. The only thing in it was the white felt tent and the dark-haired woman looking at it.

"Amazing, isn't it?" she said. "And totally weird."

He had no idea who she was talking to, but he answered anyway. "Yes."

She whirled around and their gazes met.

He knew about time. It didn't really stop, not without help from a multibillion-dollar power source within a containment field the size of Rhode Island. But time stopped for him without any technological help as he looked into her dark brown eyes. Wicked eyes, a mouth made for kissing, a body meant to be caressed. And a slow smile that was probably identical to his lifted those magnificently kissable lips as she looked him over as thoroughly as he did her.

He'd forgotten what he'd come for. He took a step forward. "I'm Bas. You must be—"

He found himself looking into those wicked, brown eyes once more. Time was still playing tricks on him, whirling around in circles instead of standing still this time. No, not circles, but a horrible downward spiral that reached out to engulf him. She was there, one sure, solid thing in the center of a black, hideous whirlpool. He reached out, desperate for a lifeline. He called out.

"Olivia!"

17

Olivia Elizabeth Wolfe Bailey held her husband in her arms and was delighted with her given name for the first time in her life. Everyone called her Libby, everyone but Bas. Her Bas, who was holding her so tightly she thought her ribs might crack. She didn't mind. She held onto him as tightly as he clutched her. She desperately needed the contact. It was still wonderously new to her that he was real and alive. And she loved him so much she would be glad if they held each other so close they melded completely into one another.

She rocked him in her arms and made stupid, soothing noises and tried not to be terrified that he'd fallen into incurable madness instead of finding his way out of it.

"Please," she whispered. "Please be all right."

After a long time he said, in a dead voice, "I played God, and got punished for it."

He let her go. The world went cold when they stopped touching. She reached for him, but he was

◇ **253** ◇

already on his feet, removed from any comfort she had to offer. She watched as he turned and walked away. Her throat tightened with tears as she got up and followed. She didn't think he knew where he was going. She wasn't sure he cared. She only knew she couldn't let him out of her sight ever again. So she trailed behind, desperate with worry, but not knowing what to do.

When branches whipped at him as the path narrowed she flinched. The defensive, defeated slope of his shoulders made her own hurt. When he made a stifled sound something like a sob she could no longer keep the tears that nearly blinded her from spilling down her cheeks.

Eventually he stopped walking. It seemed like hours before he turned to face her. He didn't meet her eyes. "I'm sorry, Olivia," he said. "Desperately sorry and ashamed."

Libby saw that they'd reached the clearing by the river where they'd watched the herons. How long ago had that been? One day? Two? The journey back to being Bas and Olivia had gone on far too long. She wiped her face with the embroidered edge of her sleeve. She sniffed. "What? What have you got to be sorry for?"

"Designing the TDD. Insisting you be part of the Lilydrake team. Worse." He pushed up his right sleeve to show a faint line of scar, an ugly white mark on his already pale skin. He came closer. "Look at this."

She ran her fingers along the puckered skin. He shivered beneath her touch. "A knife wound?"

He nodded. "I cut myself." His other hand reached out to grasp her chin in a tight grip. He pulled her face up so that his furious, green gaze bored into hers. The fury was directed inward. "I nearly bled to death, but it worked."

She blinked rapidly, refusing to give in to tears again. "What did you do? What worked?"

"Don't you know what I did, Olivia?" His voice sounded far too calm. "Don't you know why I wasn't transported back to headquarters with you and the others?"

"The medical sensor? You cut out the sensor implant?" He nodded. "Why?" she shouted. "What the devil did you do that for?"

"I had to," he said, and let her go.

He started to turn his back on her again, but she grabbed his arm—his sore left arm—and refused to let him move. While he winced she said, "I'm sick of enigmatic bullshit, Sebastian." She pointed a stern finger under his nose. He looked down at it, cross-eyed. "You've had an hour to feel sorry for yourself. Time's up, babe. Just tell me what happened and we'll work it out."

His bitterness and anger with himself was almost palpable. "You don't understand what I did."

"Then explain it to me."

"You'll hate me."

"I won't."

"How can we work out what I—"

Since it didn't look like he was going to be reasonable she did the only thing she could. She kissed him. With such force that they tumbled backward onto the grass together. He grunted as he landed on his back, but she didn't let his lips escape hers.

Olivia Wolfe Bailey did not do personal demons. Well, she'd often told him she did do one demon, and it was him. Bas might hate himself for all his wretched

faults, but she wasn't likely to let him get away with it
for long. She never did. A woman of action was Olivia
Bailey. Light to his dark. He supposed he might as well
relax and let her work out the devils that plagued him
with her sweet, hot touch.

"You're one hell of an exorcist, woman," he said,
when she let him up for air.

She leaned over him and stroked her fingers down
his nose, traced his cheeks and lips. Her smile was full
of sensual promise. "Welcome home, wizard."

He touched her face, gently, tentatively as he memo-
rized her all over again. He touched her collarbone, the
base of her throat, skimmed his hands over her shoulders
and her back. She arched into his touch, bent her head
forward so that her thick, dark hair brushed across his
cheek. His fingers worked at the cord fastening the top of
the dress she'd been given at Blackchurch. When he was
done she pulled the gown off her shoulders and down her
arms.

Bas looked at her for a few moments before he said,
"You know what I like about the Middle Ages?"

She tilted her head to one side. "No bras?"

"No bras."

She got to her knees, undid her belt, and worked
her dress down over her hips, slowly, teasing like the
best stripper, while he watched with growing arousal.
"No underwear, either."

"How—convenient."

She was not one of those flat-chested, hipless super-
model types. His wife was wonderfully curved in all the
right places, with long, long legs, and muscles like steel
under the satin smoothness of her skin. He loved
watching her move. He loved her stillness as well, he

loved the feel of her body as she curled around him in her sleep. He loved looking at her, touching her, making love to her. He loved her.

"Oh, lord," he said, throat and groin both tight and aching from wanting her.

He held out his arms for her. She moved into the circle of his embrace and helped him out of his own clothes. She caressed his naked skin in intent silence, but her hands made urgent demands that his own explorations mirrored.

Libby reveled in rediscovering her husband, in the tactile memorization of the changes in his muscle and flesh. She wanted him with a need so sharp it was painful. Every part of her ached for his touch, and when he touched her her senses raced, fire spread through her. Where she touched him she found delight and wonder.

She discovered that he was the same man she loved to make love to, and subtly different. He'd always been lean and wiry. Months of hard living had pared his already beautiful body into taut strength. The man was definitely buff.

Strong or not, he still had an injured arm. She remembered that just in time when he lifted himself over her to enter her. As urgent and ready as she was, she still pressed her hands against his dark-furred chest. "Bastien, wait," she said. "Let me."

He gave a ferocious growl, then a ragged laugh when she rolled him onto his back; the sound held need as well as frantic amusement. She straddled his erection and paused to savor the barest moment of anticipation. His green eyes flashed at her, command more than entreaty. She obeyed, and joined her body with his. Soon she lost track of the way their bodies moved together. She became aware only of the fast, hard rhythm that raced through her heart and blood and being. Details simply blended into pure, white-hot sensation. Sensation that eventually, beautifully, inevitably—as inevitable as her love for Sebastian—peaked and brought her the completion only he could bring her.

"I love you," she told him, and happily collapsed on his sweat-matted chest. She didn't rest for long, though. "So," she said when she had her wits back about her, "just what were you so upset about?"

He ran his hands up and down her spine. It tickled. As he helped her to sit up he said, "And here I thought you were using sex to divert my attention."

She looked him in the eye. "Would I do that?" Sebastian nodded. "Not divert, defuse. Besides, we have six months to make up for."

"I've missed—my wife—so much." Bas cupped her cheek with his palm. "It was the only thing that kept me going."

Libby wished she could say the same. She hadn't missed him because she hadn't known he existed. At least not consciously. She wondered if her coming back looking for outlaws had been some subconscious quest to find the man she'd lost. Outlaws were the ultimate outsiders in the ordered society of the Middle Ages, and Sebastian Bailey trapped in the past would be an outsider indeed.

"I'm just happy you survived at all. You don't have to be guilty because you did, you know."

"That's not it." He looked away. It disturbed her to realize that none of his tension had been dissipated by their making love. He was gazing up at the sky when he went on. "No, that's part of it, I suppose. I did feel guilt for surviving when I thought my wife had died. I still feel guilty. I am guilty."

She didn't shout this time. She asked sympathetically, "For what?"

He looked back at her, expression carefully schooled to stillness. His voice was flat as he said, "You don't remember my leaving you, do you?"

Actually, she did. Not in detail. "It was all very confusing. There were people everywhere, and the fire. Then there was this horrible whining, screeching, howling, piercing noise that made my head feel like it was being twisted off from the inside. Was that your prototype being switched on?"

"No," he answered. "It was not."

"That's what we were told at what little debriefing we had. The shrinks told us that the amnesia was probably caused by the prototype not working properly. If they had any other explanation Joe, Ed and I obviously didn't have a high enough clearance to hear it."

"You probably didn't. Though I doubt anyone suspected. No, your father's a suspicious man. I think what happened was that Warin quite literally used a time bomb as well as the outlaws to disguise his stealing the TDD prototype."

"A time bomb?"

Bas nodded. "He was very clever. Should I speak technobabble to you to explain how I think he created a time vortex that disrupted the local temporal field and somehow managed to shield himself and the outlaws from it when he set it off?"

"I'd rather you didn't."

"I thought as much. Then I'll put it in simple layman's terms."

"Which is?"

"We were screwed, Olivia."

If Bas said so, even in layman's terms, it was true. She nodded. "I suppose that they were trying to keep any suspicion of sabotage very quiet, to keep Elliot Hemmons from calling for an investigation if nothing else. The man will use any opening to take over Time Search for himself."

"Maybe he's not beyond bribing Mark Warin to sabotage an important project."

Libby brightened at the thought. "You think so? Think we could nail him?"

He shrugged. "There had to be some reason behind what happened at Lilydrake. Maybe it was just greed on Warin's part. Maybe he was going to sell the prototype and his services to somebody who wanted the technology for themselves. Maybe the somebody was Hemmons."

"I guess we'll never find out now that Warin is dead. By the way," she added, "nobody bothered to mention your existence. I got four years of my life sucked out of me and since we'd only known each other three and a half you weren't part of my memories. You held onto more than I did, if that's any consolation." She fought back tears. "I didn't know what I was missing."

He touched her hair, then cupped her face in his hands. "I am so sorry."

She put her hands over his. She wasn't going to cry, she was going to rejoice in having Sebastian Bailey back. "You have nothing to be sorry for. You were the one who got hurt worst of all in this."

"No more than I deserved."

"Bullshit."

His wide mouth lifted in a slight smile. "Eloquent as ever, my love."

"Just using simple layman's terms. So what did you do that was so bad?"

"I left you."

"Not on purpose."

He pulled her close and held her for a long time before he answered. "On purpose."

She felt enveloped by his strength, her senses were alive to the play of his muscles against hers, to the softness of his hair on her cheek and the distinctive male scent of him. She wanted just to be near him. She didn't want to listen to confessions and explanations. She wanted to say that she understood, and that it didn't matter. But she didn't, and it did.

"You were with me, I remember, when the acci— the time bomb detonated. The world went all weird, but you were there." She blinked. "Then you weren't there." She pulled away from him. "I remember your running—"

"Following Warin," he told her.

She scrubbed her hands across her face. She felt like a knife was twisting in her heart. "You left me."

"You begged me not to."

She remembered that now. She'd remembered it the night she got her memory back, but had suppressed her confused bitterness in the joy of finding him. "You had to have a reason," she said. "You damn well better have had a reason."

"Getting the prototype back was more important than you," he answered. "It shouldn't have been. I left you to die."

"I didn't die."

"I didn't know you wouldn't. I was feeling the effects of the time bomb. I knew what it was doing to you. I thought it was going to kill us, but I didn't even try to get you to safety. I could feel myself going mad, but I had to get the prototype back. So, just before the medsensor alerted the automatic recall I ran after Warin."

"Getting the TDD back was the most important thing," she defended him against himself. "You did the right thing." She believed it, but she didn't know if he would. She not only believed him, she was proud of him. Oh, it hurt, but she tried to convince herself that was just selfishness on her part. It was just a narcissistic longing to be the most important thing in her man's life and she should be ashamed of herself. Recovering the prototype of a time machine more powerful than the one her father had invented had been his first responsibility. "You did what was necessary, Bas."

He gave a caustic laugh. "All I did was get lost in the past with my brain fried."

"And Warin let you stay that way." She shook her head angrily. "He let you believe you were Bastien of Bale while he tried to dig information out of you. He put you through six months of hell, babe."

"I put myself through it when I didn't return to the future with you."

From the stubborn, haunted look in his eyes Libby realized that it was going to take quite a while to work this out. From the ache still deep in her heart, she knew she wasn't as sanguine about the correctness of his actions as she should be. At least it was out in the open. They'd made a start. They'd work it out, but it didn't look like it was going to be today.

She looked toward the inviting coolness of the river. "Come on. Let's take a bath."

He nodded. "You're just filing this away for future discussion, aren't you?"

"You know me too well." It healed and helped her to know that he knew her so well. The way she knew him. She thought they'd been born to be together. Six months' separation and questions of his being too devoted to his work shouldn't be able to tear them apart. She prayed they wouldn't, at least. "Let's go swimming."

They got up, scooped up their abandoned clothes and went down to the water's edge. The water was steel gray, reflecting the clouds building up overhead. It was also cold, Libby discovered when she waded in. It took a certain force of character to completely immerse herself, but she managed it.

"Wish I had some soap," Libby said as she came up from ducking her head. She shook out her wet hair. "And a comb. Come on in," she called to Bas who remained on the shore. "Or you could stand there while I admire the magnificence of the scenery."

He blushed, and she did admire the sight as deep color spread across his throat and cheeks and his flat, hard stomach. She would have sworn the water temperature went up several degrees when he jumped in.

He splashed over to her and stood braced against the current as he took her in his arms. "I can't get enough of kissing you."

She threw her head back, and gave a throaty laugh. "So kiss me."

He did, starting at the swift pulse in her neck and working his way slowly, inexorably up to cover her soft lips with his. It was a demanding kiss, full of possessive passion. He didn't deserve his good fortune in having her, he thought as he slid his hands over her water-slicked body. Her sleek flesh was like silk under his knowing hands.

It didn't matter what he deserved, he couldn't deny his need for her. She was his. He didn't have to think about that. He knew it, his body knew it, and right now his body demanded he hold and have what was his.

Their coupling was as swift and powerful as the current, and nearly as exhilaratingly dangerous. They ended up tangled together on the riverbank, half drowned, breathless with satisfaction and laughter at the foolishness of their reckless mating.

When she stopped laughing, she gave his good shoulder a half-hearted swat. "I thought we were going to take a bath!"

"You got clean, didn't you?" he countered. "All that agitating of the water we just did must have gotten off some of the grime."

She rolled onto her back. "I don't know where we got the energy, babe. I'm starving."

"Abstinence," he told her. He leaned up on his elbow so he could look down at her. It left one hand free to play with her breasts. She didn't object as he made swirling patterns on her sensitive skin. "Abstinence makes the heart grow fonder—or something."

"I don't know about the heart, but it certainly makes for stamina in other places." He flattened his palm over her breast and she put her hand over his. "Dr. Bailey, you are driving me to distraction. And why are you looking at me like that?"

"Like what?"

"With your brow all furrowed and a distinct glint of suspicion in your eyes."

He smiled. "Oh, just being jealous."

She tapped him lightly on the nose. "Wondering if I was abstinent, were you?"

"Something like that." She grinned, obviously pleased at his possessiveness. "Don't preen, woman. We have a modern marriage, and jealousy is politically incorrect."

"Not in my opinion, it isn't."

"Mine either. You *were* abstinent, I take it?"

She laughed. "Certainly. I was saving myself for the right man."

"Who just happened to be Bastien of Bale."

He'd said the words as a joke, but as he spoke them he knew how awfully, horribly, frighteningly true they were. He was Sebastian Bailey.

His wife was in love with Bastien of Bale.

18

"You're in love with Bastien."

Libby didn't understand why all the light went out of Sebastian's eyes. Or why he suddenly got to his feet. His back was rigid with tension as he got dressed. She didn't know what was wrong, but she refused to face the crisis naked while he was fully clothed. So she hurried to get dressed, then turned to face his stony silence. It wasn't just the silence that was stony, the man was as still and cold as a statue.

She spread her hands in front of her. "You've got an objection to my being in love with you?"

"You are in love with Bastien." He pronounced each word very carefully. "Bastien," he went on when all she could do was stare at him. "Not me."

"Of course I'm in love with you. You're my husband."

"I haven't forgotten." He gave the faintest of wry smiles. "Not in the last few minutes. We better get back," he went on as if he hadn't just made some extraordinary statements.

Libby sat down on the riverbank. "Get back where?"

"Lilydrake. You do have a working timegate at Lilydrake, don't you?"

"Joe and Ed were supposed to set it up, but—" She shrugged. "With all the locals hanging out at the castle I doubt if they've been able to get to it."

"Oh, yes, the castle repairs." He ran his hand down his jaw. "I worked on them myself for a few days."

She wondered if she should mention that she knew, if she should remind him of the sensor belt he had made for her. She wondered if he was talking just to avoid discussing what was bothering him.

"I suppose we'll just have to return to the nearest working timegate," he went on. "Is Downs Tower still in use?"

"That's where we arrived. Why do you want to go to Downs Tower?" She wished she hadn't answered his question, or asked him one. She should not let him create this verbal diversion. "What do you mean I love Bastien?"

He took a few steps toward her so that his shadow touched her even though he didn't. She didn't think he realized he was looming over her. "We have to return to Downs Tower so we can go home, Olivia."

She crossed her arms. "I'm not going anywhere."

"We have to return to our own time." His expression became very bitter. "Unless you'd rather stay in the greenwood with your outlaw."

She got to her feet. Face to face with him, she said, "You are my outlaw. Besides, the greenwood's full of bugs." When he didn't respond to her attempt at humor, she added, "And people with sharp, pointy weapons."

"Then you agree that it's safer for us to go home."

"I didn't say that." She touched the dagger at her waist. "We have sharp, pointy weapons too."

"And no inclination to use them."

"You're perfectly capable of—"

"I'm a dweeb, Olivia!"

His angry shout sent her stumbling backwards. She just barely managed not to fall into the river. He followed her, and continued to loom despite the fact he wasn't that much taller than she was. It was an attitude thing. "Bas?"

He grabbed her arm and pulled her away from the water's edge. "Sebastian Bailey is a techno-dweeb, a geek, and happy to be one. I'm a scientist, not a soldier."

"Bas—"

"Listen to me, Olivia. I live for my job—and my job is not being a sword-wielding hero."

"But—"

"I understand technology, I understand science, supercomputers and temporal displacement theory. I understand hot showers and fast food and e-mail. I even understand how to program that holographic virtual reality chamber you insisted we buy last year. I do not understand this time, these people or anything about this society," he told her. His grip hurt, and he'd never looked more dangerous even while his words belied what he was doing. "And I don't want to."

"You've done all right." She realized she sounded sullen, and looked away. She was beginning to understand what he meant about her loving Bastien.

"I have not done all right."

"You ran an outlaw gang," she pointed out.

He heard the admiration in her voice, and hated it. She was seeing him in a romantic light that he neither deserved nor wanted. He wanted to go back to his safe, sanitized world and lock away the beast the last six months had brought out in him. It terrified him to think that the beast was the man she wanted.

"It wasn't a glorious adventure," he told her. "I loathed every minute of it. You wouldn't have, but I did."

"What do you mean by that?"

She tried to pull away from him, but he wouldn't let her go. "What do you think I mean? You love adventures."

She shook her head. "I'm not that reckle—"

"Oh, yes you are. Who was the one laughing that time we were getting shot at by Mongols?"

"We shouldn't have been so close to their camp. Besides, I was covering you while you repaired the remote sensors."

"I know what we were doing. I was performing my job while you were in a fire fight."

"I did not enjoy it."

"Who was laughing?"

"I always laugh when I'm scared. You know, bravado."

"You've seen too many movies."

"You've given me this lecture before. Damn it, Bas, you've been through survival training. You're good at it."

"But I don't like it."

"Of course you don't like it. Nobody in their right mind really likes adventures."

"You do." After a significant moment of silence, she looked away. "Bastien did," he admitted when she wasn't looking. He let her go. "But he's dead now."

She rubbed her arm. "And you think I'm in love with him? Instead of you?"

"Aren't you?" He wished he hadn't asked.

He wished he didn't want to know. Nothing could be the same between them once he knew. But, then, how could anything ever be the same after the last six months? She'd always been wild and free and reckless, and he'd loved her for it. She'd known when to drag him out of his lab, out of the intricate puzzles that absorbed him. She'd made his life exciting, made him feel alive. Now all he wanted was to get back to the quiet life offered by his work and never come out again. What place did she have in the restrained environment he craved? What place did he have in her world? Maybe he should have asked years ago.

"Things and people change," she said, as though she'd read his mind. "But how I feel about you hasn't."

"I wish that were true."

"Damn it, Bas!"

"Stop hedging, Olivia."

The man was being relentless, and she almost hated him for making her analyze her feelings. She turned to look at the water, and her reflection in it. He came to stand behind her. When he put his hands on her shoulders, she leaned her head back against his chest, and the couple in the water mirrored their actions.

"This is very hard," she told him.

"I know."

He was right about Sebastian Bailey being a technodweeb, though she preferred the term wizard herself. She loved him the way he was. Sebastian needed her. Bastien had been dangerous, exciting, incredibly sexy. Bastien had needed her, too.

"I love Bastien," she told her husband. "But no more than I love you. You are Bastien." She wasn't sure if he believed it. She wasn't even sure she did, but she did think it was the truth. It had to be. She hoped. Because she didn't want to have to cope with having betrayed her husband with the man she loved. Who just happened to be her husband. "This is too weird, babe," she said. "Let's go on to something else, shall we?"

He stepped back, and rubbed his hands across his face. Even his reflection looked exhausted. "Let's go home," he said as she turned to him.

"We can't."

"You said you came in through the Downs gate. If it's operational—"

"It is," she interrupted. "But we can't go home yet."

She could tell he didn't want to ask. He did not look like he wanted to be calm or reasonable, but he managed. "Why?"

Libby didn't answer immediately. Instead she marched up the bank and started along the path they had taken to the ford the day before. Had it only been the day before? No wonder she was exhausted, they'd napped a bit after they'd reached the forest from Blackchurch but not enough to be truly rested. It wasn't just the emotional upheaval. She hadn't had a decent night's sleep since they'd made love in the abandoned hut. What was that, three days ago? Or closer to four? Maybe Bas was being so difficult for the same reasons she was, with the added inconvenience of his sore arm to deal with along with the sleep deprivation.

"You're just being cranky," she muttered as she turned her head to find him following close behind her.

"Where are you going?"

She took a deep breath, and prepared for one more argument. "To get your time machine back."

He grabbed her arm and spun her around. "What?"

"It was stolen by Sikes. You said Sikes's camp is somewhere across the river. We have to find his camp."

"Why?"

"We have to get the time machine back."

Bas was almost quivering with anger. "Don't be ridiculous."

"I'm not being ridiculous. I'm being a Wolfe. Time Search is our responsibility. Wolfes do not screw up and then not fix it."

"It was not your responsibility."

"As I recall, the reason we used to get me assigned to the Lilydrake team was my ability to deal with local problems. A time machine that someone might figure out how to turn on could create a massive local problem."

"That isn't going to happen."

"We don't know that. We don't know what Warin was doing with Sikes's band. He might have trained some apprentices. He might have been close to getting the thing to work. When it does all of time is going to belong to the person who controls your temporal displacement device. Do you want it in the hands of outlaws? These aren't those little guys out of *Time Bandits*, babe."

"No one but me is ever going to get the TDD to work."

"Can you be sure?"

He glared at her, and she glared right back for a good long time. Eventually, he gave a jerky nod. "Conceded. It's possible Warin was able to work out some of the bugs. He was getting information from me, I think. You're right, the device does have to be retrieved from Sikes."

"Then let's go get it."

His hand landed heavily on her shoulder. "No. We are returning to our own time and turning the problem over to competent professionals."

She bristled. "We're competent professionals."

"I'm not."

He sounded so adamant about his lack of abilities that she wanted to kick him. But that would be uncivilized, and he'd just be smug about the effects of living in the Middle Ages on her already fierce nature. She kicked him anyway.

He winced but didn't move. "Feel better?"

"Aggression often makes me feel better."

"I know. It could also get you killed. That's why I'm not going to let you do anything as stupid as confronting Sikes on your own."

"You're not going to *let* me?" Her indignant shout echoed through the forest.

It had to be exhaustion that was making her act so irrational. She knew that she was not normally so close to hysteria, or incapable of reasonable discussion. She did admit that she was prone to violence when angry, but she could normally control that too. There was nothing wrong with having a temper, it was just using it that was stupid. And with that in mind, she decided that it would be wiser not to physically assault her husband anymore.

She took a deep breath and said calmly, "I'm not going to confront Sikes on my own. I'll have you with me." She was surprised when Bas threw back his head and laughed. "What?"

He pulled her into an embrace. His chest still vibrated with laughter as he hugged her. "Darling, what do you expect me to do? Challenge Sikes to a duel? My laptop versus his broadsword? I don't think so."

Put that way, as a confrontation of a civilized modern man versus an unprincipled barbarian, his argument sounded logical. Instinct told her they didn't have time for logic. That there was a missing piece to what had happened that they hadn't considered. That something awful was going to happen, and soon. "We have to try."

Sebastian could tell he wasn't going to be able to talk her out of this insanity. He wondered if he should just pretend to go along with it and divert her somehow. After all, she didn't know her way around the forest the way he did. Or perhaps she did, now that she had her memory back. Her knowing the area had been another excuse for accompanying him back to Lilydrake when another historian should have been assigned to the project. He wished he hadn't wanted her with him so badly that he'd gone along with it. His unprofessional behavior had gotten her hurt. He wasn't going to let her get hurt again.

He was glad when she didn't continue the argument immediately. She leaned her body against his and rested her head on his shoulder. He wished he could hold her in the protective circle of his arms forever, but he knew his Olivia. He was proud of her fierce sense of responsibility. In a little while she would try to dash away to do what a woman had to do.

He needed a diversion, something that would give him time to talk her around to a sensible course of action. When his own stomach rumbled with hunger, he smiled. Sheer necessity was on his side for once.

He told her, "We're not going anywhere until we get some food in us."

Libby stepped away from him and looked around them. "I am starving." She hated to waste any more time, but she was tired, she was hungry. Sebastian was no better off than she was. "We're near the ford. I think I saw watercress growing there."

Bas made a gagging noise. "I hate living off the land. Besides, I was thinking of something a little more nutritious than a salad. I think a little hunting is in order." He rolled his left shoulder, then lifted his arm. "I can use a bow. Thank God for modern emergency medicine."

Libby looked him over from head to foot. "Bow?"

He realized his weapons, bow, quiver and quarterstaff, were missing as she spoke. He knew where he'd left them, in the same place he'd gotten his memory back. Bastien would have automatically taken them with him when they moved on to the river. It had never occurred to him to do so. Well, Sebastian Bailey still knew how to hunt with a bow. Hours and hours and endless wretched hours had to be spent in primitive survival training for all Time Search personnel. He'd hated every moment of it and had firmly drawn the line at learning to use a sword. Those hacking weapons were meant to maim and kill, which he contended was the ultimate interaction with the local population. He had gotten rather good at archery, however.

"I better go get my bow," he told her.

"Then a rabbit," she answered.

He closed his eyes and dreamed of pepperoni pizza. Extra cheese. "Whatever."

"I'll wait by the ford, with the watercress and a fire going."

He looked at her suspiciously. "You're not going to do anything stupid are you, Olivia?"

She was the picture of false innocence when she replied, "Not without you, Bas."

"Promise."

She grew serious. "I do promise. I'm not going anywhere without you ever again."

He believed her. He kissed her cheek. "Fine. I'll be back as soon as I can."

In the end he didn't shoot a rabbit. He didn't even use his bow, but managed to catch a pair of hedgehogs. He didn't feel like a particularly mighty hunter as he made his way to the ford, and was rather pleased that he didn't. He was not Bastien. He could live with not being Bastien. He just hoped his wife could.

He smelled wood smoke in the air before he stepped out of the woods. He called a greeting as he reached the ford, but no answer came back. He supposed the noise of the river muffled the sound of his voice, or that she didn't hear him because she was away from the fire she'd built.

"Gathering watercress." He grimaced as he stepped into the open. The fire was a welcome sight as it glowed and crackled. A pile of dark greens lying on a flat rock near the fire showed that she'd been busy playing gatherer to his hunter, but she was nowhere in sight. "Olivia?"

As he walked down to where the small campfire burned near the water's edge he saw that she was indeed not in camp. And she had been very, very busy. The body sprawled in the bushes testified to that. Sebastian knelt by the man and touched the jeweled hilt of the dagger buried in the stranger's chest. His dagger. The one she'd carried since she'd been found by Rolf.

He stood, and turned slowly as his gaze took in many footprints and the signs of a struggle. She was gone. He'd only wanted to protect her, but she was gone. He'd left her, just like he'd left her before, and she was gone.

19

The sight of the dead man didn't disturb him. It should have, but it didn't. He stared at the body for a long time without thinking, without moving, without even feeling. He was numb, blank. Empty. The fire burned down and the day wore on and Sebastian Bailey stood in a frozen stance over a corpse as the life he thought he'd regained proved to be as insubstantial as any other nightmare.

No, the nightmares had been easier to live with.

At some point he bent down and removed the knife from the man's chest. He spent a long, careful time cleaning it. Then he took a stone that was wrapped in a bit of oiled cloth out of his pouch and began to sharpen the blade. His actions were precise, automatic, and had very little to do with the logical, rational world of Sebastian Bailey. Anger built in him as he sharpened the dagger, it came up from the depths of his soul in a slow, dark wave and burned away every bit of civilized veneer he'd been so eager to resume. When he looked up a savage stared out of his eyes.

When he was done he was sure of one thing. His wife was right, he was as much Bastien of Bale as he was Olivia's wizard. And Bastien was very good at following a trail. Especially a trail as obvious as the one taken by his wife's kidnappers.

His wife's soon-to-be-late kidnappers, he thought as he ran through the swiftly moving water of the ford. He was going to get her back, and the men who had taken her were going to die.

"Where am I?" Libby had learned that this was the first question people tended to ask after blacking out the hard way, back when she'd woken up in the Time Search medical facility with a good chunk of her memory missing. Now she knew exactly who she was, she even remembered how she'd gotten here. The hitting on the head part had resulted from one last attempt to escape after being dragged through the forest by her three captors. She supposed she'd been carried the rest of the way here. She just didn't know where here was. So she ignored her painfully throbbing head, sat up slowly and opened her eyes.

The first thing she noticed was that her hands were tied—no, manacled—in front of her. She tried to ignore this rather alarming development for the moment and took in her surroundings. She appeared to be in a wide-mouthed cave. A couple of torches burned in brackets hammered into the stone walls, but plenty of the light came in from the entrance. There were rolled-up sleeping pallets stored against one wall, along with baskets and bundles, and something large and lumpy covered by a threadbare tapestry against another wall. She was sitting on a pile of bracken covered with a deerhide blanket at the back of the shallow cave. There was a woman standing in front of her, looking at her with an expression of deep concern. The woman was attractive, though not young, with a great deal of gray hair in her thick red braids.

"I know you," Libby said. "You were with the outlaws that came to Lilydrake." The woman nodded. "I thought you were Bastien's wife."

The worried looking woman smiled, and she became beautiful. "I'm Berthild," she said. "Sikes's wife." She laughed softly. "Though I'm told this Bastien lad is the handsomest man in the forest, I'm content enough with my own man." She patted Libby on the head. "I served your mother once, when she was chatelaine at Passfair."

Libby smiled at the woman. "She's mentioned you often. She's always been very concerned that you were taken by outlaws and never found."

"It's worked out well enough, my lady," Berthild said as she looked behind her.

Libby looked up when Berthild glanced back toward the entrance of the cave. A broad-shouldered man filled the entrance. He looked like a Saxon recruiting poster, all blond braids and beard and blue eyes. He came up to Berthild and put his arm around her shoulders. There were fine lines around those cold, blue eyes and a bit of softness around his waist, but he was handsome and dangerous despite his age.

"Sikes?" Libby asked.

"That's me, my lady." He gestured around the cave.

She knew that he was called Old Sikes by the other bandits of Blean Forest, but the term was misleading. "How do you like your fine quarters?"

Libby was tempted to tell him that the place wasn't much worse than the first apartment she and Bas had shared, but she didn't suppose he'd appreciate the humor. "I've had worse," she said instead.

He smiled, but his eyes didn't. "That's a lie, my fine, well-fed aristocrat."

"Well, close."

"How are you feeling?" Berthild asked her.

"She's not here to be pampered, woman."

"I'll not have her ill treated." Berthild was not in the least intimidated by the formidable outlaw. "She's my lady's child."

Sikes scowled. "She was Bastien's prisoner, and now she's mine to ransom as I choose."

"Which is no reason to be impolite," his wife countered. She smiled at Libby.

"Thank you." Libby smiled at the helplessly annoyed look on Sikes's face at his wife words.

His annoyance deepened as he looked back at her. "You and Bastien have been chased all over the forest by the Normans these last few days. You'll not be going anywhere while I hold you captive. No Normans will be coming to your rescue."

She tried not to show any emotion at the sound of her husband's name. The less these people knew the better. "Why did you bring me here?" she asked instead of asking if Sebastian was all right.

"I got tired of waiting for that young fool to bring you to me. No doubt the delay was so he could make merry with you in private."

"Sikes!" Berthild's fair cheeks reddened. "How can you think Lady Jehane's daughter would be a wanton?"

Sikes let out a deep, rumbling laugh. "Bastien's a man, isn't he? Of course he's bedded the girl." He squeezed his wife's shoulders. "What was the first thing I did when I kidnapped you?"

Berthild's blush deepened, then she giggled. The kidnapping had obviously worked out to their mutual benefit.

Where was Bas? Libby wondered desperately as she watched the couple exchange a quick kiss. She prayed the men who'd captured her hadn't attacked him as well. She prayed even harder that he hadn't been injured. Or killed. No, she wouldn't let herself consider the outlaws having killed him. She hoped he was on the way here to have a long talk with the older outlaw about letting her go. Actually, she would prefer if he'd march in and bust some heads, but he would think that diplomacy was the better part of valor. And he'd be right.

With that in mind she carefully and slowly made her way to her feet. "Bring me to you? Why? I thought Bastien sent his people to you for protection."

"His womenfolk are welcome, but his men are too loyal to be of any use to me. You're the one who's useful to me. Your ransom will make me rich enough to take Berthild and leave the forest forever."

So, he wanted to take the little woman and retire from the brigand business. Libby had an image of Sikes settling down in a condo in Florida. Yeah, right next door to Don Corleone and Jabba the Hutt.

"I'll bring you some food and ale," Berthild told her and bustled out of the cave.

"There's a man willing to pay a high price for the Lady of Lilydrake," Sikes went on after his wife left.

The manacles were heavy and tight. They were going to chafe her skin badly if she tried moving too much in them. She held her hands out toward Sikes. "It's going to take a while for my father to pay any ransom, so maybe we could dispense with these."

"You killed one of my men."

True. She wished she could say she was sorry, but she'd been terrified and at the end of her endurance when she'd been attacked. The man had grabbed her from behind and she'd reacted on instinct. The only honest answer she could give was, "I didn't mean to kill him." She held her hands out again. There were only about five inches of thick, rust-crusted chain between her wrists. "Please."

"While I do like hearing you beg, I don't think those cuffs are coming off."

"I wasn't begging, I was asking nicely," she said before she realized that it wasn't Sikes who had spoken, and that the language hadn't been Saxon. Or Norman French.

The man who walked into the cave to stand beside Sikes had spoken in modern English. Shock ran through her as she stared at the newcomer. He was a small man, wearing little more than dirty rags, but the rags were pinstriped. A heavy beard and badly cut hair obscured a familiar, sharp-featured face. Amber gold eyes looked her over with an unfamiliar manic hatred.

Her throat went dry, then she swallowed hard and croaked, "Hemmons?" She would have put her hands angrily on her hips if she could have as she demanded, "Elliot Hemmons, what are you doing here?"

"Holding David Wolfe's daughter prisoner," he answered, with a very unpleasant smile.

Libby felt like she'd been punched very hard in the stomach. A lot of things that had happened recently made very little sense, and seeing one of the richest men in the world in a thirteenth-century outlaw camp was the most insane twist of all. It wasn't that Hemmons didn't belong among brigands and thieves, but his usual haunts were boardrooms and Congressional committee hearings. She'd met him a few times, at the sorts of official parties where one had to be excruciatingly polite.

She was glad she didn't have to be polite now. She didn't ask him again what he was doing in the past. He was the man who wanted to turn time travel into some sort of interactive Disneyworld attraction. What was that line from *Jurassic Park*? Something about when the Pirates of the Caribbean breaks down the ride doesn't eat you, wasn't it? Hemmons looked like he'd been chewed up pretty badly by the reality of the Middle Ages. She began to laugh.

She didn't stop until he slapped her. "What's so damned funny?" he demanded.

"You," she said, after she'd wiped off blood from a split lower lip with her sleeve. "Have you enjoyed the ride?"

"What are you talking about?"

The irony didn't seem to be as self-evident to him as it was to her. "Welcome to Medieval World," she told him. "How many people have you seen die since you got here? Are you enjoying the mud? The accommodations? You look like you've lost a few pounds, so the cuisine must agree with you." His eyes narrowed dangerously. Libby figured she was about to get hit again, but she couldn't stop needling him. This was the man responsible for putting Sebastian through hell. She wished she had something more lethal than words to use on him. "How about the lawlessness, Hemmons? No, you probably do enjoy that part."

He didn't hit her. He smiled, and that was worse. "What are you babbling about, woman?"

"You're the one who wanted to turn the past into a theme park. You've been living here for the last six months, haven't you? Has it been fun?"

The smile turned nasty. "Some of it has. Especially the lawlessness." Now he hit her. "There's a certain satisfaction in being as unpleasant as I like to anyone I like."

"Anyone smaller and weaker than he is," Sikes interjected. "He's a nasty little rat, my lady," the outlaw went on while Hemmons glared at him. "You better learn to mind your manners with him."

Libby was actually rather appreciative of the man's advice. She didn't suppose he'd interfere in anything Hemmons might do, but he was thoughtful enough to give her the warning. "Do you work for him?" she asked Sikes.

"As long as he has gold to pay me," was the answer. "And he always seems to have more gold."

Berthild returned then, with a loaf of dark bread and a wooden cup filled with ale. She shook her head sadly when she saw the marks on Libby's face, but she didn't protest. Instead the older woman helped her sit on the tapestry-covered lump and handed her the cup. Libby drained it quickly, before she could actually taste it, and then took the bread. Libby stuffed the food down, since she was ravenous. She would have begged for more, but Hemmons was pacing agitatedly in front of her and she thought it was best to get her attention back on her captor.

"What?" she asked as he scowled down at her.

"Aren't you going to ask? Aren't you interested in how I outsmarted your old man? Don't you want to know why?"

Libby had some pretty good ideas about how Hemmons had gotten into the past. She already knew why, but he seemed to crave an audience. He wanted to brag about the brilliance that was Elliot Hemmons. He was acting like a bad movie villain, the kind that gloated over their victims just long enough for them to work free of their bonds and take the villain captive in turn. She'd always hated that sort of plot device. Besides, she wasn't getting out of these manacles anytime soon. The best she could hope for at the moment was for Bas to show up and save the day. Personally, she had infinite confidence that he could prevail against an entire camp full of bad guys. Sebastian, however, was sensible to his core, and did not share her taste in movies. Oh, well, he'd think of something.

Meanwhile, she gazed steadily at Hemmons and said, "I'd very much like to know how you got yourself stranded in the past." Since she and Hemmons were speaking English she didn't think anything he told her would mean anything to Sikes and Berthild. So at least she wouldn't be breaking any non-disclosure rules.

"Wouldn't you like to know how many people I've got on your father's staff?"

"None anymore," she answered. "Or you could have gotten back through the Downs timegate."

He laughed. "That's where you're wrong. I didn't go back because I didn't want to. Not yet. But we're getting ahead of ourselves. I was sick of all the legal maneuverings to get at the technology your father developed. How he got the government to agree to letting him own his own patents I'll never understand. Suffice it to say, David Wolfe has Time Search too neatly locked up for me to take over."

"Not that you haven't tried."

He ignored her. "So I was very interested when Mark Warin came to me with information about the Bailey TDD. He said it would open up all of time instead of the puny two hundred–year window Wolfe's device can cover." He made an expansive gesture. "All of time. The possibilities are endless. The profits will be staggering. I knew I had to control the TDD, so I bought it from Warin."

"You bought—" Libby's indignation was boundless, as much as Hemmons's greed and stupidity. "It wasn't exactly Warin's to sell."

"But he got it for me." Hemmons patted the tapestry-draped object she was perched on. "He contacted Sikes and arranged the diversion. He brought me through the Lilydrake timegate while the rest of you were drugged."

"Why risk coming back yourself?"

He laughed. "I'd been wanting to time travel for the last twenty years. I wasn't going to miss the chance to be in on this."

"And you didn't completely trust Mark Warin," she guessed.

"Warin's an eggheaded, netsurfing computer dweeb. He means well, but his mind's not in the real world."

"Neither is the rest of him," Libby said. "Not any-more. He's dead."

Hemmons did not look grieved, he looked angry. "Damn. I needed that fool. What I really needed was Bailey. We should have just killed the others in their sleep and taken you and Bailey hostage, but Warin told me that wouldn't be necessary. Warin said he could complete the work without Bailey."

"Apparently, he was wrong."

"That's for damn sure. The plan was to make it look like an outlaw attack, and that the injuries from Warin's sabotage would make it look like the effects of the TDD were too dangerous to continue its develop-ment. Bailey was not supposed to get out alive. The 'accident' was supposed to give me the ammunition to get the project scrapped by Time Search while I went ahead with the real thing."

"So what you did to Joe and Ed and Bas and me was just a policy decision?"

Her words had been seething with anger and sarcasm, but he took no notice of either. "Essentially." He cast a glare at the indifferent Sikes. "The locals destroyed the timegate when they plundered the hall. Warin wasn't as clever with Bailey's machine as he thought."

"Why didn't you use the Downs gate? You'd have been retrieved if you'd used the emergency signal."

Hemmons's laughter filled the cave for a long time. When he stopped, he wiped moisture from his eyes and looked at her as though she was the stupidest thing he'd ever seen. "Warin suggested that a few times. I vetoed it. I wasn't going to go begging to David Wolfe. A little inconvenience back here is worth more than spoiling all my plans."

"Not to mention the jail term all those plans would get you back in our time." He nodded. So, he'd lied about having people on Time Search staff that would sneak him back to the future. She smiled, but didn't point out the man's prevarication to him. "I see your point in not using the authorized channels to go home. But how were you hoping to get back?"

"This."

He twitched back the covering. Libby scooted off from where she was sitting. The device looked to be imbedded in a solid rock casing, but she recognized some of the indicators and circuitry and bells and whistles of Sebastian's time machine. This contraption looked like a high-tech gargoyle.

"Very nice. Blends in with the decor."

"Warin's been working on it for months," Hemmons went on. "Made progress, too, with what little he's been able to worm out of Bailey. If Bailey didn't think he was Robin Hood the work would go even faster." He gave her a very nasty sneer. "Too bad your husband's completely insane."

"He's not," Libby said hotly. "He's got his memory back." She could tell her hasty defense of Bas had been a mistake the moment she spoke.

Hemmons's eyes lit up with a very feral glow. "Oh, really?" he asked, and grabbed hold of the chain that bound her.

20

"By Saint Thomas, Bas, you gave me a fright!"

Bas had climbed a tree when he'd heard the three men coming, and dropped out of it behind them as they'd passed. They'd whirled at the sound of him landing and stiffened with alarm at the sight of the arrow he had aimed at them. Cynric had recognized him within a heartbeat, and very nearly shouted the words he'd just spoken.

Odda and Harald relaxed visibly, but Cynric remained alert. "You can lower that arrow, lad."

His aim didn't waver. "Whose men are you? Mine or Sikes's?"

Cynric laughed, the others joined him. "Whose do you think?"

"That's no answer."

"We follow you, Bas. None of us have women or babes to worry about," Cynric told him. "So we had no reason to turn to him for protection when you sent the others."

"Then what are you doing patrolling the perimeter of his campsite?"

"Looking for you," Odda spoke up. He gave a gap-toothed grin. "But you found us first."

"That's why he's the leader," Cynric told the others. They nodded in agreement. "Now that we know where he dwells, what do we do about him, Bastien?"

Bas slowly relaxed the tension on the bowstring, then put the arrow back in his quiver. He flexed his left arm, glad to know that he could shoot with it if he must, and equally glad he wouldn't have to use it yet.

"Sikes has Lady Isabeau," he told his men. "I've come to get her back." No need to try to explain the truth of the situation.

The men looked at each other, then back at him. Cynric spoke for them, "You plan to rescue her?"

"I do."

Cynric looked thoughtful. "For ransom? Or do you plan to marry her?"

Bas didn't know if the old outlaw was more interested in matchmaking, or if Cynric was longing to rest his old bones around the winter fire at Lilydrake. Not that it mattered. "We're already married," Bas answered.

Cynric gave a cackling laugh. He clapped Bas on the shoulder. "Well, you've had a busy few days, haven't you, lad? Then it's a proper rescue we need to plan. What do we do, Bas?"

"Can four men take Sikes's camp?"

Cynric laughed. "No."

"I didn't think so." He shrugged. "I suppose I'll just have to walk in and claim my property back from the old bandit."

"Aye, you can walk in. But will he let you walk out?"

*   *   *

Sebastian walked into Sikes's camp alone. Sentries had tried to stop him, but without success, and without having time to shout out any warnings. He came under cover of darkness with a load of firewood in his arms and a hood pulled up to shield his face. He walked stooped over like any tired peasant eager for his meal and a place at the fire. That his bow and quiver were slung on his back was no different from any other man in the outlaw camp, either. Sikes had many men, and they all went armed. He'd left his quarterstaff with Cynric to mind for he couldn't manage it and the wood, but he still had the dagger at his belt. He reasoned that his best weapon was the cover of night.

No one took notice of him when he left his load of sticks at the first fire he reached and moved deeper into the campsite. The place was more like a bustling village than the temporary, easily abandoned sites of hovels and firepits where he'd lived with his own band. Sikes's village covered much of a clearing between a small stream and a rise of low hills. There were cattle pens, vegetable patches, a smithy and storage sheds; rows of tents and huts were intersected by well-worn paths. It looked like Sikes had built himself quite a prosperous little fief in the hardest-to-reach stretch of the king's forest.

Bas moved cautiously through it, intent on finding where his wife was being held and trying not to attract any attention. The darkness and the hood and the dinner hour helped. People glanced his way as he moved from one patch of firelight to the next, but no one stopped him. Gradually he moved out of the main part of the camp and toward the path that led up the hill.

When he looked up and saw the cave mouth that made a gash in the side of the chalky slope he decided he'd found the right spot. A fire was lit outside the mouth of the cave, and two men armed with spears stood before the blaze. It was the presence of the guards that told him there was something valuable inside. The chalk cave was probably where the old outlaw stored his most precious loot. A prisoner being held for ransom would be considered treasure worth guarding.

When he heard someone coming up behind him, he slipped off the path. He thought himself well hidden by the dark shadow of a tree, but the woman must have seen him move, because she stopped only a few feet from where he stood. After several silent moments in which Bas forgot to breathe, she stepped closer. Though he could barely make out her features, there was something familiar about the small woman.

"You'd be Bastien, then," she said. Her emphatic tone brooked no denial. "Come for Lady Isabeau, you are." She came closer and looked him over head to foot as he stepped away from the tree. "Push back your hood, lad, and let's have a look." She peered sternly up at him. "Well?"

As Bas yanked back the hood he said, "I am, and I have." Admitting to her conjectures seemed better than throttling her and leaving her in the bushes.

"You're as fine-looking as I've heard," she went on after she'd inspected him. "Though the brow's a bit heavy and serious for my taste. I'm Berthild," she added. "You'll have to talk to my man about taking the lady away, but I'll take you to her for now."

Bas gaped at the woman as she walked on up the path. Gaped, and followed, because there wasn't anything else he could do to get his wife out of that cave without violence. He didn't want to worry about fighting until he was sure she was safe.

When they reached the guards, Berthild merely waved them aside. They didn't question her authority, or even look at him twice as she stood back and directed him inside. Bas gave her a look of gratitude, and went into the shallow cave.

The place was well lit and dry, high enough for him to stand upright in, but small and full of stuff. Among the stuff, seated next to a block of stone, was his wife.

His breath caught in his throat at the sight of her, and a pain loosed around his heart as well. It had been so hard and heavy and so much a part of him for so long that he didn't realize until this moment that he truly hadn't lost her at Lilydrake. She was really alive, and not a dream. They were together. They would get out of this, somehow. He was never, ever going to leave her side again. No matter what happened, he could not bear to part with her again.

She looked up as he hurried toward her, and her dark eyes lit with pleasure. Then, with a sardonic twist to her smile, she said, "Will I sound absolutely stupid if I say, oh, darling, I knew you'd come?"

"Yes." He knelt beside her.

He wanted to say all he was feeling, vow his love and undying devotion. But he could tell by the way her eyes glowed at the sight of him that he didn't need to say what they both knew. What they both felt. So, he answered her the same way she'd greeted him. "What you should say, is, oh, darling, did you bring the bolt cutters? You have noticed that you're chained to a rock, haven't you?"

He took her face between his hands then, and kissed her before she could answer. It was a hard, swift kiss, full of passion and relief. He couldn't afford for the kiss to last too long, but he felt much better for having done it. "So," he said as he looked deep into her eyes. "Is this what you wanted?"

She looked confused. "Getting captured?"

He ran his hands down his tunic as though he were modeling his Bastien persona for her. "This. This heroic coming to the rescue sort of thing. What do you think? Is it me?"

She managed, though her arms were chained to a metal bolt driven into the rock, to just barely cup his cheek with her manacled hand. "It's you. When it has to be."

Bas put the subject aside. This was really no time for it, and besides, she was right. "Man's gotta do what a—Why are you chained up like this?"

"Well, Sikes didn't take kindly to my killing one of his men. And I think the other guy's a kinky little bastard."

He ran his fingertips across her swollen lower lip. "Who hit you?"

"The other guy."

His eyes narrowed to dangerous green slits. "I'm going to kill him."

"Fine with me."

"I'm in love with a barbarian."

"So am I." His answering smile was thin-lipped and dangerous. Libby wondered if she should explain about Hemmons now, or if they should get on with the escape and discuss other problems later. "One crisis at a time," she said. "Did you bring the bolt cutters?"

"No." He stood up and finally took a good look at the rock. After a while he said, "This is the TDD."

"Um—yes," she agreed. She couldn't twist around enough to see him, but she heard his hands as they moved over his creation. The whisper of his touch sounded like caresses, and his voice as he commented on bits of circuitry was full of wonder. She had a feeling he'd forgotten temporarily about her predicament. She only minded a little; she'd known what the job entailed when she'd married a genius. Geniuses tended to get distracted by their work. "Excuse me, Mr. Wizard, but—"

"Who integrated it into this kind of mineral sheath casing?"

"Someone with a literal definition of the word hardware?"

"Olivia."

She almost laughed at his reproving tone. "Warin, of course. He'd been working on the thing. He stole it, remember? And probably wanted to make sure nobody got the chance to steal it from him."

"It's going to take hours to get it out of this box. And other than solving the miniaturized power source problem he's—"

"So happy to see you approve of the new energy utilization design, Dr. Bailey."

"That's all I appro—" Bas broke off as he realized the speaker had not been his wife.

When he looked up he saw a bearded man standing nearby. Several things about the man seemed out of place—his stance, the cut of his clothing, the language he'd used. The easiest anomaly to pin down was the gun he was holding.

"This is a Kalishnikov KU-49." The man sounded smug, and as though his words were self-explanatory.

Bas looked at his wife. "Olivia?"

"It's a fully automatic assault weapon capable of firing a thousand fully jacketed 9-mm explosive rounds per minute. It also fires laser packs, in case you just want to permanently blind your target," she rattled off details about the weapon without a pause. "Charming little accessory, isn't it?"

Bas didn't know whether to appreciate his wife's expertise in certain areas, or to be appalled at learning far more than he wanted to know about the gun the man held on them. He decided to simply say, "Oh. And he is?"

"Elliot Hemmons," the man answered. He gestured around the cave. "Welcome to your new laboratory, Dr. Bailey. And welcome back to the real world."

"Real world? You call this the real world? We're in—what year is it, Olivia?"

"Never mind," Hemmons answered. He smiled, in a very unpleasant and calculating way. "I'm told you have recovered from your little psychotic episode and are fit to work. You can take off the bow and arrow, Bailey," he added. "You look silly in that Robin Hood getup."

Sebastian returned to crouch by his wife after he'd laid his weapons on the cave floor. "What's he doing here?" He looked at the dark bruise on her cheek and her swollen lip while she explained how Hemmons had caused all their troubles and gotten caught in them himself. Bas hadn't cared for the man before he heard the explanation. He hated him by the time she was done. Her current treatment at Hemmons's hands sent a sharp, burning anger through him.

He stood up and spoke to the man with the gun. "Let her go."

Hemmons shook his head. He jerked a thumb toward the darkness beyond the cave. "There seems to be a battle going on outside," he told them. "Your band of outlaws coming to your defense, no doubt."

That had not been the plan. His men were only supposed to take out the sentries, then guard the path back to the river. Bas glanced briefly at Olivia. He could hear dogs barking in the distance. And shouts, and the clash of weapons. She lifted her brows in question. Apparently, she hadn't arranged for the cavalry to arrive either.

Before he could comment, Hemmons stepped closer and went on, "Sikes isn't putting up much of a fight. In fact, I think he and most of his people have decided that discretion is the better part of valor. They have hiding holes throughout the woods. Better to let their village be burned than be taken. So, your people might make it to the cave without too much trouble. But I still have the gun."

"So you have nothing to be concerned about," Bas agreed.

Hemmons nodded. "After you've sent your people away, or I've killed them, you can get to work. On second thought, get to work now. Warin said it was almost operational. I want it operational tonight."

"Operational? The TDD? You want me to get it working for you?" He laughed. Once again Hemmons nodded. "No," Bas said. "I don't think so."

"I intend to own time, Bailey."

"No one can own—"

"I own David Wolfe's daughter," the man interrupted harshly. Bas took a menacing step toward Hemmons, but the man's next words stopped him. "I have the key to those manacles, I have the gun, so I own Wolfe's daughter and your wife. Through her I own David Wolfe. And I own you. You'll both give me what I want."

"Why?" The question came from Olivia. "Why should he give you what you want?"

Bas turned to look at her. "Because I love you."

She smiled at him. The warmth of it melted some of the cold fear that twisted through him. There was a layer of steel underneath the warmth, however. "I love you too, Bas," she told him, "but that doesn't mean I would—"

"Shut up," Hemmons cut her off before speaking to Bas again. "I should have done something like this years ago. I can't imagine either of you romantic fools sacrificing the life of someone you love. So tell me I don't own time, Bailey."

Bas didn't want to tell the man anything. He wanted to get the gun, and the key that held his wife locked to the time machine. He did not want to give Elliot Hemmons access to the most dangerous technology any damned fool curious scientist had ever devised. There was only one thing he could think of that he could do about it.

He looked at his wife and said, "I'm sorry."

Her eyes widened in alarm. "What? You're not giving him what he wants, are you?"

"Yes," he said, and went to the bank of controls at the front of the TDD. He removed a panel, then flexed his fingers, and set to work.

He couldn't see Olivia from where he was, but he felt the explosive silence that emanated from her side of the rock. Finally, she said, "Sebastian?"

"Yes."

"Tell me you aren't doing this to save my skin."

"I'm doing this to save your skin."

"I told you not to tell me that."

"I know."

After a short silence, she said, "Thank you."

"You're welcome."

"But I really wish you wouldn't."

There was a hum coming from the TDD now, and a group of lights were going from green to amber to red in the sequence he wanted. "I know," he said again.

She sighed. "Bas, think of what Hemmons will do with a time machine. He can't change his own past, but he can mess up everyone else's."

He heard the man with the gun come a little bit closer, as though he were curious to hear the answer. Bas said, "He'll use it for plundering the past and controlling the future. He'll use it to make himself CEO of the world. It can't be helped, Olivia."

"Yes, it can! Just don't do it!"

Sebastian didn't let his concentration waver from the controls he was so delicately adjusting as he answered, "Can't stop now, sweetheart."

Hemmons laughed. The triumph in the sound was galling.

The TDD was more than humming now. The sound was closer to a screech, a fingernails-on-slate rasp just on the edge of hearing. The noise didn't seem to come from the machine, it was more like the machine was pulling the noise out of the air. Bas knew it was the protesting sound of time being sucked out of the world. Pulled, twisted, distorted, and turned into a weapon. The timefield generated by the TDD was growing, soon it would encompass the area of the cave.

Bas's head was beginning to throb with pain, but he wasn't worried. He was used to this effect, not immune, but practice with the madness would help him fight it. It would have to, because he had to make himself function for as long as it took.

He vaguely heard the clink of metal against metal as Olivia tried to move. She groaned. "My head hurts."

"I'm sorry, sweetheart."

"What are—" Her words stopped on a sharp gasp. "Ah," she finished. It was a small sound, but it hadn't been one of pain. It had held a great deal of understanding, not to mention savageness and pride. He knew that despite her distress, she was smiling.

"Room's spinning," Hemmons said. There was a strain of fear and confusion in his voice. "That damn thing's giving me a headache."

"Good," Bas whispered under his breath.

"What's happening?" Hemmons demanded as he made the mistake of taking another step closer.

Hemmons hadn't noticed the dagger when he'd made Bas disarm. Or if he'd noticed it, he hadn't thought it was any use against a weapon from the twenty-first century. Bas waited a few more moments, holding on hard to his sanity and self-control as the field continued to build. He whispered a prayer as he heard his wife moan, and slipped the dagger from his belt.

Hemmons's skin was ashen, his brow furrowed and his eyes squinted nearly closed in reaction to the drain from the timefield. He hunched forward in agony, just as Sebastian grabbed for the gun with one hand and thrust the dagger up under his ribs with the other. Hemmons was dead by the time his body dropped heavily onto the cave floor.

Even through a red veil of pain Libby heard the clatter of the gun as it hit the ground, followed by a thud a moment later. The sounds sent a shiver of terror through her that had nothing to do with the disorienting agony. "Bas," she called frantically. "Are you all right?"

"Fine," he called back.

She sagged against the cool stone in relief. "Thank God."

"Damn. I can't find the key."

"What key?" Since the world insisted on spinning, she closed her eyes and ignored it. She fought the disorientation as well. It wasn't as if she hadn't had practice. She knew what was happening, and wasn't going down into the darkness without a fight.

"The key to those cuffs."

"Sikes locked me into these things."

"You mean Hemmons didn't have it?"

"No. Bas, turn off the time machine before it gets us. We'll worry about the key later."

He swore. She heard him move, but the machine was not turned off. He came to kneel beside her instead. "Olivia, I have some bad news."

She opened her eyes, and concentrated hard on his face to keep the swirling background at bay. That was all right. She didn't really want to do anything but look at him anyway. "Why can't you turn it off?" she asked, before he could explain that he couldn't. Why question the obvious?

He put his hands on her shoulders. "Because Warin was getting instructions on making the thing work from a madman. All he succeeded in doing was creating another time bomb."

Sharp needles drove into her mind, and fighting off darkness was becoming harder. "It's happening again." She didn't have time to say the things she wanted to, or to ask any more questions. She was about to lose her memories once more, maybe even her life, but there was something she had to make sure of first. "Get out of here," she told her husband. "Get away right now, before it gets us both."

Instead of getting up, he pulled her close. With his arms tightly around her, he whispered into her ear. "No." He cradled her protectively.

She welcomed his strength, his closeness. She didn't want to face the cold emptiness alone. "Please go," she begged. "I don't want you to go through hell again."

"I won't. Not while we're together."

There was actually a smile in the damn fool's voice. She might have hit him if her hands hadn't been chained. She did start crying. Not in fear of the impending tragedy, but because he was the most wonderful man in the world. Also crazier than a loon to put himself through this for her. And she was crazy, too, because she knew she would have done the same thing for him.

She supposed there was nothing more they needed to say. So she turned her head into his shoulder, and pressed herself as tightly to him as she could. Together they waited for a storm made of time to smash them down into the dark.

"Are you sure they're up here?" Marj asked as she followed Reynard toward the cave mouth.

In answer he pointed at the sleek deerhounds who raced up the path ahead of them. The dogs had explored the settlement while she, Reynard and Bastien's men had seen to emptying the place of Sikes's outlaws. The outlaws had been easy enough to rout once they knew it was the sheriff who attacked them. Stopping Bastien's men from fleeing when they'd first approached them had been the hard part. Promises of pardons for their help had worked wonders, and the battle, such as it was, had been joined. Now that the action was over, the dogs had set about their quest once more.

"I suppose Luke and Leia know where they're going," she agreed with Reynard.

He still had his sword in his hand, and he walked at a brisk, determined pace. She tried not to let the pain of knowing she was going to have to leave him as soon as Libby was rescued stab at her. She tried to just concentrate on getting Libby back, and not on leaving the man she'd come to desperately love. It was hard not to think about him though, as she watched the spare grace of his movements.

"Damn," she muttered to herself as a mingled ache of love and pain shot through her, only to be replaced at her next step with a disorienting wave of dizziness. She stopped as nausea hit her. "What the—" It felt like her head was being twisted off from the inside.

Reynard grabbed her arm. "Don't go any closer," he said. Then he ran toward the cave mouth. He was hurrying toward some awful danger, and she suspected she knew what it was. So she raced after him, whether to warn him or just to be with him, she didn't know. It got worse with every step, but she wouldn't let him face a monster from her own time alone.

He was standing in the cave entrance when she

reached him, his sword held before him. Like a cross in front of a vampire, she thought as she saw the way he gripped it. The disorientation flowed out from the center of the cave. It hit with almost solid force. Like waves, she thought, like an inexorable tide. It hurt.

In the distance, like looking through a wall of glass, she could see Bastien. Libby was with him, though hardly visible in the shelter of his embrace. "Are they dead?" she wondered.

She didn't think she had the strength to brave the tide to find out. She had another obligation more important than Libby's safety. She had to get Reynard away before he was injured. She couldn't allow a local to be exposed to danger that emanated from her own time. Besides, she loved him.

But when she put her hand on his arm he ignored her. She had to focus hard through the growing disorientation, but she was able to see that he was doing something with his sword hilt. He was performing a magic spell, she thought, or a prayer for some saint's aid. As he pressed the jewels set in the steel one at a time, she managed to say, "Religion isn't—"

"What's going on here," he said, as the merciless, mind-rending waves abruptly stopped. The hideous, subvocal screeching she hadn't noticed before ended as well. In the sudden, dead silence he hurried into the cave.

The dogs, who had sensibly stopped when they'd hit the invisible wall, raced in behind him. Marj didn't move for a few seconds. She couldn't. She watched from the cave mouth as Reynard pushed the animals aside to get to Libby and Bastien. He carefully separated them, gently laying Bastien on the ground. Libby, she saw, was handcuffed to the heavy stone in the center of the floor.

Laser cutter, she thought absently at the flash of green light when Reynard touched his dagger hilt to the chain and it separated as if by magic. One by one he checked their pulses.

"Are they alive?" she asked in a voice she didn't recognize when he was done. The dogs began to lick and nose worriedly at the unconscious pair.

"They're alive," he answered. "I just hope they're sane. We'll have to wait until they wake up to find out." He'd spoken in English.

Of course. That made sense. One had to be conscious to judge whether or not one were mad. Marj wished she wasn't conscious, because she certainly thought she was crazy. No, she wasn't crazy. She was confused, and she was beginning to be angry, but she was sane enough.

"Who are you?" she asked as he came to stand in front of her.

"Not the Sheriff of Elansted," he answered.

"I guessed that much."

Before she could say anymore, Libby groaned and Bastien sat up, and she and Reynard raced to their sides. Marj settled next to Libby. "Are you all right?" she asked anxiously. "Who am I? Who are you?"

Libby ignored the headache. She wanted her husband, but she answered the questions. "I'm fine. You're Marj. I'm Olivia Bailey. Where's Bas? There's a dog licking my toes."

"Who's Olivia Bailey?"

"I am. I got married while you were in Carmarthen." She looked around anxiously. "Bas?"

"Here," he answered. He had to push Marj aside to do it, but he swept Libby into a tight embrace. "Are you all right?"

Marj stood up and exchanged glances with Reynard while the couple on the cave floor checked to make sure they had all their fingers and toes and brain cells in working order. After a few minutes of listening to them, she pointed at Bastien and asked, "Who is he really?" She wanted to know the same thing about Reynard, but one thing at a time.

Reynard ran a finger along the edge of his mustache, and explained. "Somebody Time Search security thought was dead, which is why I wasn't briefed on what he looked like. Sorry, Sebastian," he apologized to the man who probably wasn't an outlaw. "I would have hauled you in sooner if I'd connected Bastien of Bale with the fellow in the wedding video Libby's mom sent me. That church was really too dark to shoot a video-tape in, by the way." While everyone stared at him in consternation, he went laconically on. "Libby'd already run off with you by the time I figured out who you were, so I let things take their course for a while. Sorry for the inconvenience," he said as he looked at Marj.

"Inconvenience," Marj repeated. Then she blinked, and shouted, "Who the hell are you?"

"Sam Wolfe," Libby answered. Bas helped her to stand. Then they leaned against each other, for support and the sheer pleasure of touching. She squinted in the torchlight as it flickered over the craggy-featured, gray-ing man. He smiled, showing deep dimples. "That is you, isn't it, Uncle Sam?" He was twenty years younger than her father, but the resemblance was there just the same. She hadn't seen him since she was ten, and he'd left to work as a Federal marshal on the Mars colony. She still wished she'd made the connection sooner. "What are you doing here?"

"Came home on leave and your dad recruited me. Wanted somebody he could trust to look after his little girl. I should never have let your mom train me in all this medieval crap when I was a kid." He brushed his finger across his mustache again. He gave a quick glance at Marj. "Playing Reynard's been kind of fun, though."

"You've been teasing me," Libby accused.

He nodded. He smiled at Marj, as well. "Shamelessly."

"You kept telling me I ought to get married—when you knew I already was," Libby accused.

He looked from her to Bas, and grinned. "Just trying to jog your memory. Thought the shrinks were stupid not to let anybody tell you your past. Something started itching in the back of my head when I saw you with Bastien. It seemed right for you two to be together, rules or no rules." He spoke to Marj again. "I'm truly sorry I couldn't tell you. I was tempted. More than tempted about a lot of things. He took her hands as Marj began to blush. "You know how tight security is."

"I know," Marj said. Libby thought that Marj looked angry, but relieved as well.

"I didn't want to hurt you, Marjorie. I love you."

"I know you do," Marj answered. "I love you. And I'm also going to make you pay for every minute you spent pretending to be Reynard of Elansted."

He was not intimidated. "I can play payback, too, *Lady* Marjorie."

"Wait a minute," Bas said before Marj and her uncle could go off into a corner to discuss their future. "You saved us, didn't you? How?"

In response, Sam tossed his sword to Bas, who easily

caught it by the hilt. *Macho men,* Libby thought, and exchanged a smile with Marj. *You gotta love 'em.* Bas took his arm from around her waist and began examining the sword. "Well?" she asked after he'd played with it for a while.

"Looks like your dad solved some of the flaws in my design while I was playing Robin Hood."

"Yep," Sam said. "Sent that little thing along with me just in case I ran into a stolen time machine. He suspected sabotage all along." Sam looked down at the body of Elliot Hemmons. "Or at least since this fool disappeared. Come on, we have to talk," he said, and led Marj out of the cave.

Libby didn't want to stay in the cave with Hemmons's body any longer, either, but she took the time to take the sword from Bas and lay it on the dead time machine. She put her arms around her husband once more. "You weren't playing," she told him. "If you'd been playing you wouldn't have saved my life half a dozen times."

"I wasn't playing," he agreed. "Maybe I'm not the mild-mannered sort I thought I was."

"Of course you're not."

"I guess not. But I never want to do this again." He took her face between his hands and smiled into her adoring eyes. "But, so help me, if you try to program this adventure into your virtual reality chamber, I'm getting a divorce."

"Oh, no," she told him, and turned her head to kiss his palm. "I think this will just have to stay an adventure for us to remember. Forever and ever and ever."

"Promise?"

"I swear by the sun, the stars and the Great Khan Temujin."

He rubbed her temples with his palms, then he smiled. "Sweetheart, you've spent too much time in Mongolia. Let's go home."

Let HarperMonogram Sweep You Away!

You Belong to My Heart by Nan Ryan

Over 3.5 million copies of her books in print. As the Civil War rages, Captain Clay Knight seizes Mary Ellen Preble's mansion for the Union Army. Once his sweetheart, Mary Ellen must win back the man who wants her in his bed, but not in his heart.

After the Storm by Susan Sizemore

Golden Heart Award–Winning Author. When a time travel experiment goes awry, Libby Wolfe finds herself in medieval England and at the mercy of the dashing Bastien of Bale. A master of seduction, the handsome outlaw unleashes a passion in Libby that she finds hauntingly familiar.

Deep in the Heart by Sharon Sala

Romantic Times *Award–Winning Author.* Stalked by a threatening stranger, successful casting director Samantha Carlyle returns home to Texas—and her old friend John Thomas Knight—for safety. The tender lawman may be able to protect Sam's body, but his warm Southern ways put her heart at risk.

Honeysuckle DeVine by Susan Macias

To collect her inheritance, Laura Cannon needs to join Jesse Travers' cattle drive—and become his wife. The match is only temporary, but long days on the trail lead to nights filled with fiery passion.

And in case you missed last month's selections . . .

Dancing On Air by Susan Wiggs

Over one million copies of her books in print. After losing her family and her aristocratic name, Philipa de Lacey is reduced to becoming a London street performer. Entranced with Philipa, the dashing Irish Lord of Castleross vows to help her—but his tarnished past threatens their love.

Straight from the Heart by Pamela Wallace

Academy Award–Winning Author. Answering a personal ad on a dare, city girl Zoey Donovan meets a handsome Wyoming rancher. Widower Tyler Ross is the answer to any woman's fantasy, but he will have to let go of the past before he can savor love's sweet bounty.

Treasured Vows by Cathy Maxwell

When English banker Grant Morgan becomes the guardian of impoverished heiress Phadra Abbott, he quickly falls under the reckless beauty's spell. Phadra is determined to upset Grant's well-ordered life to find her spendthrift father—despite the passion Grant unleashes in her.

Texas Lonesome by Alice Duncan

In 1890s San Francisco, Emily von Plotz gives advice to the lovelorn in her weekly newspaper column. A reader who calls himself "Texas Lonesome" seems to be the man for her, but wealthy rancher Will Tate is more than willing to show her who the real expert is in matters of the heart.

Harper Monogram

Echoes and Illusions
by Kathy Lynn Emerson

Lauren Ryder has everything she wants, but then the dreams start—dreams so real she fears she's losing her mind. Something happened to Lauren in the not-so-distant past that she can't remember. As she desperately tries to piece together the missing years of her life, a shocking picture emerges. Who is Lauren Ryder, really?

The Night Orchid by Patricia Simpson

In Seattle Marissa Quinn encounters a doctor conducting ancient Druid time-travel rituals and meets Alek, a glorious pre-Roman warrior trapped in the modern world. Marissa and Alek discover that though two millennia separate their lives, nothing can sever the bond forged between their hearts.

Destiny Awaits by Suzanne Elizabeth

Tess Harper found herself in Kansas in the year 1885, face-to-face with the most captivating, stubborn man she'd ever met—and two precious little girls who needed a mother. Could this man, and this family, be her true destiny?